ANDRE GONZALEZ

Keeper of Time

First published by M4L Publishing 2020

First edition

ISBN: 978-1-951762-09-4

Cover art by ebooklaunch.com
Editing by Stephanie Cohen

This book was professionally typeset on Reedsy.
Find out more at reedsy.com

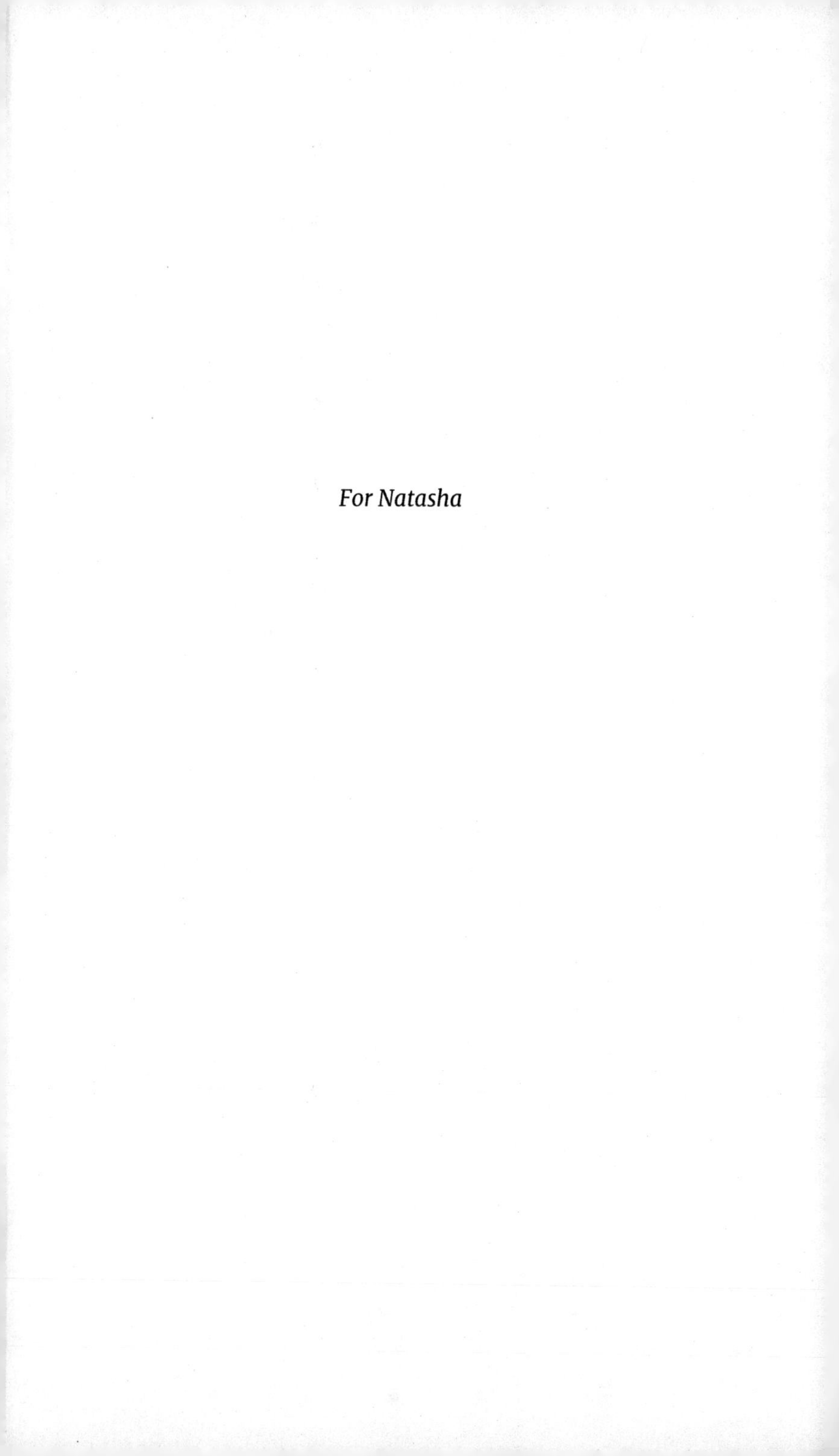

For Natasha

"Sometimes it's not the people who change, it's the mask that falls off."

Contents

GET EXCLUSIVE BONUS STORIES!

Connecting with readers is the best part of this job. Releasing a book into the world is a truly frightening moment every time it happens! Hearing your feedback, whether good or bad, goes a long in shaping future projects and helping me grow as a writer. I also like to take readers behind the scenes on occasion and share what is happening in my wild world of writing. If you're interested, please consider joining my mailing list. If you do so, I'll send you the following as a thank you:

1. A free copy of *Revolution*, a prequel story that goes back in time before Chris Speidel ever knew about the mysterious world of time travel.
2. A free copy of *Road Runners*, a prequel story that visits the origination of the Road Runners organization.

You can get your content for free, by signing up HERE.

https://dl.bookfunnel.com/zb03c72679

I

The Journey of Martin Briar

1

Chapter 1

Chris Speidel paced back and forth in his office, a coy grin plastered to his face, mind and body consumed by a pulsing urge for revenge. Duane Betts, his longtime right-hand man, sat in the chair facing Chris's desk, a steaming cup of coffee in one hand, a pen in the other as a clipboard rested across his lap.

Chris had been rambling off the names of each location he could think of where the Road Runners housed one of their underground offices, the list stretching across forty different cities.

It had been a whole week since the Road Runners attempted to bomb the mansion in Barrow, Alaska, and so much had happened since then. Commander Strike was now in the basement, the lone prisoner, as they had freed everyone in exchange for her.

The mission to kill Martin's mother Marilyn had been executed flawlessly, the only disappointment being that Chris wasn't there to see the look on that ungrateful bastard's face when he arrived home. Speaking of Martin, the sly snake who had managed to slither out of this very mansion, he was *missing*. No one had a tail on him, although Chris presumed someone within the Road Runners did, as rumors had spread that he fled the country that same night after finding his murdered mother.

No matter what Chris had to focus on—authorizing torture against Commander Strike, or recruiting new members for the Revolution, among many other daily tasks—Martin remained stuck on his mind, like a fungus that refused to leave.

"Anywhere else, sir?" Duane asked, taking a sip of coffee.

Duane's voice sounded distant to Chris, his brain again occupied with the never-ending TV show that was Martin Briar. Sure, he had made plenty of mistakes in his life, both as a man and the Keeper of Time, but nothing paled in comparison to the blunder of trusting Martin. To be fair, the mistake entirely belonged to Chris and no one else. He had acted on emotion—a forbidden choice—and actually felt sympathy for Martin when they had all arrived at the mansion. Chris had rescued him from the trap being laid out by the Road Runners, dragging the poor guy through different modes of transportation and different eras of time to dodge the group of madmen chasing after them. He had no reason to think Martin was anything less than grateful for the help.

Briar had always been a curious fellow, asking a ridiculous amount of questions, so Chris thought nothing of it when Martin asked if he could roam the grounds around the mansion. He figured it would be one less list of questions to personally answer, saving him an unnecessary headache.

"That's all I can think of, Duane," Chris said, returning to the chair behind his desk. "If you wouldn't mind researching these locations and finding out which are the easiest to access, furthest away from the regular population, and which ones house the most Road Runners."

"Yes, sir."

Ever since the bombs had dropped on the mansion, everyone around Chris seemed to have grown more obedient, Duane included, something that made Chris uneasy as he typically relied on Duane to challenge his ideas, playing devil's advocate in search of any flaws. But the bombs had sparked tension for those within the mansion. They had felt the rumbling of the building they called home, and many confronted their own mortality for the first time in years. Only Chris was immune to death; even if the bombs broke through the steel barrier and shattered his body, it would eventually form back together like a puzzle, returning him to normal.

"I want to move quickly on this," Chris said. "And I want to force their dirty hands to make a choice between their own buildings and Ms. Strike downstairs. We need to place calls to every fort we have bombs stored. It's a long list, so I'll help out. I'm thinking we can have something ready to execute in about three days. Does that sound feasible?"

Duane nodded. "Yes, sir."

"When this is all said and done," Chris continued, "I don't want the Road Runners to know up from down, let alone know who their leader is, or what their plans are to move forward. Whichever buildings we decide to blow out, I don't want a single life remaining. Blast them to the fucking moon. Do you understand?"

"Yes, sir."

"Do you have any other responses besides 'yes, sir'?" Chris had grown more irritated with each passing day since the attempted bombing. Even after killing Mama Briar, he still felt unfulfilled. Now, any little thing seemed to set him off.

"What do you mean?" Duane asked in his calm, flat monotone, unfazed by no one.

"You've just sat here the last couple of days, agreeing with everything I say."

Duane gazed into Chris's eyes and shrugged his shoulders. "I haven't had anything to disagree with. This is a pretty straightforward matter. They bombed us, and we need to retaliate."

Chris frowned. "I agree, but I'm confused. You always try to force us to take the higher ground. Why the sudden love for revenge? Is something bothering you? You seem distant."

Duane's eyes welled with tears, his lips quivering uncontrollably. "I'm sorry, Chris." His words came out shaky and nearly inaudible. "I know this is probably the most crucial time for the Revolution, but I need to go home."

"Home?!" Chris gasped. Duane was from Clearwater, Florida, a whole 5,000 miles away from Barrow.

"My mom's been diagnosed with terminal cancer . . . six weeks to live. Five, since I received the news last week."

"Duane, I'm sorry to hear this, but you do know I have access to the cure for cancer. All I have to do is make a phone call and we can have it by tomorrow."

Duane shook his head violently. "That's not the point. This whole thing has got me thinking. It's karma, for all the bad shit we've done."

"Karma? You don't expect me to believe such a thing. I virtually run the world."

"You don't," Duane said sharply, regaining full control over his stern voice. "Someone who rules the world doesn't get bombed. If you truly ruled the world, then you would know *everything* that's happening."

"No, that's like assuming the CEO of a company knows the janitor's schedule. The person at the top can't possibly know everything that's going on inside the building."

"Chris, you're not understanding. Me and those men out there who are willing to sacrifice their lives for you," Duane said, pointing toward the hallway where guards roamed, "We don't see you as a CEO, or even a leader. We see you as *God*."

The word tickled Chris. He'd never been called God before, but dammit, he certainly felt like it on plenty of occasions. Toying with lives like a puppeteer pulling strings. Making things go boom in the night, causing people to drop dead, exposing the ugliness that lay dormant within innocent souls, and turning that same horridness into a weapon of war.

"God?"

Duane nodded in silence. "It's wrong to think of anyone like that."

"Are you having some sort of come-to-Jesus moment?"

"I don't know what's going on with me, honestly. I haven't felt like myself since I received this phone call. It's like I'm living in a dream. A nightmare."

"Is 'karma' really the reason you don't want to save your mother?"

"All Martin Briar was trying to do was save his mother. Then we killed her. And now this has happened to me."

"The world doesn't work like that. Your mother would have come down with her cancer regardless of what we did to Briar's mom."

"We don't know that." Duane spoke with the most authority that Chris had seen in years.

"Do you have a problem with me?"

"No, of course not. I don't have a problem with *you,* I have a problem with the things we've done—the things *I've* done. You forget that you're the one in the unique position. You have nothing to lose. You killed your wife for this life. Your daughter hates you. Your actions no longer have an emotional effect on you, if they ever did to begin with."

"So now you think you're better than me?"

"That is *not* what I said. Our situations are just . . . different."

"You haven't had a single thought like this the entire time we've worked together. And that's been fifty years, in real time."

"I have. I just buried it all. This has brought these feelings to the surface, and now I don't know what to do with them. I've killed with my own hands, authorized mass executions and have been by your side for every decision you've made in leading this organization. All to kill people that have done me no harm. People who were just trying to live their lives before this war ever started."

"*THESE PEOPLE SPEND EVERY DAY PLOTTING MY DEATH!*" Chris snarled, spittle flying from his lips like a spray bottle. "They've killed us, we've killed them, it's a *war,* for fuck's sake! Are you a Road Runner sympathizer now? Is Strike brainwashing you down in the basement?"

"Of course not. I just need some time away – my mind is too occupied to focus on the things we need to do. I want to step away *for* the Revolution. They deserve me at my best, and that's just not something I can give right now."

Chris crossed his arms that had been trembling with hot rage, brows furrowing as his eyes bore into Duane across the desk. They sat in silence for what might have been an entire minute, Duane keeping his gaze to the floor.

"Fine," Chris said. "Go home, take all the time you need. Come back refreshed when you feel ready."

Duane raised his head and met Chris's gaze with a cocked eyebrow. "That's it?"

"What do you want from me?"

"I thought for sure you'd throw me in the basement, or maybe even shoot me right here in the office. At the very least, deny my request."

"Am I really seen as that big of a monster?" Chris asked.

"You're ruthless," Duane replied, matter-of-fact.

Chris frowned and leaned back in his chair. "I'm sorry you felt you couldn't bring this up to me sooner. You are my closest confidant, and your loyalty has never wavered. A lot of our success is thanks to your hard work behind the scenes. I can't deny you a simple request like this. I think you've taken one vacation since we started working together. Though the timing is unfortunate, and it puts a lot more on my plate—I don't trust another soul with the work you do. If this is what you need to do, then you must."

Duane stood up, his face pinched into confusion. "Thank you, Chris. I don't know what to say."

Chris raised his bony, fragile hand. "You don't need to say anything. We'll be here when you're ready to come back. Just promise me you'll stay in touch."

"Absolutely. And if I'm feeling up to it, I might see about doing some work while I'm out there."

"I can see you sipping piña coladas on the beach, plotting how to deploy these bombs."

This drew a soft laugh from Duane, who stuck out his hand to Chris. "Maybe you'll come join me."

"I've never been one for sunshine. Why do you think I chose

this place for my mansion?"

"Fair enough."

"Take our jet, relax on your flight, and please get your mind cleared. We'll all be thinking of you."

"Thanks again, Chris, really. This is so generous."

"Get out of here before I change my mind."

Duane grinned and nodded to Chris before turning to leave the office, closing the door behind him.

Chris stared at the ceiling and let out a long exhale, completely overwhelmed for the road ahead.

2

Chapter 2

Martin walked through the sand, a cold Mai Tai in hand, the ocean water rushing in miniature waves up to his ankles before falling away. He was on the northern shore of Crooked Island, a small Bahamian paradise an hour flight south from Nassau.

He had arrived four days ago, having fled Denver immediately after finding his mother slaughtered in their home. He had caught a flight to Miami, the furthest destination available when he arrived at the airport. After spending a couple of days in Miami, dragging his depression up and down the crowded beaches, he decided a small island would make his trip more enjoyable.

Crooked Island provided him the sense that he was in a whole new world, a floating mass of picturesque land where there were no such things as Revolters or Road Runners (except for the two Road Runners trailing him like secret service agents in the background). With a population of 400 and minimal tourists, Martin had the beach to himself most of the time, and today was no exception.

He used his time to reflect on the life he had left behind in

Denver, and all that he had been through over the past month. Not a day passed where he didn't think of Izzy, her body finally resting in peace after two decades in the bottom of a lake. His mother, Marilyn, had encouraged that he take this wild journey with the Road Runners, one that may have led to her very death.

Numerous times each day, Martin had to fight away the thoughts of Chris Speidel and how badly he wanted to wedge a machete through the old man's throat. Chris had turned his world upside down after Martin wandered back into his fake antique shop, falling into a trap that led him to this exact moment, alone on the beach in the middle of nowhere.

He wasn't sure if he had fallen into his old habits of alcoholism, but he certainly enjoyed the numbing sensation all of the rum on this island provided. He felt out of touch with reality, as if Izzy, his mother, and Chris never existed. Never mind Sonya, who the mere thought of turned Martin into a crying, hysterical teenager.

They were all in his past where they'd stay, minus Chris. That brainwashing lunatic surely wouldn't rest until he had Martin dead or in his possession. But they'd never find him on this island while he plotted the next steps of his life.

The Road Runners weren't going to give up their relentless pursuit of him running for the commandership when he returned to the U.S. The thought of taking on such a heavy responsibility disturbed Martin. He lacked leadership experience and had only been an official Road Runner for a little more than a week.

He'd eventually call over the two men who followed him around all day. They dressed like tourists, blending into the background whenever Martin took his long walks on the beach, or sat down at the local bar. He had pulled out his phone to make a call before leaving Miami for the island, but realized he had no one to call, neither personal or professional.

Bill and Julian were dead, and Commander Strike might have been dead, for all anyone knew, trapped inside the walls of Chris's mansion on the other side of the world, leaving the organization with no actual leader.

It's not my problem, he reminded himself. *I don't owe a thing to these people. Sure, they helped me obtain the cure for my mother, but where were they when Chris slipped in and killed her? They tried to get me to kill the only woman I've loved since Lela. Why should I bend over backwards to help them?*

The whole situation made him feel like he needed a hot, steamy shower. What bothered him was how they expected him to be honored by such a request to lead the Road Runners, as if he should jump at the opportunity. He didn't even know what the job entailed. Would he have to move to a different city? What exactly did he have to do on a daily basis? How many lives were affected by his decisions? How far did his control even go? What happened to his life after the two-year term?

If he could leave the world of time travel behind forever after serving his term, he'd fly back right now and start campaigning. But they surely wouldn't allow someone who served in the highest office of the organization to simply disappear into the night like they never existed.

He had many questions that needed answers before he considered running, because as of right now, he still toyed with the idea of finding a way to slip away from the two Road Runners tailing him. Vanishing to a new country—perhaps in a different year—and never looking back. He even considered just walking into the ocean and letting the water take his body where it may.

But you're a Warm Soul, or have you forgotten? It's your destiny *to kill Chris. No one else can. If you can't see the writing on the walls, then you need to open your eyes.*

Martin tipped back the last of his drink, his fingertips and face turning numb. He started back toward the house he had rented, a beachfront property that cost him $400 per day to rent, hardly putting a dent in his bottomless bank account.

It was time to make a much-needed phone call, one he had been putting off for too long. He pulled his cell phone out and dialed the name he never thought he'd type.

It rang four times to an unknown location. *He could be anywhere in the world,* Martin thought.

Just as he was about to give up, a man answered. "Hello?" the voice asked, both familiar and unfamiliar at the same time. Martin's stomach sunk at the sound, and he was suddenly dizzy with nostalgia.

"Daniel?" Martin replied, knowing very well it was his brother on the line, but wanting to test his voice now that a lump had swelled within his throat.

"Martin . . . this is a surprise. Is something wrong?"

"What? I can't call my loving brother to see how he's doing?"

"Okay," Daniel replied, his voice dripping with confusion, panic, and a bit of curiosity. "How long has it been?"

"Well, I haven't seen you since 1996. Did Mom ever tell you we had a funeral for Izzy after they found her body in the lake?"

"She did."

"Oh, well thanks for calling to check on me."

Stay calm, Martin told himself, but his other inner voice got the better of him. *Fuck this guy, don't ever forget what he did to you. Drag this call out and make him as uncomfortable as possible.*

Martin smiled at this thought, kicking the sand beneath his feet while an ocean breeze rushed through his graying hair.

"I'm sorry, it's complicated," Daniel said.

"Complicated? Why? Because you *fucked* my wife?"

The line fell deathly silent, the gentle waves the only thing Martin could hear.

"How did you find out?" Daniel asked, his voice deflated.

"Hmmm, Mom must have not had the chance to tell you that Lela's in prison. Did you know that?"

"Prison?!" Daniel gasped, sounding genuinely surprised. "What the hell for?"

"For murdering Izzy. The same night you fucked her. You don't even know what happened, do you?"

"What?! No. I left. Izzy went missing and I already had so much guilt. The emotions were too much, so I packed my things and drove across the country."

Hearing this sent chills down Martin's back. Had he not just done the same thing? Is that not why he was on Crooked-fucking-Island in the middle of the Caribbean? He and Daniel were clearly cut from the same cloth if this is how they handled problems at home.

"Izzy knew what you and Lela had done that night. She was in middle school, for God's sake—she wasn't some oblivious child. Did you two even think this through before you started making my wife moan in the room right next door to my daughter?"

Silence.

Martin continued on. "Izzy came out of her room after you left and called out Lela for what had happened. They got into a big fight, and it ended with Lela chucking a frying pan at Izzy. It hit her in the head and she died on the spot."

Martin wanted to let these words linger, remaining silent as he waited for Daniel to reply. It might have been ten seconds or ten minutes that passed before Daniel spoke. Martin would never know as his body tensed with steaming rage.

"I don't know what to say, Marty."

"Don't call me Marty. You've lost that right."

"I'm sorry. None of this was my intent. It was a bad lapse in judgment. I was young and dumb."

"Well, it affected so many lives. I hope you realize that. I've been suffering through depression for the last two decades, drinking myself within an inch of my life. Have you ever put a gun in your mouth, little brother?"

Martin knew Daniel hated when he called him 'little brother', which is exactly why he said it. *Fuck him.*

"I'm sorry, Martin. Really. I don't know what you want me to say."

"Mom's dead." Martin decided this would be a good time to drop that bomb.

"What do you mean *dead*?" Daniel gasped, all the life returning to his voice.

"She died earlier this week. Her body is being cremated and the ashes are being delivered to me."

"What? Where are you? What's going on? How did she die?" Now he spoke with the urgency of a teenage girl telling her friends about her crush.

"How long has it even been since you last spoke with her?"

"It's been a month or so. That's about how often we talked, though."

"Did you even know she had Alzheimer's?"

"She had told me she thought she might have it. But I never heard back, so figured nothing of it."

"Son of the year. You are impressive. Well, it was very advanced and it finally took her."

Martin had no intent on sharing the actual truth. The truth wasn't believable and would take hours to explain how they had all arrived to this exact point. And Daniel didn't deserve hours from Martin. Never.

"She probably forgot who you were, let alone remember to call you," Martin said.

"I need to come home. I'll catch the next flight."

"Oh, now you want to get involved. Save it. I'm handling things just fine. You keep living your life."

Martin was dying to ask Daniel where he lived, what he did for a career, and if he had a family. He was sincerely curious to know what kind of life his little brother had carved out for himself. But asking him would show that he cared, so he pushed the questions to the back of his mind.

"I'm coming home," Daniel declared as if no one could stop him.

"You can come home, but that's not where I am, and that's not where Mom's ashes are being sent. You don't even know where we live in Denver."

"I can find out."

"Good for you. Do whatever you need."

"Tell me where you are, dammit!" Daniel snarled, and Martin pictured his brother's face turning bright red. The thought made him snicker.

"I'm in the Bahamas."

"What the hell do you mean? Mom dies and you take a vacation?"

"It's not like that. I just . . . had to get away."

"Real rich coming from you after all the accusations of

calling *me* the bad son. You're so full of shit—"

"I'll explain another time, maybe in another life. Until then, enjoy the rest of your life."

Martin hung up the phone, arms still shaking with anger.

He stormed off the beach, dashing across the sand like an angry crab, and barging into his house where he'd have a drunken crying session for the next hour.

3

Chapter 3

"What are we doing with Briar?" Councilwoman Murray asked her colleagues. Her eyes drooped over a notepad, gray hair twisted into a swaying ponytail. They had gathered in their New York office, pressure mounting from the Road Runner community as they needed an actual leader for guidance in these trying times.

"His mother was just murdered, give the man a break," Councilman Uribe said, his dark brown eyes gazing at Murray. Uribe served as the Chief Council, the leading member of this group of seven unofficial leaders of the organization. He had served on the Council for the last forty years, twenty as the Chief, where he presided over all debates brought to their attention.

"I understand, but we don't exactly have the luxury of time right now," Councilwoman Murray fired back. "We are running around like headless chickens." She had never been a fan of Uribe, the two clashing on nearly every decision.

The Council was loosely structured after the United States Supreme Court. Members were appointed by commanders as positions opened. All terms were lifetime, but seeing as time travelers could essentially live as long as they'd like, most councilors bowed out after twenty years or so of service. The Council served as the only real checks and balances against the commandership, able to overturn any decision made by a commander by having a simple majority vote.

However, it was rare for them to get involved with a commander's decision, seeing as a commander represented the population of Road Runners, no matter how controversial. They did not get involved with Strike's decision to attempt an assassination on Sonya Griffiths, but did intervene when Julian Caruso found himself thrust into the position of commander and promptly authorized the bombing of Chris Speidel's Alaskan mansion. That particular day might go down as the most chaotic in the history of the organization, and the Council had no choice but to pump the brakes on such a drastic decision by a freshly inaugurated commander, one who had not been elected, but rather succeeded due to Strike's capture.

Everything about that situation had felt slimy as they voted unanimously to halt the bombs. Julian proceeded anyway, and the rest of the story was history. In the days since, more evidence rose to the surface that uncovered Julian's secret operation to overthrow the commandership and put himself in the position of power. They had traced the history of Julian's tracking device, finding a couple of trips to Chris's mansion, one that included him going inside the mansion. The timing aligned with the random—at the time—release of Road Runners from Chris's control. From there, it wasn't difficult to figure out that he had negotiated with their sworn enemy to exchange Commander Strike for the prisoners.

"We haven't even decided how *we* want to proceed with

our government," Councilman Pierre said, stroking his pencil mustache. He was the newest addition to the Council, and the youngest at the age of 38, now serving in his seventh year.

"He's right," Uribe said. "Julian exposed a major flaw in our system for succession to the commandership."

"Not to mention he *murdered* Bill," Pierre said. "Assuming we don't have any more murderers in our organization, our current system is fine. He was being impatient, if you ask me. He could have had an easy go at the commandership in the next election. That's why we only have two-year terms, to keep the ideas fresh and ensure that no one settles too comfortably into their position of power."

The room fell silent, the topic still a sensitive matter. Julian's actions were one thing, but the biggest fault was the fact that someone like Julian had made his way into the Road Runners to begin with. Even for an organization with millions of people across the world, each holding strongly to their opinions, nothing like a murder had ever been reported. It was simply something the Road Runners did not do.

"I've said it time and time again," Councilwoman Lewis said from the opposite end of the table, brushing back her strawberry blonde hair before throwing her hands in the air. "We need to put caps on membership. Our population has soared, but our resources and government have not. It's all about scaling, and that's something we have never done in our history. My proposal is to break our continent into regions and appoint separate, regional governments to run things."

The Council also held the power to create laws for the organization. Globally, the Road Runners were divided into different governments across each continent and had no sort of international leader, although they did convene twice a year to make sure priorities were aligned.

"Lewis, you've been calling for regions for years and no one has ever sided with you," Murray said. "It's not going to happen."

"Then what's your solution? Nothing, like always?" Lewis snapped.

"Stop it right now!" Uribe barked. "All of this bickering will get us nowhere. Lewis, the issue we run into with regions is trying to figure out how it will all work. We'd have to lay out the initial groundwork and rules."

"But we wouldn't—and that's the point," Lewis said. "We create regions and let each region decide how to approach things for their population."

"That only takes us down the dark road of the government structure used in many countries across the world," Murray said, much more reserved. "Eventually, it will all lead to local governments: states, counties, cities. Just a bunch of power-hungry fools clamoring over themselves to get ahead and push their agendas. When that many people get involved with power, it leads to corruption. Road Runners are still human beings, don't forget that."

"Corruption like Julian Caruso?" Lewis asked, burning a glare across the table to Murray. "Fear is not a reason to *not* do something. Don't feed me all of this bullshit about how it will spiral out of control. *We* are still in control over this continent. We already have regional chapters who run things smoothly."

"Under *our* guidance," Murray said. "*Not* through their own power."

Councilwoman Thrasher cleared her throat. "I'm willing to vote with you, Lewis," she said shyly, dropping her gaze to the table, fidgeting with her ring-covered fingers. "We need something new, and this just might be it."

"And what has changed your mind?" Murray demanded.

"Our current state. I've thought this over plenty. Toyed with the idea of developing a congress, but it's too messy. Maybe we can discuss having a separate election for the lieutenant commander instead of letting the commander decide who fills that role. I don't know, but we need *something,* especially with our growing population, and we're beyond the point of putting caps on membership. Even if we halted any new members from joining for the next five years, our membership will continue to grow through childbirths, and we'd still be outbalanced to govern all of North and Central America."

"Those are all good ideas to discuss," Uribe boomed with complete authority. The bright lights of their chambers gleamed off the growing bald spot on top of his head. "If you recall, though, my question was about Briar. We can discuss these matters tomorrow, but we have to figure out the plan for Briar and the election."

"Two weeks," Murray said. "He's in the Bahamas all by himself, surely he'll be ready to come home in two weeks and we can start the election process."

Lewis shook her head, another common clasher with Murray, despite the two being best friends outside of the walls of the Council.

"Anyone oppose or have a different thought?" Uribe asked.

Everyone sat in silence as Uribe scribbled notes on a pad of paper. "Okay, let's put it to a formal vote. In two weeks we will have Martin Briar brought back to the country and will begin the election. Election preparation typically takes another two weeks, so we can plan for election night exactly four weeks from now, let's say November 19, 2019. All in favor?"

All Council members said, "Aye."

"All opposed?"

Silence.

"That settles it. We'll announce the election date tomorrow to the Road Runner population and allow any candidates to begin the nomination process and campaigning immediately. We also must inform Briar so that he knows to not get too comfortable. This session is adjourned."

Uribe plucked the glasses off his face and tossed them on the table before he stood and left the room, the other members breaking into casual conversation as if they had not just had a heated debate. They all shared the common desperation of getting a new commander elected as soon as possible. Not one of them enjoyed the responsibility of guiding the organization while it lacked a leader.

Little did they know the one month window of time would be plenty for Chris to interject and cause a new wave of chaos never anticipated.

4

Chapter 4

Chris wanted to wait—he really did—for Duane to return before moving forward with any of their previously discussed plans. But his lifelong advisor was gone without a set return date. And if he had to sit around one more day in this mansion plotting out the next steps, he might actually snap. That would be catastrophic for everyone.

Duane offered up a name he thought might be a good replacement while he was on leave, longtime soldier Sherman Wilkes, a brainwashed man who lived for the sole reason of shooting Road Runners.

"Sherman won't challenge any of your thoughts," Duane had explained. "But he knows our systems and can assist you with anything that might arise."

Chris didn't want to call this mindless robot into his office, but it was time. He needed to broadcast a live stream into the Road Runners' programming network, and had no clue of how to do so. Sherman did.

He pressed his skeletal finger on the intercom button. "Sherman Wilkes, please report to my office immediately. Thank you."

Chris rapped his thumbs on his desk while he waited. He knew all of his soldiers well, directly recruiting each and every one of them to his team, but it had been so long since he'd had the chance to check in with them, swamped with these trying times of constant, difficult decisions.

Heavy footsteps clapped from the hallway, approaching the office, the floor creaking and whining as the door swung open and revealed the behemoth of a man known as Sherman Wilkes. He towered at just a couple inches under seven feet, with broad shoulders that could break through a brick wall, and a jaw so thick that it could certainly absorb thousands of fists. Sherman wore his dirty blond hair in a buzz cut, his piercing green eyes immediately locking with Chris.

"Good afternoon, sir. Are you in need of assistance?" Sherman asked in his mindless baritone.

If Chris had a human soul, he might feel bad for what he had done to these people. When they had met, Sherman was a gentle giant who enjoyed playing cards with friends and sharing a good laugh over a glass of scotch. But after a hurricane in Florida had taken his entire life and family with it, Sherman fell into dark times, in need of intervention and guidance.

Chris pulled him out of the darkness, and within six months, had himself a dedicated soldier, ready to jump at any command.

"Good day, Sherman, how have things been?" Chris asked. The least he owed the man was some small talk after what he'd been through.

"Very good, sir, thank you for asking. How can I help you?"

Good boy, Chris thought. He had hypnotized these soldiers

into staying focused on their cause, their minds unable to be distracted. This instance was no different; Sherman was here to serve.

"I'm needing to broadcast myself to the Road Runners' network. Do you know how to get me in there?"

"Yes, sir. Duane has shown me everything."

"Just curious, how long ago did he start teaching you all of this?"

Sherman kept a stern expression, but looked up to the ceiling, a robot's apparent way of thinking. "About a week ago."

Duane, you sly dog. You had this planned all along.

Chris wanted to get upset, but Duane had covered his bases, leaving as smooth of a transition as possible.

"I see. Do you need to use my computer?" Chris asked, pushing himself away from the desk.

"Yes, sir."

Sherman shuffled his tree trunk legs around the desk and crouched over the computer, the mouse and keyboard miniature in his giant hands. His expression never changed, remaining laser-focused on the screen that splashed blue light across his pale face. He clicked around for a couple of minutes before standing up and taking a step back, holding an arm out for Chris to return to his place.

His screen showed a new software open, revealing a livestream of the Road Runners' network, currently featuring a news broadcaster updating the status of their precious Commander Strike, but a 'Breaking News' side bar scrolled along the bottom, announcing a future date for their election.

Chris smirked, proud to be throwing a wrench into their organization just weeks before they were set to elect their new leader.

Divide and conquer, he reminded himself, a basic, yet complex strategy he and Duane had been discussing for the past several months, but now ready with the proper ammunition to carry out the plan. *Pit all of these people against each other, and I can swoop right in and appeal to those who start having doubts about the Road Runners.*

Chris let out a childish giggle, his senses throbbing at the thought of ending his enemies' existence once and for all.

"Just click on the green button when you're ready to go live," Sherman said. "Wait about five seconds for our feed to override theirs—you'll see it there on the left. Once you see your face you can start talking. The same button will turn red, and you click on that when you're done broadcasting."

"Perfect."

Chris sat back in his chair and wheeled forward, sliding on a headset as he liked his voice to project as clearly as possible, while providing a solid noise-cancellation environment. He cleared his throat and ensured he was facing the screen straight on before clicking on the green button to start the broadcast.

It lagged, and the anticipation swelled within Chris, a sensation he hadn't felt in many years. The Road Runners' broadcast cut out and was replaced with Chris's grinning face.

Damn I'm looking old, he thought, not having looked in a mirror in months.

"Good evening, my lovely Road Runners. I hope I'm finding you well today."

He paused, and always imagined the people at the Road Runners office scrambling in a panic as they tried to figure out how the hell he hacked into their system once again.

"We're at an interesting time in this ongoing war, wouldn't you say?" Chris continued, maintaining a wide grin while he spoke into the camera. "What a time to be alive! I have your only leader in my basement, and you people are floundering with what to do next. It truly brings warmth to my heart."

He paused, poured himself a glass of water from a canteen on the edge of his desk, and took two long gulps. He didn't care for dramatics, unless dealing with the Road Runners. Having their undivided attention aroused him in a way unmatched by anything else.

"To celebrate this delightful occasion, I want to make an offer to you, Road Runners. My ask is simple, and if interested, please send someone to my mansion to discuss the logistics. I promise you will not be harmed.

"My offer is to release Commander Strike back to you—in good condition—in exchange for Martin Briar. Bring me Briar, and you can all return to your happy little lives with Commander Strike to lead the way. I have been betrayed by Mr. Briar, and I want nothing more than to have a *word* with him in person."

Chris paused and ran through his same antics of sipping water—something he didn't actually need to survive.

"I will give you fine people seventy-two hours to make a decision. Like I said, if interested, come to the mansion and we can work out the details. If I hear nothing in three days, Commander Strike will be publicly executed on this live stream for you all to watch. It's her blood on your hands. Choose wisely."

Chris leaned back in his seat and stared into the camera, trying to peer into the souls of those millions of Road Runners watching around the world. For the first time in his life, he actually felt like a villain. He'd done plenty of bad things during his time, unforgivable actions that normal people would never think of. But he'd never delivered such a gut-wrenching ultimatum before. He had always played the long game, believing that "one day" the opportunity would arrive for him to make a move and send the Road Runners into complete chaos.

Through all the years of strategizing, refining, and planning, that "one day" had now arrived. He had just tipped over the first in a long line of dominoes, starting a chain reaction that would lead to his ultimate goal of gutting the Road Runners of their unity and common sense, characteristics that had kept them such a sound and strong unit in the past, bending but never breaking at all of the difficulties Chris had thrown their way.

With one brief announcement, Chris Speidel would manage to bring the Road Runners to their knees. He had released a lone drop of his poison—his negativity—into their organization, and in a matter of weeks it would spread like a virus until some felt they had no choice but to leave the Road Runners behind.

Chris leaned forward, stopped the streaming video, and stood up while howling laughter that echoed throughout the mansion, Commander Strike hearing it from the silence of the basement three levels below.

5

Chapter 5

The Council convened an hour after Chris had made his announcement to the entire Road Runner community. They murmured to each other as they entered their private chambers underground, many looking like they had just seen a ghost.

Chief Councilman Uribe entered the room, his wide frame commanding attention and respect, and all chatter immediately ceased as he crossed to the center seat of the oval table. He sat down, pulled out a notepad and pen, and began scribbling like an angry child upset about having to finish their homework before going out to play.

No one said a word as the room remained in a deafening silence for an entire five minutes while he scrawled notes, flipped a page, wrote some more, then flipped another page. When he was done, he tossed his pencil down after turning over the notepad facedown. He rubbed his eyes and temples before planting his elbows on the table and clasping his hands together under his chin, leaning forward as he stared around the table.

They all met his gaze and looked away with relief when he

passed on to the next person. The tension was thicker than Los Angeles smog during the morning rush hour.

He took a long breath, inhaling deep like a yoga instructor, exhaling through his mouth like a vape smoker after a long hit.

"Excuse my language, but what the *fuck* are we supposed to do about this?" he asked, and immediately held up a stiff, thick finger. "Before anyone speaks, I need you to know that no bickering will be tolerated like our last session. This is a crisis, folks. I'm all for a healthy debate, hell, call it an argument if you like, but no bickering like schoolchildren. No personal attacks, no dirty looks across the table. If you do any of that, see yourself outside and come back when you're ready to be an adult. Am I clear?"

Uribe was typically a calm, level-headed man who rarely displayed emotion, but in this particular instance, he showed why he was chosen as the Chief Councilman, putting his authority on the table for everyone to see, and dare to challenge.

The councilors nodded in silence as they looked around at each other.

"This is a highly sensitive decision. I expect strong arguments for both sides of this issue, and you should expect that, too. This is a lose-lose situation for us, and either way we choose will leave a certain group of our population highly upset. There is not a correct decision in this scenario, and the sooner you all understand that, the sooner we can arrive to a peaceful, unified decision. Now, that all said, who would like to go first?"

They stared around the table, most turning their attention to Councilwoman Murray, who seemed to always speak up first. But she offered nothing, returning a gaze to Uribe.

"Do the Bylaws help us in any way with this choice?" Councilman Pierre asked.

The Bylaws were the Road Runners' version of a constitution, rules written in place with amendments added since their initial conception as an organization. The Council's responsibility was to guide the Road Runners under their fairest interpretation of the Bylaws.

"I'm afraid not," Uribe said. "Our founders never bothered making rules based on our commander being held hostage by an enemy. The only Bylaw that applies to this situation is regarding the death of a fellow Road Runner: 'No Road Runner shall ever be executed or enslaved for any reason whatsoever. Imprisonment or banishment is only allowed if a Road Runner has committed treason against the organization."

"This isn't an execution or enslavement," Pierre replied, a thin eyebrow cocked in confusion.

"How is turning Briar over to Chris Speidel *not* an execution?" Uribe asked. "Or best case scenario, enslavement? If we hand him over, it's his blood on our hands. We don't have to do this, and according to the Bylaws, this would be a direct violation, in my opinion. Commander Strike is already in his possession, kidnapped right from under our noses. At this point, there's nothing we can do. The rescue teams have come up with nothing for getting inside that mansion. Strike is at the mercy of Chris."

"Couldn't you argue that doing nothing to rescue Strike is a direct violation of the Bylaws?" Councilwoman Murray asked. "We are knowingly *not* taking a chance to get in there and rescue her, essentially choosing to let her die."

"This is where the law is up for interpretation," Uribe said calmly. "Thoughts?"

"I think we have to save Briar," Councilwoman Lewis said. "We can't turn someone that valuable over to Chris. He'll turn right around and use him against us."

"I don't even know anything about the guy," Councilwoman Thrasher said. "What's the big deal?"

"He's a Warm Soul," Lewis explained. "The only Warm Soul we've ever had on this side of the ocean, and quite frankly, our best hope for taking out Chris and ending this war."

"Does the public know this?" Thrasher asked. "I'm just trying to view our eventual decision from all angles."

"I don't believe so," Uribe said. "He hasn't announced his candidacy yet, so he's still very much an unknown player within our organization."

"Well, I certainly didn't know this," Thrasher said. "All the times we've discussed Briar and *that* was never mentioned. I thought we were just playing nice for the guy because of what happened to his mom. But this . . . this changes everything."

"Would it be appropriate for us to announce his candidacy on his behalf?" Councilman Ryan asked. Ryan was the second-most junior councilor. "Even if it's a brief press release, we can announce him as a Warm Soul and the newest candidate."

"Who's endorsing this guy?" Thrasher asked.

"Europe and Asia. And I believe South America is on board, too," Uribe explained. "The election is basically his."

"We need to make this decision in the membership's best interest," Murray said. "Tension is already high among those who feel nothing is being done to save Strike. Rumor is, a group of people are forming their own coalition to try and break her out."

"That's suicide," Thrasher said.

"I know," Murray continued. "But these are the things we have to keep in mind. If we decide to save Briar and leave Strike to be publicly executed, those people will lose their minds. They might even take their anger to the streets. Does anyone have a good pulse on exactly what percentage of our membership is hell-bent on saving Strike?"

They all turned their heads to Councilman Ryan, his face scrunched in deep thought as he ran his hands through his light brown hair, for he studied membership trends and issues. "It's impossible to measure the extremes of this matter," he said. "Overall, ninety-eight percent of the population supports rescuing Strike—that's the general number, essentially an approval rating. When asked if they support rescuing her, even if it means other Road Runners will be sacrificed, that number falls to fifty-two percent."

"She won her election in a landslide," Uribe said. "Seventy-two percent of the votes. She's popular and still remains a key figure in the eyes of the public."

"And she's certainly more popular than Briar," Murray added. "If we rescue her, we don't have to hold a special election."

"So you're suggesting that if we get her back, Briar becomes irrelevant?" Uribe asked, his voice borderline accusatory.

"Please don't put words in my mouth. All I said was that we won't need a special election next month as currently planned."

"Martinez, you haven't said anything," Uribe said, turning his attention away from Murray.

Councilman Martinez was typically reserved, and this heated discussion was no different. He sat with his hands folded on the table, a blank, emotionless gaze as he looked around to his fellow councilors.

"I think our choice in this debate is a simple one," Martinez said, taking a moment to clear his throat. "*We* don't make the decision. Let the community vote on what we should do."

"An immediate special vote?" Murray gasped. "Impossible. We only have seventy-two hours."

Martinez raised his thin hand in silence. "It's more than possible. We can set up a ballot – it's a simple question with two possible answers. We can have the poll up and running within two hours, we just have to push the word, keep a scrolling message at the bottom of our network, send out emails, text messages, social media . . . we have plenty of ways to get the word out over the next twenty-four hours."

"It does make good political sense," Uribe added.

"Indeed it does. Quite frankly, I don't think this is within our purview to make this decision. I understand that the Bylaws state that we're in charge and can act with complete power under the circumstances, but should the seven of us be the ones to decide the future for millions of people?"

"I don't feel this decision will affect the people," Murray argued. "Sure, everyone has an opinion, but regardless of the choice we make, life will still continue on, either with a return to Strike's reign, or under a new leader after our election."

"I'm afraid it's not that black and white, Councilwoman," Martinez said. "This is the kind of topic that sparks pure rage. On one side we have people with a sworn loyalty to Commander Strike, and on the other, people who swear on our Bylaws like the Bible. That's not including the people who are genuinely split on the issue."

"Will any segment of our population act out in any way? Depending on the decision?" Pierre asked. "Do we have anything to reference in our history?"

"The election of 1978," Martinez said. "We were a much smaller organization back then, maybe a few thousand across the continent, but the election was so close the ballots had to be recounted three times."

"Three times?" Thrasher gasped.

"Yes. The first results came back with the decision in favor of Commander Collins by a whole six votes. The recount showed Commander Lincoln as the winner by two votes. A third and final recount was agreed upon, and ended up giving the election to Commander Collins by a heavily disputed three votes. It is still the closest election we've ever seen, and probably ever will see. The couple thousand people who had voted for Lincoln boycotted the organization for three months, refusing to carry out missions or have any involvement. Some ran to the Revolution, citing us as a corrupt organization. We got most of the boycotters back—it doesn't take long for sensible people to realize how slimy the Revolution is—and life continued as normal. My fear this time around is how many more members we have. We already have a group threatening to break out Strike on their own. What if there is a group on the opposite side wanting to bring Briar back home, or do anything to defend their interpretation of the Bylaws?"

"There could be riots," Thrasher said. "People taking it to the streets to protest."

"I like to think the Road Runners know better than to bring our issues into the public world," Uribe said. "That's one thing I know we've never had an issue with."

"This might be the tipping point, Chief," Martinez said. "People are already on edge, paranoid for themselves and their families. Combine that with something as traumatic as watching their own commander get battered like a piñata on live television – it's hard to say what the reaction will be."

"This is one option I want to come back to," Uribe said. "I

like it a lot. Is anyone in favor of saving Briar and sacrificing Strike?"

Councilman Ryan raised his hand slowly, but confidently. "I don't like the phrase 'sacrifice', but I do think what's best for the long run is to move forward. We lost Strike, and that's something we have to live with as an organization for the rest of our existence. A rescue mission will risk too many Road Runner lives. It's just not worth it for the remaining half of Strike's term."

Murray shook her head in disgust, but others nodded around the table. Uribe showed no emotion and continued writing on his notepad.

"I'm calling for a formal vote," Uribe announced. "We have three options: Strike, Briar, or let the people decide. Due to the sensitivity of this subject, we'll cast our votes anonymously, myself included, so that the public record will not know who voted for which option. Strike will be option number one, Briar two, and a deferment to people, three. Please write your vote on a piece of paper in the form of tally marks. You have five minutes to cast your vote and place it in our ballot box. Time begins now."

Before the advances of technology, this exact method was used by the Council to settle their votes, an old school action that Uribe brought out from the woodworks. Safety was key. Not that a Council member had ever been assassinated, but Uribe had no intent on being the Chief to oversee such a crime. They had no interest in making these swaying decisions for the organization, being in their positions to provide fair checks and balances. A vote of this nature could cause immediate death threats for any members of the Council if their votes reached the public.

He cast his vote and slid the paper into the drop box in the center of the table, waiting for the others to follow suit.

6

Chapter 6

Chris made his way down to the basement using the stairs. He could have taken his private elevator for a quicker trip, but decided now was probably a good time to mingle with the many soldiers who had stayed by his side. He might need them now, not quite sure how exactly the Road Runners planned to respond to his threat. Surely they had entered an instant state of chaos.

He hadn't visited Commander Strike in three days, and imagined she must be recovering from the last round of torture. They had tried everything from electric shocks to Chinese water torture, but she refused to give any information. Chris had given up, but authorized some new form of suffering every few days just for fun. It wasn't often that you got to welcome your sworn enemy with a twisted hospitality.

Knowing she wouldn't be in the basement for an extended time, Chris took a different approach to the ambiance, keeping the lights on full blast, compared to the dimness they had when fifty Road Runners were held prisoner. His goal was to keep her from sleeping easily, the brightness comparable to that of a sunny day on Miami Beach.

A guard sat behind a desk at the front of the deserted basement, Commander Strike a lone fish in the ocean of space that spanned a couple hundred yards. The guard stood when Chris opened the basement door, a sign of respect that he had been brainwashed into every soldier who worked under him. His muscles bulged as he saluted the old man.

"Good day, Mr. Reynolds," Chris greeted as he approached the desk. "How is our little butterfly today?"

"Good afternoon, sir," Reynolds said, meeting Chris with a confident stare. "Ms. Strike slept in late this morning, hasn't said a word since she woke up around eleven o'clock, and picked at the food we brought her for lunch."

"I see. I want us to take good care of our lovely commander over the next few days. No more pain, and I want her back in the best health possible. Turn the lights off at night for bedtime, take requests for what meals she would like to eat."

"I don't understand, sir."

"We're in a position to win this war, and it will require a healthy commander."

No matter what the Road Runners decided, Chris needed Strike back to full strength. If they agreed to turn in Briar, then they expected her back in good condition. He fully expected them to turn in Briar. He had only been a Road Runner for a few weeks. Why would they side with a man they barely knew over their own leader?

"Understood, sir. Is there anything we need to get ready for a potential release?"

"No, let's hold off on anything official. I want her ready just in case—we still don't know what will happen yet." Chris nodded before turning and shuffling toward Strike, sitting on the ground with her ankles shackled to a hook.

"Good afternoon, Commander," he said, her eyes slowly working their way up from his feet until she met his piercing blue gaze. She said nothing. "I thought you might like to know what's happening. I just got off a live broadcast to your little Road Runner network, and let's just say I've done something very naughty."

Chris giggled, waiting for a response, but Strike only watched him.

"Have a little fun, darling," he said, reaching down and squeezing her cheeks like a grandparent gushing over a baby. "I've made them an offer, and now we get to see what your lovely group really thinks of you. I gave them three days to decide if they want to exchange Briar for you. If they do, you can walk right out the door and I'll never bother you again. If they decide they value Briar instead, then you and I will be going live on television where I will personally execute you. Either way, I get to have a good time."

Strike shook her head, eyes brimming with a rage that she had so far managed to keep under control. "You're sick. One day you'll get what you deserve."

Chris grabbed his stomach and let out a howling laugh. "Oh, Commander, I think I've heard that exact threat three hundred times. I appreciate your determination, but get in the back of the line!"

"It's only a matter of time. You can't actually live forever. There are *prior* Keepers of Time, you do know that? They all eventually died."

"The Keeper has always been a member of the Revolution, and that is one thing that will never change."

"They said the Roman Empire would never fall. Everything

comes and goes. It may take longer for certain things to happen, especially with our time travel abilities, but everything ends."

"You are correct, Commander, but I'm afraid it's going to be *your* organization that ends. What do you think they will decide? Is it even a difficult decision?"

"They'll find a way to ensure both me and Martin are safe. We aren't afraid of your bullshit anymore."

"I love when you talk dirty to me." Chris bent over and planted a kiss on Strike's sweaty forehead. "Now, tell me, Commander, who do you honestly think they will choose? Pretend I have a gun to your head and you have to give me an answer. I can get a gun, if you'd like it to feel more realistic."

Chris made a pistol out of his first two fingers and pointed it at Strike's face. She scrunched her expression into a look of disgust, shaking her head.

"C'mon, Commander, flatter me. I'm merely curious."

She looked down to her shackled ankles, apparently giving the question serious thought.

"I think they'll choose Martin," she said flatly.

"Briar?!" Chris gasped. "You don't say. Why?"

"Martin has done nothing wrong. Therefore, turning him over to you would be considered treasonous against our organization."

"You people never stop amazing me. They would let their leader die over ethics? *Ethics*?!"

"You should try getting some. Being a good person might change your life."

"I *am* a good person," Chris said. "I've built this life for myself and have taken care of those who support me. I've never harmed anyone for the sake of pleasure—it's always a calculated reason, just like when I'll be killing you for the whole world to see."

"You're a psychotic dictator," Strike said calmly.

Chris giggled. "Oh, Commander, your flattery never gets old. Now, just so you know, I've authorized some changes for your care down here. No more torture. No more bright lights at bedtime. I want you relaxed and comfortable. Eat whatever you want, sleep in peace."

"Gotta get me all fattened up before killing me on TV? What a gentleman."

"Not the first time I've been called that, and it certainly won't be the last. All that said, is there anything I can do to make sure you're happy?"

Strike pursed her lips and looked to the ceiling before dropping her gaze to Chris. "Yes, one thing actually. If you could go fuck yourself and die, I'd like that a lot."

Laughter erupted from Chris, toppling him off-balance on his thin legs that looked more like sticks, his bony hands grasping his stomach. His face turned bright red as he gasped for breath. "Commander," he said in between breaths. "You must stop. Your humor is. . . contagious."

Chris shot a look behind him toward Reynolds, who had settled back behind the desk. "Isn't the Commander a hilarious woman?"

"Yes, sir," Reynolds called back, unimpressed.

Chris returned his attention to Strike. "I'm sure in another life you could've been a stand-up comedian. I really do hope your people choose to turn in Briar. A, he's what I really want, and B, you're just too much fun. I'd hate to see you leave this world."

"Then don't kill me. No one ever has to know. Send me into

the forest and I'll never come back."

Chris howled another laugh. "Commander, if you only knew how many times I've been made that offer. As if sending you into the Amazon is somehow a fair trade-off. Nice try, but I won't be postured, especially by Road Runner scum."

Strike spit a wad of saliva into Chris's face, hitting him square on the nose, while another clump dangled from his white eyebrow. He appeared stunned at first, but after wiping it off with his sleeve and examining the liquid, broke into another hysterical round of laughter.

"Oh, Commander, you're too precious."

Chris turned with nothing further to say, disappearing through the same door he had arrived, leaving Strike alone in the basement where she'd wait with sickening anticipation over the next three days.

7

Chapter 7

Chief Councilman Uribe stood behind a podium in the Council's chambers, the rest of the councilors watching him from across the room. A camera focused on him as an aide patted a light layer of makeup on his face.

"We're on in one minute," the cameraman called out, prompting Uribe to straighten his tie and pat his gray hair to ensure everything was in place. He took a deep breath and held it in his lungs for a few seconds before blowing it out through his lips.

The votes came back with a five to two decision in favor of their upcoming announcement, and the final step was to explain those results to the general public.

The cameraman held both hands in the air and started counting down from ten, one finger dropping with each passing second until he pointed to Uribe with a thumbs up.

"Good evening, Road Runners of North America, and to any others watching around the world," Uribe started, his speech now broadcasting live to millions of private streams across the globe. "As you know, Chris Speidel made us an offer to release

Commander Strike in exchange for Martin Briar. The Council has spent the last three hours discussing this and looking at the possibilities from all angles. It's been a trying day, and we appreciate your patience as we worked toward a decision.

"We had many disagreements, as you might expect, but one thing became clear that we agreed on: this is too delicate of an issue to let seven Road Runners decide. We will be launching an impromptu ballot later tonight where you can cast your vote. We want to hear from you, the people, and will let democracy decide our best course of action. Even though you'll only have twenty-four hours to vote, we encourage you to take time and seriously reflect on the question at hand. As I stressed to the Council, there is no right or wrong answer. Whichever way this goes will provide its own unique set of challenges for us moving forward. We are giving you twenty-four hours because we will need another day ourselves to ensure all the votes were collected fairly and are reflected correctly in the final count. With just under seventy hours until Chris Speidel moves forward with his agenda, we felt this was the best course of action.

"In about two hours, you will each receive a unique link to cast your vote. We will send the link to all means of communication we have available, but it will only let you cast one vote. I want to thank you in advance for partaking in this crucial decision for our organization. I look forward to returning to you tomorrow night to announce the results. Thank you."

Uribe held a stern expression to the camera until the cameraman waved his arms and yelled, "That's a wrap!"

The decision was officially set in stone, and Uribe felt a wave of relaxation flow throughout his body as he stepped away from the podium to return to the rest of the Council waiting for him.

"You looked good up there," Pierre said with a wide grin.

"Thanks. How did it go?"

"You delivered the message flawlessly. I can't imagine people getting too upset over this," Murray said with a nod.

"Great," Uribe replied. "Are we ready to head out for dinner?"

The Council had reserved a private dining room at Wolfgang's Steakhouse in New York City. They planned to eat and drink the night away after the horrendously stressful day, knowing the next twenty-four hours would swing the organization to new, uncharted territory.

"Let's get out of here," Martinez said, being the first to stand and leave the chambers.

* * *

They all agreed to spend the night in the office after wrapping up dinner. Thousands of dollars of wine flowed throughout the evening while hundred-dollar steaks were consumed without a care in the world.

Each of their offices came equipped with a pullout queen-sized mattress, providing ample comfort. The entire office that the Council called home was built to serve as an underground fort should the world above ever become destroyed. Hidden pantries housed a six-month supply of food for each Council member, while an entire room was dedicated to storing a mountain of bottled water.

The Council had a staff of assistants, each carefully chosen based on their age and gender, just in case the future responsibility of repopulating the world fell upon their shoulders. This same staff maintained the pantries to ensure no expired food remained in the building—the last thing they would need during a time of crisis was to deal with food-borne illnesses.

The Road Runners were planners, ready for the worst of any situation that arose, which made the events of the last twenty-four hours push the entire population out of their comfort zone. They had never planned for a scenario where their leader *and* both successors were unavailable to serve in their roles, and they certainly had no game plan for negotiating Road Runner lives with a known madman. After the dust settled from the upcoming vote, laws would be put in place to address these exact matters. The last thing any Road Runner would do is make the same mistake twice.

When they woke up the following morning, none of the councilors—who had studied everything throughout history—had a clue what would come in the days following the announcement. They already sensed a shift in attitude across the organization, but figured it was the natural ebb and flow of fresh blood and a new generation coming into their lives as time travelers.

A divide had begun, starting as subtly as a chip on a car's windshield, nearly invisible, but ready to expand with each passing day until a massive crack spread from side to side.

They met in their chambers as breakfast was served. Another long day waited, seeing as the polls wouldn't close until seven that night, exactly twenty-four hours after they had gone live for everyone to vote. The votes would come in by each country in North America, and with everything electronic, the Council would receive updated poll numbers at the top of every hour. They planned to keep close eyes on the results, trying to get ahead of the decision and have a fully prepared statement for Uribe to deliver later that night. They hoped it would be a landslide decision one way or another, but didn't hold their breath for that result, considering how split they had been among themselves.

The official population of Road Runners across North America was just under 4.8 million people, and by the time Uribe called for the first results of the morning, more than two million had already cast their votes overnight.

It was 10 A.M. when Uribe scanned over the polls on a special tablet synced with their voting software. "Roughly two million votes in," he announced to the Council. "As of now, fifty-two percent in favor of rescuing Strike, forty-eight in favor of Briar."

Councilman Martinez shook his head. "This is gross," he said. "This is essentially a vote for the commandership without people fully realizing it."

"What choice do we have?" Councilwoman Murray asked. "And it's not a vote for commander, it's a vote for the Bylaws and how the public interprets the laws. At least, I hope that's how they're viewing it."

"It's not a vote for commandership," Councilman Pierre said. "If it was, Briar would have no chance against Strike—no one even knows his name. These early results already tell us that people are voting based on the Bylaws."

"I agree," Uribe said. "Now, it looks like this isn't going to be easy on us. I was hoping for something a little more decisive, but if half the population is this undecided, I don't see one side pulling away. Let's dig in for the long haul today. We have nine hours until the polls close, plenty of time to draft up two different speeches in preparation for tonight. With that, we also need to plan for both outcomes. If Strike wins, how do we go about getting Briar delivered to Chris? Who is going to the mansion to have this discussion with Chris? And what will the hierarchy and structure look like if Strike assumes her role again?

"And if Briar wins, do we make a final attempt to break out Strike? Or do we let her go? People will have questions, and we need all the answers. We might want to have some of our staff reach out to the general public and see what issues are pressing their minds in this matter. That will help us prepare."

The Council nodded in agreement.

"How many votes are we expecting to be cast?" Council-woman Thrasher asked.

"I'd imagine close to four million," Pierre said. "We'll know in the next hour. If we see another 250,000 have voted, that trend will likely carry throughout the day. We did deliver this message around dinner time here on the east coast, and I'd assume many people wanted to sleep on their decision and make a sound vote today."

"Let's get started on everything I mentioned," Uribe said with authority. "It may sound like a long time, but these next nine hours will fly."

They had all wanted to speculate on the polls, make predictions, follow the trends, but Uribe had to keep them on track. They had a reputation as the most prepared segment of Road Runners, and he'd be damned if gossip would get in the way of that.

8

Chapter 8

The Council put their collective heads down and worked diligently over the next several hours. With each passing update, it was growing clear that the results wouldn't be finalized until the polls closed. The polls came in as follows:

11 A.M. had Strike pull ahead with a 55% to 45% lead

12 P.M. saw that lead shrink to 53% to 47%

1 P.M. brought them to their first tie of the day

2 P.M. Briar took his first lead, a slim margin of 51% to 49%

3 P.M. Strike regained control at 51% to 49%

4 P.M. Briar back in the lead at 52% to 48%

5 P.M. Briar still ahead 51% to 49%

When six o'clock rolled around, the results hadn't changed since their last check. Pierre had been correct with his projected vote total. They had 3.8 million votes counted with one hour to go, and the results still a virtual split, Martin Briar leading by an entire 30,000 votes.

They had spent all day tracking these numbers, writing speeches, making phone calls to ensure matters were in place for whatever decision was reached. Both speeches were crafted and finalized at three o'clock, and both were read over by Uribe. The speech for a Briar victory sent chills down his back, reminding him of a recently released speech transcript that President Nixon had just in case the moon landing had ended in failure and death.

Uribe didn't *want* to read either speech, and was dreading how close of a call this would be. The real question that rose to the surface was whether or not to share the final numbers, or leave it vague by simply announcing the winning result.

"How can we honestly be this divided?" Uribe asked as they waited for the final, decisive results at seven o'clock. "I've never seen anything like this."

"I hate to say it," Councilman Ryan said. "But I think Chris may have won the war. He backed us into a corner with no easy way out. He stuck a dagger right into the fabric of our organization."

"You're being dramatic," Councilwoman Murray said. "We always unite and move forward."

"This isn't normal," Ryan added. "Did none of your staffers share what they heard speaking with the public?"

Everyone looked around at each other in silence.

"You're either in the dark or afraid to admit the truth," Ryan continued, slightly snarling as he spoke. "Bad things are headed for us. I don't know where all of the rage has come from, but it's strong right now. People are threatening to leave the organization, burn buildings down, even kill in the name of Commander Strike."

"It's true," Councilwoman Lewis said. "I heard the opposite. People will be outraged if we hand over Briar, baffled that we would violate our own Bylaws, especially to give in to Chris's demands."

Uribe let out a long sigh, shaking his head. "These are trying times, but I believe we will prevail. We may be divided, but we're still united against Chris. I don't see how either result changes that fact. People aren't going to magically start liking Chris to spite us. Road Runners have always recruited intelligent individuals and free thinkers. A simple vote shouldn't make our people irrational all of a sudden."

"I agree," Murray said. "I think emotions are high, but no one is actually going to leave us. And if they do, they become an enemy to the organization where we can promptly take care of them."

Ryan shook his head, but kept any additional words to himself.

They reached the point in the night where there was nothing left to discuss, no speeches to write, no plans to prepare, only a time to wait. A thick cloud of tension hung over them in their underground chambers, and they had no idea of the current mood around the continent. The news coverage on their private network ran all day, full of tons of speculation and debates on what to do. They had watched it for an entire two minutes in the morning before deciding it was best to turn it off for a somewhat peaceful day.

The clock on the wall ticked past 6:30, and no one said a word for the next thirty minutes.

* * *

When seven o'clock struck, Uribe stood from the table and paced circles, fidgeting with his fingers, removing and replacing the wedding band that had left an indent on his ring finger.

Every hour throughout the day, a staffer had dropped in to inform Uribe that the voting software had successfully refreshed its data, prompting him to update the room with the results. Now they waited for the final confirmation.

When 7:03 struck, Pierre cried out, "What the hell is taking so long?"

"Relax," Ryan said, raising a hand. "The final vote takes an extra minute or so to calculate. The system goes back and sweeps every country for any straggling votes it may have missed, then does a recount to ensure the results we see are set in stone."

At 7:05 a young man with greasy black hair entered the room, his face and eyes exhausted. "The system has updated, and the final poll results have been uploaded for your review." The young man, who Uribe believed worked for Thrasher, disappeared back out the door.

"No matter what's on here, I want you all to know that I have full confidence in this group to maintain a peaceful future for our organization," Uribe said.

The tablet throbbed in his trembling hand. Uribe couldn't recall a time he had ever felt nervous since joining the Council, but there were apparently firsts for everything. He swiped his thumb across the screen, already loaded to show the poll results.

The others watched, eyes glued to his every movement.

He lay the tablet on the table before bringing it back to his eyes for a closer look. He skimmed over the screen, which showed nothing but a final vote count for each option, a time stamp, and a special asterisked message in big red letters that said FINAL.

"Our results are in, folks," Uribe said. "If you didn't think this was an important issue to our people, then think again. We topped 3.9 million votes, meaning nearly one million members did not cast a vote."

"That's the biggest voter turnout in the history of this organization," Ryan said.

"And each vote was worth it. I can't imagine this being any closer."

"So what speech are you going to deliver?" Murray asked, impatience dripping from each word. It was the nicest way of her asking him to hurry up and share the damn results.

Uribe looked around, as if paranoid they were being listened to. "I'm not going to say aloud, just for the sake of sensitivity." Instead, he placed the tablet face up on the table and slid it across to Murray. "Read it and pass it along. Let's keep this completely confidential until it's announced."

The answer made its way around the table while Uribe crossed the room to the podium to prepare for his upcoming speech.

9

Chapter 9

"Commander Strike was so close to killing that piece of shit and if they forget about that, we'll have to free her ourselves."

Stephen DeVito stood at the front of a room filled with thirty other Road Runners. They were underground, of course, and had been having these nightly meetings for the past week. They met under no official name, just a shared passion to rescue Commander Strike. Each night they discussed possible ideas to save their beloved commander.

Stephen had been a Road Runner for eighteen years, having lived through nine different commanders, and never seeing one of them make an actual attempt at taking Chris's life.

Until Strike.

This sparked a stronger passion than usual toward a commander, making her an instant favorite among those who sought justice for Chris Speidel's wicked ways. Everyone had their preference of what a commander should focus on. Some preferred them to strengthen the lives of Road Runners by allowing more missions and giving a sense of purpose to the population, others liked a commander who sought a peaceful end to the war with the Revolution. And then there were people like those gathering in the basement every night, believing the execution of Chris should be the only priority for the organization. They felt the Road Runners would forever be shackled to him as long as he existed, not allowed to fully grow into their unlimited potential. Chris was a monster with a Road Runner body count that made World War II look like a walk in the park.

Stephen had an imposing appearance, standing tall, wide, and a facial expression that seemed stuck somewhere between pissed-off and contemplative. He had lost his mother and grandmother directly at the hands of Chris, an event that sparked his thirst for revenge for the rest of his life. As long as Chris lived, he'd never experience joy. He wanted nothing more than to tear the old man apart, limb by limb, maybe even throw the bastard on a grill and eat him just to make certain that his body no longer existed.

"Whatever news is delivered tonight is great news," Stephen continued to his crowd of eager onlookers. He paced from left to right as he spoke and all eyes followed his every movement like a tennis match. "If the people vote for saving Strike—which they should—then our government will *finally* get off their ass and get her out of that hideous mansion. Who the fuck is Martin Briar, anyway? Has he ever posed a threat to Chris? He's just some nobody, disposable. We can make the sacrifice and never look back, because Strike will be too busy looking *forward*."

A few people clapped, but it was far from a resounding applause. They liked to get rowdy at the end of these meetings instead.

"And if the people vote to save this Briar scum—and they'd

better fucking not—then *we* get to make the trip to Alaska and bust Strike out ourselves. The government will be sitting back and moving on to whatever nonsense they want to worry about next. That'll leave a wide open window for us to swoop in and get our woman. It's the least we can do if the people really want to leave her to die with no dignity in that mansion."

"Mr. DeVito," a man sitting in the front row called out, half-balding as the lights gleamed off the top of his head. He stood and pushed his glasses up the ridge of his nose. "Have travel arrangements been made, just in case? I ask because that's a very long trip from here in Iowa. And we only have two more days until Chris said he would kill her."

"Mr. Frazier, I appreciate your concern, but we are well on top of these logistical matters," Stephen said. This man had been a Road Runner for only six months and got dragged to these meetings by a friend, ending up a passionate member of the cause and always chiming in. The man sat down and returned his focus to Stephen.

"Has everyone completed their practice for the week?" Stephen asked, receiving dozens of nods in return. Everyone in this coalition was assigned various tasks to practice in their anticipated journey of breaking out Strike. They spared no expense as they prepared for a seemingly impossible task. Some spent all day at the shooting ranges, becoming comfortable with various guns. Others studied espionage and stealth, while some hit the gym and bulked their bodies to look like the Incredible Hulk.

They still didn't have an exact approach for getting into the mansion, but they wanted all of their bases covered, leaving no potential weakness for exploitation.

"Good," Stephen said to the room, energy rising. "This

group works harder than anyone else in our lazy government in trying to get Strike back. I'm proud of each and every one of you. I really hope it doesn't come down to us having to take this on ourselves, but if we must, I can't imagine a better team to hit this motherfucker's mansion."

This caused the crowd to erupt—standing, clapping, whistling, and howling like savage loons.

"Are you ready to get our commander out of that fucking hellhole?!" Stephen shouted, met with more thunderous applause. When the room returned to silence, Stephen continued in a much more relaxed tone. "In about fifteen minutes, Councilman Uribe is going to come on that TV screen and announce our fate. Tonight all our planning will go into motion. If we're traveling to Alaska, you know what to do. I don't want any emotional reactions. We need to carry ourselves with class and go about our business. For now, the bar is set up in the back of the room – enjoy some snacks, enjoy the evening. Thank you."

One final round of applause and everyone stood from their seats, either chatting in the rows or making their way to the back of the room. The bald man worked his way to Stephen, causing him to sigh while he turned to grab a bottle of water off the table behind him.

"Stephen, do you have a moment, please?" the man asked.

"Ah, Mr. Frazier. What can I do for you?" Stephen asked, promptly sticking the bottle in his mouth.

"I know I'm new, but I really want to be on the flight to Alaska if it comes to it."

"Mr. Frazier, we have policy in place for a reason. You need to be a Road Runner for at least one year."

"I understand that, but why does that matter? It's not like

this group is an official part of the Road Runners. We're just a group of Road Runners taking a matter into our own hands."

"We put that measure in place to ensure we have experienced time travelers going on these dangerous missions."

"If I may, who cares? If danger is the question, what does experience matter? I'm willing to risk my life for this cause. Shouldn't that be enough?"

"It's not that simple."

"No, *you're* not making it simple. I would think for a task as grave as this you would want all hands on deck. Anyone willing to go should be allowed to."

Stephen stared at Frazier, trying his best to get a read on him. Everything the man said seemed honest. He really wanted to go to Alaska, and Stephen couldn't think of a valid reason to not send someone willing to go on a virtual suicide mission.

"Remind me what you've been training for?" Stephen asked the leech of a man who wouldn't leave him alone.

"Survival and combat."

Who the hell assigned him those two fields, if he's not even supposed to be going on the trip?

Stephen was cornered and didn't see a way out of this jam now. "Do you know someone?" he asked. "I just don't understand how you got assigned to those two training programs to begin with."

"I only know Darnell. He brought me here for the first time, and I can't get enough."

Darnell was a longtime member of the Road Runners and had participated in this coalition since its formation. Stephen didn't know Darnell on a personal level too well, but had witnessed his strong advocacy for saving Strike.

"Stephen," Frazier continued. "You have no reason to hold

me back. I have the skills you need. I can shoot, I can lift impossibly heavy weights, I can kill a man with my bare hands. Not to mention, I can survive weeks without food and water, know how to build a fire in the wild, and can hold my breath for just under three minutes. But most importantly, I have the balls to walk right up to that mansion and knock on the front door. I don't give a shit about Chris—he can't hurt me any more than I've already been hurt in the past."

Frazier spoke with such conviction that Stephen felt himself lured into his story, now intently curious as to what this man had gone through that led him to this precise moment in life. Every Road Runner had a heartbreaking story of how they were sucked into the world of time travel—often tricked by Chris—followed by the breaking point of learning it was Chris who had turned their worlds upside down for his own gain. But something about the murkiness with which Frazier spoke made Stephen suspect his past had taken some seriously dark turns.

He studied Frazier's brown eyes, a buried rage swimming beneath them, trapped like a caged predator ready to pounce on its prey.

"Okay," Stephen said. "I'll give you a shot."

"Really?!" Frazier's eyes shifted from focus to gleeful in the matter of one second. "I promise you I won't let you down. I've been dreaming about this moment since my first day here. I'll admit, the rules you had mentioned sucked the life out of me, but I knew if I just worked hard it would pay off."

Frazier spoke like a chatty teenager at a thousand words per minute, but Stephen held up a hand to silence him.

"Look, you can't say a word to anyone about this. If they find out I'm bending the rules, then everyone will want a rule bent for them. Just go about your business and act like you've been part of the plans all along."

"Don't you worry, I won't say a word," Frazier replied, giddy and radiating an energy that was too much for Stephen to handle at the moment.

Frazier had a wide grin but held up his index finger to his lips to show his lips were sealed regarding the matter.

This guy gives me the creeps, Stephen thought.

"Glad to have you on the team," he said, sticking out a hand to shake. "I really do need to step away for a second before this announcement comes. Pardon me."

"Thank you, I look forward to helping."

Stephen nodded and stepped past Frazier, immediately wondering if he made the wrong decision.

10

Chapter 10

Martin sat at the bar, having knocked back a couple shots of some island specialty that was fruity in his mouth, but tingly on the way down. Two empty beer steins stood in front of him as the gentle sounds of island music poured out of the speakers.

He had managed to completely unplug from society. Getting away wasn't enough. He left his cell phone powered off—except for the call he placed to his brother—didn't use the internet, and refused to turn on the TV in his rental property. Instead, he lazed around, reading books, playing solitaire, and drinking alcohol until the world spun and the emotional pain was numbed just enough for him to make it through the days.

Crooked Island welcomed random waves of tourists, and this particular night was a busy one, the bar crowded with at least forty patrons, mostly Americans, drinking booze, puffing cigars, dancing in the sand, and not having a single care in the world.

Martin envied them, watching them from a distance, wishing he could let go of all the issues weighing on his mind, but they would never truly leave him. While on the island, the shock of everything had finally worn off, leaving ugly bouts of grief.

His mother was gone. During a brief trip into the future—where only ten minutes passed in real time—Chris had managed to slip into his new house and turn his world on its head. Martin had mentally prepared to die on the dangerous mission, leaving his mother to succumb to the deadly grasp of Alzheimer's in her final days. But never did he expect the scene he arrived back home to.

He wanted a rage so overwhelming that it forced him onto the next flight to Alaska where he could end Chris once and for all, but that emotion hadn't settled in. Not yet. The starvation for revenge would come soon enough, but for now he had to adjust to life without the woman who raised him. The woman he had dinner with multiple times a week.

The woman who led you into that thrift store.

He didn't blame his mom; she was simply doing what she enjoyed by wandering into a store with intent on buying something she probably didn't need. He had followed her into thousands of stores throughout his lifetime, leaving him no reason to reflect on this particular trip as something he could have changed.

Martin asked for another mystery shot and slammed it back without hesitation.

"Mr. Martin, what is the occasion?" the bartender asked. Martin had spent enough time at the bar to befriend the young man, Javon, who served alcohol to pay his way through college in Nassau.

"Drinking for my mother," Martin said. "She passed away recently, and it's been a hard time. That's actually the reason I came out here."

Javon had never asked, likely assuming the older American

was out here for a getaway vacation like anyone else. But Martin trusted the kid, especially with the amount of alcohol flowing throughout his body.

"I'm sorry to hear that, Mr. Martin," Javon said, pulling out a clean shot glass and pouring from his unmarked bottle. "Here, on the house. For your mother."

Martin pursed his lips as he stared at the shot glass, nodding as he picked it up. "You're a good kid. Thank you."

He raised the glass to Javon before tipping it back.

Javon grinned and left to tend to some other customers, and Martin felt the liquor swirling in his stomach. He hadn't stood up in two hours and was now afraid to do so, the shift in balance a guarantee to feel exactly how much alcohol had been consumed.

He thought back to the old days in his Larkwood apartment, and wondered how he was still living. His liver had taken a twelve-round beating every single night. His lungs absorbed packs of cigarettes. And his stomach handled the pills to give him just a bit of a high to feel like he could float right off his balcony like Peter Pan. How his body survived that decade of constant abuse was beyond him, but here he was, healthy and strong despite being emotionally wrecked.

Martin had no clue of the ultimatum Chris had delivered to the Road Runners, the vote, or the pending chaos surrounding the announcement. One of the guards wandered into the bar and sat in the open stool next to Martin, dressed in khaki shorts and a Hawaiian shirt to fit in with the rest of the tourists.

He had met the two men briefly before taking off from Denver, and they promised to stay so hidden in the background that he'd forget they were even there. Which they did, as Martin rarely sensed their presence, barring a couple of late night walks on the beach under the glowing moonlight. He remembered their names were Antonio and Everett, but couldn't remember who was who.

Martin shifted in his seat at the sight of the guard, a sudden panic settling over him as his mind kicked into high paranoia.

The guard looked to be in his fifties, like Martin, judging by the gray stubble forming around his jaw.

"I need to have a word," the guard said. "In private."

Martin's stomach sunk and he hoped whatever he was about to hear wouldn't sober him up in an instant.

"Where?" Martin asked.

"Just outside of here. It's too noisy."

The guard stood up and left, and Martin trailed behind, pushing through the drunken crowd of adults acting like children. Even though the bar itself was outside on the beach, they had to pass through the indoor dining room to exit the building. They stepped out to the soothing sounds of distant ocean waves, the setting sun glimmering off the water's surface in the distance.

"What's going on?" Martin asked, his mind definitely sobering up as adrenaline started to fill his veins. The guard still felt very much a stranger despite being on the island with Martin the entire time. They hadn't said a word to each other after the Denver airport, and Martin could only assume this man wanted to talk with him because of something important.

"Mr. Briar, I'm sorry to interrupt your evening, but I have some information you might be interested in hearing."

Please don't tell me my mom's ashes are missing, Martin thought, unsure what else could be so pressing that they had to pull him out of the bar.

"Back in the States, Chris has offered to release Commander

Strike."

"That's fantastic news," Martin replied, a wave of relief sweeping over him. "What made him want to do that?"

Sober Martin would question everything about this news, but drunk Martin was just glad to hear, not suspecting anything sinister from Chris.

"Well, Mr. Briar, that's what we need to discuss. Chris said he'll release the commander if we turn you over to him. If we don't, he's going to kill her on a live broadcast."

The guard paused and let these words settle. He surely knew Martin was drunk and would need a few more seconds to process the words coming out of his mouth.

Martin's expression shifted from pensive to terrified as the realization came to fruition. He opened his mouth to speak, then closed it, unsure what to say.

"There's a vote taking place," the guard continued. "And they are expected to announce the decision tonight."

"A vote by who?"

"The whole organization. Chris made his announcement on our network, so the whole world saw. The Council gathered to make the decision, but decided it was best to leave it to the people."

"So he's trying to make it a contest between me and Strike?"

"I'm afraid so, sir."

"Well, who did you vote for?" Martin asked, knowing damn well it wasn't polite to ask such a question, but his emotions and common sense were shattered beyond recognition at this particular moment.

"I voted for you, sir. We don't negotiate with lunatics."

"Do you have any idea what the voters are deciding?"

"No. Only the Council knows how the votes have trickled in.

None of that information is shared until the polls are officially closed at seven o'clock."

"Okay. So what does this mean for me exactly?"

"We figured, at the very least, that you should know. Our leadership team back home urged us to not tell you, in case the results come back in favor of Strike. They didn't want you running off. But I couldn't do that. It didn't feel right. So Everett and I made the call to tell you."

Martin had thought this man was Antonio, but hadn't been sure, grateful for the unintended confirmation.

"We think you should stay close to us," Antonio continued. "Regardless of the outcome. If the votes come back to send you to Chris, we're ready to do our best to hide you. Do you already have the tracking device in your arm?"

Martin nodded.

"Everett knows how to cut those out. He has quite the steady hand."

Martin trembled at the thought of cutting his arm open to pull the device that was attached to muscles like a suction cup. It also reminded him of Sonya and the final encounter they had in her house, right when she committed to going into the future and staying there forever. A life that seemed so far back in time that it was impossible to believe it ever happened.

"And what if the votes are for me?" Martin asked, unsure exactly what emotions he was feeling.

"If that happens, we definitely want to ramp up security. We might even have you stay with us. The way we see it, if Chris is this desperate to get you, he's going to try. If we don't give you up, he's going to kill Strike and still come for you. Considering he has a knack for just showing up in the most random of places, we'd expect to see him on this island soon enough. There are people in high positions who don't want to see you handed over like a bargaining chip. They've offered us any assistance we need to ensure your safety."

"Wow, who said that?"

"A few people, but I'm not dropping names. Just trust that regardless of the outcome, people in the right positions want you alive. They view you as our next commander, you know?"

"Yeah, I'm aware. I can't say I'm interested in that job, but they haven't really given me a say in the matter."

That's it. That's who's talking to Antonio. Commander Blair, Commander Quang. Those two are waiting to endorse me and basically force me into the position.

"I can't speak to that," Antonio said. "All I know is that I will not violate my oath to uphold the Bylaws. If they expect me to turn you over to Chris, they're gonna have to bring a lot of backup to pry you out of our possession."

"And Everett feels the same?"

"One hundred percent. We're frontline soldiers by trade. Our whole purpose is to ensure that the Road Runner Bylaws are upheld and enforced."

"I'm sorry, when did you say this announcement is coming?"

Antonio stuck his arm out and checked his watch. "Expecting it in about thirty minutes. Polls close in fifteen minutes, and they should come on the TV shortly after that."

"You have this streaming in your room?"

"Sure do. We've been up all day, watching and waiting for any sort of update. None has come—they really want to drag this out."

"I'd like to go watch, please."

Antonio nodded and they left the bar behind, Martin unaware

he'd never return.

11

Chapter 11

When Chief Councilman Uribe stepped behind the podium, he felt the world fall silent. The camera wasn't yet rolling, but he knew all eyes around the globe were glued to their TVs in anticipation of his speech.

The rest of the Council watched him, some excited about the results, others with their faces scrunched in disappointment, as if they had been betrayed by the people.

The staffer who served as the unofficial cameraman was fiddling with the camera, making sure it was lined up just right to capture this pivotal moment in Road Runner history.

"Are you ready, Councilman Uribe?" the young man asked, a slight crack in his voice.

He shuffled through his speech and took a long inhale. "I'm ready."

"You're on in five . . . four . . . three . . . two . . ." The cameraman pointed at Uribe and fell silent with the rest of the universe.

"Good evening, Road Runners," Uribe started. "I'm Chief Councilman Francisco Uribe. I want to start by thanking you all for your participation in these last minute polls. As we suspected here at the Council, this issue was too sensitive for us to make the final call. You all responded by setting a new record for voter participation.

"Over the last twenty-four hours, we all made a decision on how we want to proceed from this unfortunate position we've been put in. Like any democracy, there can only be one winner in a poll. It's imperative that if you're on the losing side of this vote, we must remain one and keep pushing forward. Either way, this is a dark day for us all – perhaps the darkest in our history. But there will be light, and we can only reach that light if we continue to hold each other to the highest of standards. I've heard rumors of pending chaos depending on these results. Do not let yourselves devolve into savages. We are Road Runners, and that's all that should matter at the end of the day.

"As for the results, please know this was by no means a landslide decision. Out of the millions of votes cast, this ended up being decided by three thousand votes. That said, the decision has been made to *not* turn over Martin Briar in exchange for Commander Strike. Please know that we have been proactive in making preparations for either decision, and we still are seeking ways to free Commander Strike.

"The next two days will be extremely stressful for us all. It is imperative to stay ready to help as the organization requires. We don't know how Chris will react to this decision, so remain diligent and aware. We imagine he won't stop until he has Martin Briar, so it is up to all of you to look out for yourselves and your neighbors.

"Commander Strike, if you're watching this, don't give up hope. We have not forgotten you, and are working tirelessly to free you. Thank you, and have a good rest of your evening."

Uribe nodded to the cameraman and was given the clear that the camera was now off.

"Thank you," he said. "How did I sound?"

"Very good, sir."

He rejoined the Council at their main table, where no one moved an inch.

"I can't believe this is happening," Councilwoman Murray said, shaking her head. She had remained rather silent after they passed around the results.

"I just discussed the need to not dwell on this matter," Uribe said with a clear frustration under his tone. "The real question is: what do we do now?"

"We can sit back and watch the fireworks," Councilman Ryan muttered.

"Be *constructive,* Councilman," Uribe snarled. "What has gotten into some of you? We are the highest office of the organization—we cannot act like pouty teenagers who didn't get their way. Am I clear?"

Ryan tossed his hands in the air. "None of it matters. The people have spoken, and they want anarchy."

"You're being dramatic," Councilwoman Thrasher said. "We held a vote and are honoring the results. Nothing about that is anarchy."

"We just voted as a people to *not* save our own leader, as if she never existed," Ryan snapped, standing up from his seat and slamming two fists on the table to grab everyone's immediate attention. "There was a time where we wouldn't think twice about rescuing our commander at any cost. Thirty years ago this would have been a ninety-five percent vote in favor of saving the commander—no doubt about it. We wouldn't have had to waste a whole day taking polls—that day would have been spent getting our commander to safety. Now, there's no respect for authority, that much has been made clear. I just don't recognize this organization any more. What have we become? We're no better than the Revolution."

"Don't you dare say something like that!" Councilman Martinez barked. "We are nothing like those people."

"*Those* people don't give a shit about their leadership. They blindly follow Chris. If he were to go missing, they'd just follow the next man up. Today's vote was a huge step in that direction for us."

"What do you suggest we do, then?" Councilman Pierre asked. "Because it sounds to me like this has been years in the making. Our people didn't just wake up one day and decide to change their priorities. If you saw the start of this years ago, that would have been the time to speak."

Ryan took a deep breath before speaking again, this time in a much more controlled tone. "I'm afraid a vote like this is something that can divide our membership beyond repair. There are people ready to march right up to Chris's mansion right now and get Strike themselves. Road Runners *are* smart and savvy. I wouldn't be shocked at all if they actually found a way to get her out of that place. It was hard watching you lie to the people, pretending that we have people working on finding a way to rescue her."

"We do have teams—" Uribe started.

"Save it. Those teams have been at work for weeks and haven't done a damn thing. They're no different than the teams who have been working for years to find a way to kill Chris. Just a bunch of moronic ideologists."

"Of course *you'd* think that," Thrasher snipped across the

table.

"Enough!" Uribe shouted. "We have to get on the same page. No one in this room loves the decision. And no one would have loved it the other way, either. Let's call it a night. We've been together since yesterday morning. Go home, sleep in your own bed, try to unplug from the stress we've had to endure. You may not recognize the Road Runners, but I don't recognize this Council. I'm ashamed of the behavior I've seen these past couple of days. We have work to do, a special election to manage, and new laws to create to ensure we don't get put in this position again. Take the morning off, and we'll meet here at noon tomorrow. I'll buy lunch for us and we can get back to work."

Ryan pushed his chair and walked off, muttering under his breath. Murray was the next to stand and leave without another word.

Her silence was enough to prove a point, and the rest of the Council quietly rose from their seats and departed the building. Some exchanged awkward glances with each other, but they moved about as if they had never met before.

* * *

Across the country, from the comforts of his office, Chris Speidel chucked the remote at his TV screen, shattering it into dozens of little shards.

He snapped up the phone and called down to whatever guard was on duty in the basement. "Let's make sure the commander is ready for her television special in two nights."

He hung up, threw his head back, and snickered at the ceiling.

12

Chapter 12

The vote was indeed polarizing and divisive, and definitely widened the pending divide within the organization. The following day was as lifeless of a day the Road Runners had ever seen, a virtual dark cloud hanging over the entire organization, panic spreading among groups pushed to the brink in their efforts to save Strike.

Others feared for Martin's life, both from Chris and other Road Runners who seemed to have lost their minds. No one knew what to expect in regards to Chris's promise to execute Strike on live television. They were halfway to his deadline, and it became increasingly clear that there was a target on Martin Briar's back.

Where was the mysterious and unknown Martin Briar? He had been a central focus in this offer from Chris, yet no one had heard from him. The Road Runners news ran numerous reports on Martin and why he was so important. He was a Warm Soul, and that's why Chris was so intent on getting him. This also made him a valuable weapon for the Road Runners in their mission to hopefully kill Chris and destroy the Revolution.

But he was missing in action. They discovered the story of his mother's murder at the hands of Chris, and many figured he was hiding.

Tarik Sadi, the Lead Runner of the Denver chapter, denied any knowledge of Martin's whereabouts. The people refused that answer. Briar was a Road Runner and had a tracking device just like everyone else. Someone knew where he was hiding.

A national witch hunt sparked as a result, some people just wanting to know that Martin was okay, others desiring to capture him and drop him at Chris's front door. Some speculated that he fled to another continent to hide under the protection provided there. Commanders from all around the world were contacted and denied any knowledge of their prized possession.

"It's all bullshit, folks," Stephen said, a cigarette pinched between his lips. The group heading to Alaska had gathered in Stephen's living room, their jet being fueled and prepared to make the flight from Iowa to northern Alaska, leaving within the next hour. "Briar could be dead, for all we know. Since when can our government not locate one of our own? Just another reason to not trust these people, I suppose."

The team was comprised of ten men and two women, dressed in all-black attire, loaded handguns in their waist bands, fully automatic rifles being loaded onto their jet.

"Before we get on that plane," Stephen continued, "I want to tell you all how proud I am. This is no mission for the weak. You're here because you *want* to be—want to do something good that our organization is turning a blind eye to. There's a good chance we all die tonight. Thank you for your sacrifice. We may not know the outcome of our work today, but trust that you are doing the right thing. Now, is everyone clear on their roles once we land in Alaska?"

Stephen looked around his group of dedicated soldiers who were all nodding with confidence.

Frazier raised his hand, prompting Stephen to fight the urge to roll his eyes. Instead he pointed at him. "I've been thinking, we should have a name for our group. Don't you all think?"

More nodding worked around the group.

"We've discussed the matter before," Stephen said. "But have never agreed on anything. Do you have a suggestion?"

"I sure do. I was thinking our group can be called the Liberation, which means each of us are Liberators."

"Liberators," Stephen repeated, his eyebrows raising at the good idea. "Thoughts?"

"I think it's badass," one man said, others nodding in agreement. "Good job, new guy."

"We are the Liberation," Frazier said, taking a step toward the front of the room, not stopping until he was within five feet of Stephen. He turned and faced the group. "And we fight for those no one else will fight for!"

The small team burst into applause and Stephen caught himself grinning. Frazier, the awkward weirdo, was riling up the team. Perhaps he'd need to get to know him a little better on the long flight ahead.

Stephen stepped forward to join Frazier. "Alright, Liberators, it's time to head out and do what we came to do. There are a couple of vans outside waiting to take us to the hangar. Be sure to make any final phone calls to family or friends you might leave behind on this mission. Do *not* go into the specifics of our work. This is a trying time where it's impossible to know who to trust, and that can include your own mother. Make those calls, though, come to peace with the possibility of you not returning, and let's go get Commander Strike and kill that evil sonofabitch in the process."

More howling, clapping, and slaps on the back for this team of savage brutes. They made their way out of the cramped house (Stephen never wanted to upgrade after coming into his Road Runner fortune) and filled the two vans parked on the sidewalk. They looked like a group of ninjas heading off to a convention. Stephen was the last to exit his house, and after he locked the door and patted it with a shaky hand, he stepped back to admire the home he had lived in his entire life. His parents raised him in this house, nurtured him with love and care, and always wanted him to be his best. He wondered if he'd ever get to return. If he died, he had it ordered in his will to demolish the house. If he couldn't raise a family of his own there, then no one else would, either.

He turned and jumped in the van, watching his house fade into the distance as they drove away.

* * *

Stephen might have not upgraded matters in his personal life, but he never shied away from going over the top on these special outings with the now-named Liberation. And this time, with death looming, he went well above the top. Their jet was loaded with premium steaks, bottles of the most expensive champagnes and wines, and somehow, every snack imaginable.

They drank and dined without a care in the world. It was a six-hour flight, and Stephen kicked off the party with a round of shots and trays of fancy appetizers no one knew how to pronounce. It was a mild party with wings, and everyone enjoyed every second of it.

They partied for two hours before Stephen cut off the alcohol supply. There was still a serious task awaiting them that evening, and they didn't need anyone hungover or vomiting on Chris's front steps. All Stephen wanted with the flight was for everyone to feel loose and stress-free. Some dozed off for a quick nap; others put on a movie and unwound from the long morning.

By the time they landed in the mid-afternoon in Barrow, Alaska, the group came back to life, conversation broke out, and everyone jumped out of their seats, ready to execute what they came here for.

Stephen stood at the front of the plane with his arms raised until the team fell silent.

"Don't get too excited. We're going to be on the plane for a good while. Remember, no one knows we're here. We can't exactly walk into the Road Runners office and wait for nightfall. This is our home and office for the next several hours. I want everyone to get with your partner and ensure your specific plans are completely ironed out. Everyone here has a role—make sure you're ready. We'll be having more food cooked for dinner. I wanted to go out, but decided against it because of how small this town is. We must stay on the plane – we can't afford to be seen by any Revolters or Road Runners."

As these words left his lips, Stephen realized for the first time that he might have accidentally formed a new organization to counter the Road Runners *and* the Revolution. Weren't all great things born from tragedy, though? A response to a need in the world?

It wasn't his intent to go against the Road Runners, but they were the ones making no effort to free Strike. With the knowledge and resources they had, there was no reason to not have rescued her by now. There was either something suspicious happening within the organization, or they were simply chickenshits, too afraid of Chris to make a move.

The Liberation believed the conspiracy theory that the Council was trying to force this unknown Martin Briar into leadership all because he was a Warm Soul, but not a single part of that statement had yet to be proven true.

Another theory was that Julian's death was not actually a suicide, but rather a cover-up in this grand scheme to replace Strike. The timing was rather questionable, as all of these events happened shortly after Strike's attempt to kill Chris had failed.

Like anything, the theories were never-ending, and the Liberation only discussed them with seriousness after passing a bong around and letting their minds wander to unknown depths. All that mattered in this exact moment, however, was what waited on the other side of sundown.

Everyone had broken off into pairs and would stay that way through dinner, plotting and planning for the most intense moment of their lives. When the skies turned dark, they would file out of the jet and head to Chris's mansion.

13

Chapter 13

Chris was still in his office when the sun disappeared behind the horizon – not that he ever knew, thanks to the steel barricade engulfing his mansion. It had been a long day of preparing for a public execution tomorrow. The Road Runners were surely expecting something spectacular, and he wanted to deliver.

Every hour or so, he'd catch himself shaking his head. He thought for sure they would turn over Martin. It was an offer too good to pass up, but the Road Runners decided to take a shit on their commander and leave her to rot. They continued to amaze him, somehow remaining both predictable and utterly unpredictable at the same time. Not once in his term as the Keeper of Time did he think he'd see the day where the Road Runners refused their loyalty to a commander, certain she would be the easy ticket to Martin Briar. The thought frustrated him as he plotted his next moves.

Yes, he knew Martin was on Crooked Island in the Bahamas, just as he always knew where his old friend was by a simple dive into his mind. But Martin was surrounded by two guards at all times, and Chris couldn't exactly march onto the island with his crew of soldiers without expecting some sort of gunfight where Martin could be killed. He wanted Martin breathing and at all full strength, so he could bend him to his will and have a little Warm Soul puppy to play with.

It had only been a couple of days and he already missed Duane's help and support. Surely Duane would have some fun ideas for the execution, helping Chris out of the mental logjam he now found himself in.

His computer screen flickered to life. It automatically did this if the outdoor cameras caught movement within a 100-yard radius. Chris leaped out of his chair, sending it back to crash against the wall.

"What the hell?"

A group of three people were approaching in the distance, moving at the slow, steady pace of a walk through the park. He dropped his finger on the intercom, but had no one to page. Sure, he could've called the mindless robot that was filling in for Duane, but he provided nothing of substance in a time like this.

"Goddammit, Duane, why the hell aren't you here when I need you?!" Chris snarled, his hands rummaging through his desk drawers to retrieve the headset that plugged into his computer. "All these years together, and not one single day off. Until now."

Chris plugged in the headset and opened the software that allowed a two-way conversation.

The phone on his desk rang, causing him to jump again, laughing briefly at his startled self. He snapped the phone off the hook. "What's wrong?"

"Mr. Speidel, we have visitors," the voice on the phone said.

One of the guards.

"I know. Get a team up to the main level, guns loaded. Leave everything to me, and don't make a move until I say so. They want to speak with me, and I'll allow them to do so."

"Yes, sir." The phone hung up and Chris returned to the screen where the trio was now within one hundred feet. "C'mon, you bastards. Tell me you have Briar. FUCKING TELL ME!"

Chris's emotions danced all over the spectrum. The Road Runners had announced they were not going to turn in Martin, but here they were, ready to knock on his door and make an offer.

"Good evening, folks," Chris said into his microphone once he knew they were within distance to hear. "Are you nice people with the Road Runners?"

The three, who were bundled up from head to toe in all-black clothing looked to each before turning back to the mansion.

"Sort of," the one on the left said, the voice a hoarse baritone.

"What does that mean?" Chris snapped back.

"We are Road Runners who don't agree with the announced decision. We believe in loyalty to our leaders and want to work with you."

"You're going through all of this for Strike? Half of your people disagree."

"But the other half doesn't. Everyone seems to be forgetting about the other half like we don't exist."

"Are you even able to make decisions on behalf of the Road Runners?"

Chris knew this group was clearly not official Road Runner leadership, but wanted to play along.

"No, but that shouldn't matter. We're here, humble and

willing to work with you. If we have your word about releasing Strike, we will get you Briar."

Chris grinned, ready to call the bluff. "How much time do you need?"

"Three days."

"I've already given three days. What have you been doing this whole time?"

"This isn't a simple process. Arrangements have to be made, especially since we are going against our organization's will. We have to be very careful to not get caught."

"I'll give you three days if you can tell me the exact location of Mr. Briar right now."

The man who had been responding stared blankly at the mansion for a few seconds before shrugging. "We are still working on that."

"Sir, I suggest you get off my property right now before I kill you all," Chris said calmly. "You've already proven that you're nothing but a sham. If you came here with actual details and a plan, then we'd be having a different discussion. Instead you thought you could knock on my door and try to bullshit me. Not in this universe, my friend."

"We will get you Briar. We have ways—"

"Stop while you're ahead and leave."

The man looked at his two companions and they drew their heads together to whisper under their breath. Chris couldn't make out what they were saying.

"We're not leaving," the man said.

"Excuse me?" Chris stood up from his seat, hands planted on the desk as he gawked at the computer monitor in shock.

"We came here for Strike, and we're not leaving until we get her."

Chris felt his jaw hanging, unable to believe that someone would come to his mansion and defy everything he said, threatening to camp out like a protest, as if they could actually get their way.

The group held their blank expressions, sending Chris into a mental frenzy. He had options, and wanted to make sure he made the right decision.

I can bring them in as prisoners. It's been awfully quiet since letting all the Road Runners go. Unless . . .

He wondered if these three Road Runners were former prisoners, familiar with the basement layout, and trying some elaborate plan to get imprisoned on purpose to free Strike. The Road Runners had always proven to be conniving geniuses. Chris rubbed his face in frustration, desperately wanting new prisoners, but now unsure.

Just do what's safest. Now's not the time to get cute and take chances.

"Last chance to leave, gentlemen," Chris said to the trio before taking off his headset and pushing his finger on the intercom to speak to the whole mansion. "I need all soldiers to the main floor right now. We have business to tend to outside. In two minutes I'm lowering the barricade, and we will be met with guns. Exterminate everyone in sight."

He slid the headset back on and said, "I suggest you start running."

"We're not leaving, Chris. You can kill us, but we're not going down without a fight."

I love a stubborn Road Runner, Chris thought. *Their pain tastes so much better when they die, like a juicy filet mignon.*

Chris didn't respond and removed the headset again. He was done speaking with these suicidal people and ran through the steps to lower the barricade. The entryway camera showed a dozen soldiers huddled together at the front door, guns resting on their shoulders.

"That's plenty," Chris said, and entered the code to initiate the lowering of the steel walls.

The loud humming sound filled the mansion to go along with the slight vibrations from the barricade's grinding motors.

"Oh, my Road Runner friends, what a bad choice you've made today!" Chris giggled like a child excited to open his presents on Christmas morning. He watched the screen, more people running from the woods in the distance, barreling toward the mansion like a stampede of wild animals, rifles waving in the air.

There had to be at least ten others from his quick count on the screen, but Chris grinned, laying his finger on the intercom button. "Take all of them out."

The barricade completed its descent, and Chris realized the original trio's main objective was to get the walls lowered, leaving the mansion a sitting duck. He also realized that these people were indeed not on official Road Runner business. Any Road Runner worth their weight knew a dozen soldiers were no match for Chris—he had twenty of his own to deploy. Had they arrived with hundreds, it might be a different story, but these people's work was lackluster and lazy. Why would they show up to the mansion with no way of actually winning? The thought sparked a flash of paranoia as Chris clicked through the cameras until he found the view of the back of the house. Surely hundreds of Road Runners were charging from that direction. But the screen revealed an open, snow-covered field as far as he could see.

"Let the fireworks begin!" Chris shouted to the screen,

watching as these sloppy Road Runners started to open fire on his house.

His Revolters, those trained, robotic soldiers, marched outside with no fear, their own rifles cocked and ready to take lives on their front lawn that was now a battlefield. Gunfire exploded, sounding like a series of fireworks from Chris's office. He pulled his pistol out of his drawer, ready to fend off anyone who might try to slip into the mansion—not that they would get very far if they did.

"Yes! Yes! Yes! Kill them all!" Chris howled laughter as he watched four Road Runners drop like sacks of potatoes.

The odds of killing a Revolter were slim to none. Ever since that Russian bastard wiped out Chris's entire team, the soldiers were required to wear full armor whenever the barricades were down. The people running from the woods reached the mansion grounds and were greeted by a bazooka that made the ground in front of them explode, sending their bodies back several feet. The Revolters rushed them while they were down and promptly put bullets in each of their heads.

Chris started dancing, giggling, his euphoria rupturing as he watched each Road Runner drop dead. The gunfire ceased and Chris returned to his computer for a look at the battlefield. The bodies were scattered about, and he counted twelve in total, all of them still except for one that wiggled on the ground.

Chris grabbed his pistol off his desk and made his way outside, where the cool air smacked his face, death and fear so thick it made him drool. He paused in the doorway and opened up his soul to feast on those raw emotions that his latest victims had left. He didn't like massacres – the cleanup always a bitch – but how sweet the fear tasted as he absorbed it, no different than hosting a barbecue with friends. Sure, the preparation and work afterward were horrendous, but if everyone had a good time with delicious food, wasn't it worth it?

The wiggling body was none other than the man who had spoken to Chris over the security system. Chris jumped down the steps and stood over the man, fear radiating out of his pores.

"I've got to ask, friend, why did you think you had a chance? Did you really not know how this would end?"

The man tried to speak, but could only gurgle blood.

"I see," Chris said. "It's too bad. You may have come a day too early. I plan to recruit those of you Road Runners who are upset. We're gonna have a grand ol' time wreaking havoc on the system. No commander *and* an upcoming election that we plan to infiltrate will just be the start of the fun. Your team probably would've made the perfect fit. But here we are."

Chris whipped his pistol in front of the man's face and immediately tasted a renewed wave of fear, as if someone had opened an oven of freshly baked bread. He pulled the trigger and marched back into the house.

"Don't clean up the bodies. Leave them as a reminder for anyone who thinks they can trick us with lies."

The soldiers nodded and followed him inside, the barricade ready to go back up within a few minutes.

14

Chapter 14

Martin packed his suitcase with everything he had accumulated on the island, smashing it down to get the damn thing closed. The morning after viewing the results to spare his life, Commander Blair from Europe had called to let him know that he would be freezing time to allow Martin to move in safety.

"Get ready to leave in one hour," Blair had told him. "I've already spoken with your security team, and they are also preparing for next steps. A route has been planned out, and the jet to get you off that island is already waiting for you at the local hangar. Your team will meet you at your door once they're ready."

Martin wasn't ready to leave, but understood the target on his back. There were too many Road Runners in high positions who knew his location, and no one knew who to trust. People had become so glued to their opinions in this debate, that it no longer seemed a far-fetched idea for someone to betray the organization and take matters into their own hands.

Julian had initially sparked the wave of distrust when he killed Bill, a stain that would remain on the organization forever.

With no commander in charge of North America, all other commanders had taken on various responsibilities, along with the Council, until an election sorted matters out. Commander Blair made it clear his sole focus was keeping Martin alive, and played it close to his chest, refusing to let any of his staff know the grand secret of his whereabouts.

Martin's two guards picked him up shortly before ten o'clock in the morning. Their car was ready to take them all to the hangar where the jet was running and ready for takeoff. During the quick, five-minute drive, they filled him on what was to come.

The plan was for Martin to jump around from place to place, until they deemed it safe for him to return to the United States. He felt like a fugitive on the run, especially upon hearing that he'd be in a different city every night for at least the next two weeks. Upcoming locations included Jamaica, Haiti, Dominican Republic, Aruba, and the Virgin Islands, and ended in Mexico where the team would gauge the situation unfolding in the States. From there, they would either bounce around Mexico, or return to the United States where they hoped to introduce him as an official candidate for the commandership.

"Have you ever flown a plane before?" Antonio asked while they continued to drive toward the hangar.

"No," Martin replied, his mind distracted as he stared out the window. "Why?"

"You're going to fly one today."

"Excuse me?"

"Orders from Commander Blair. He said anything that's in direct contact with you while he freezes time is immune to the freezing. We need to travel while the rest of the world is frozen, so you're going to fly the plane."

Martin let out a nervous laugh. "I don't think so. You want me to kill us all during my own rescue mission? I don't see the logic."

"Relax, you're simply going to tend to the autopilot. I'm going to get us in the air, get us at cruising altitude, and even program the plane for our destination. From there it flies itself. We just need your hands on the control wheel when Blair freezes time."

"Why can't I just touch you and not have to worry about it?"

"That rule doesn't work on other people, only objects. Trust me, we've tested this out with just about everything you can imagine."

"Where are we even going?"

"Aruba will be our first stop. Ever been?"

"No." Martin rarely traveled. This was actually his first time visiting the Caribbean islands.

"It's a beautiful place."

They sat in silence for the next two minutes until they arrived to their private jet, excessively large for carrying an entire three passengers. Antonio parked the car in a designated space, and they each lugged their bags onto the jet. This wasn't a luxurious flight like he had experienced with Chris. There was no fine dining or expensive alcohol, but the jet itself sparkled clean and looked more than capable of hosting such an event.

They walked in a diagonal line, Martin in the middle for protection. Antonio and Everett were concerned someone might try to snipe Martin from a distance, and urged him to run toward the jet.

The engine was already fired up and rumbling, and they wasted no time dashing up the stairs and settling into their seats. The whole process only took a couple minutes until Antonio pulled Martin from his seat and into the cockpit. They had called ahead to have a local pilot prepare the jet for takeoff, but Antonio was the only pilot on the island that they could trust to remain aboard.

Martin watched from behind as Antonio pushed various buttons and flicked switches on the panel.

"We're ready," Antonio said, dropping into the pilot's seat. "C'mon." He patted the co-pilot seat for Martin to join him.

"What do I have to do?"

"Let me get us in the air first, and I'll show you." Antonio checked his watch and nodded. "We're one minute ahead of schedule and need to keep it that way. Commander Blair is going to freeze time at the top of the hour, and give us two hours until he unfreezes it."

Martin wished he could be anywhere besides having to fly this plane. If red lights flashed or alarms sounded, Martin was prepared to grab a parachute that he knew was stashed in the back of the jet, and jump to save his life.

"Let's go!" Antonio barked, moving the jet forward out of the hangar and onto the narrow strip of concrete that served as the runway. He floored the accelerator, the jet gaining steam as it charged forward. "Hold on!"

Everything passed in a blur as they rumbled toward the end of the runway, Antonio pulling back on the control wheel to tip the plane upward, cruising into the sky. Martin watched as his new favorite haven disappeared from sight. The place where he had come to mourn and leave his depressing life behind was already a distant memory, a place to which he'd forever long to return.

Martin watched Antonio navigate into the clear blue sky, but had no clue what his guard was actually doing. His body had tensed up during the takeoff, arms sore as they clenched the entire time.

Antonio kept a studious expression while they elevated, his tongue pinched between his lips until they leveled out and continued forward. In a matter of minutes, nothing but the deep blue of ocean was visible below the scattered cloudline.

"This is it," Antonio said, checking his watch once more. "In one minute the world will be frozen. Grab hold of the control wheel now, and don't let go until you see me freeze."

Martin whipped his hands on the wheel, as if the world's existence depended on it.

"Relax, Mr. Briar. In fact, relaxation is going to be crucial over these next few days. It's gonna be a lot of this same routine because Commander Blair wants us to move while time is frozen."

"Why?"

"So we can guarantee to not get followed. I don't quite have time to explain—he works like clockwork. The plane is fine and will remain on cruise control for the next two hours. Don't worry about anything, since you can sit back and relax. Time will be unfrozen when we still have an hour until landing—just to be safe. I'll see you in a—"

Antonio stopped mid-speech, his lips pursed inward, leaving Martin to assume the next word coming out was *bit.*

"Yeah, see you in a bit," Martin said to his frozen guard, his glossy eyes fixed forward out of the cockpit windshield where the world kept moving by. His heart started thumping as panic settled in, the lone conscious person on this moving jetliner. If Chris somehow knew where he was—and remained unfrozen—he could shoot him down like a bird with no one ever knowing what happened. "You're okay," he whispered to himself, trying to get his heart rate under control, studying the panels with so many buttons and switches that kept him a foot away to avoid bumping into something that would send them crashing into the water.

A small screen showed their cruising speed at a steady 320 miles per hour, with exactly 998 miles remaining on the trip. Martin did quick math in his head to confirm that Antonio would indeed be unfrozen in two hours before they missed their stop.

With that to comfort him, he settled back into the co-pilot's seat and leaned back to avoid the panel. He had too much adrenaline to doze off, or really do anything else for that matter. He would sit there like a rock for the next two hours, praying Commander Blair wouldn't forget about them.

15

Chapter 15

The next morning, Martin was the furthest thing from Chris's mind. There would be plenty of time to bring his old friend back to the mansion. Today, however, was for Commander Strike. Chris knew the Road Runners were drenched with anticipation, and a few probably figured he was bluffing—those were the ones who didn't truly understand his ways. He had never told a lie since becoming the Keeper of Time. Deception, sure. Stretching the truth, most certainly. But never a lie. Never a bluff. When he said something was going to happen, it happened, plain and simple.

He waited the full seventy-two hours as promised. When the clock struck four in the evening, leaving him one full hour until show time, Chris made the call to have Commander Strike brought up to his office. Before doing so, he had covered the floor with plastic table covers, stretching them the entirety of the room. He didn't know how much blood would be shed during her execution. He hadn't actually planned for it to get this far, certain they would've turned over Martin. Now he was stuck carrying out this broadcast murder on the fly.

Well, Saturday Night Live *happens on a whim. It's what people love.*

He laughed at the thought. Maybe after Strike was dead, he could close his performance with, "Live from New York, it's Saturday Night!" That would make the stunned Road Runners at least share a chuckle, right?

Commander Strike arrived in his office ten minutes later, hands cuffed, three guards surrounding her.

"Good evening, Commander," Chris greeted. "Have you had a good couple of days?"

"I'll be happier once I'm dead—won't have to spend another second in this shithole."

Chris giggled, caught off guard by her snippy response. He imaged she'd be more quiet and nervous, but she seemed to be her usual, loathsome self. "Actually, Commander, I haven't decided where we're going to put your body. It could be here, maybe elsewhere. Perhaps in multiple places. We'll just have to see how the night goes."

"If only it could end with your fiery death," Strike snapped back. "Why don't you just do that? You're such a showman—that's what the people really want to see. I can even kick your severed head down the street. That's a nice touch, don't you think? Would be great for ratings."

Chris grinned, openly. "Commander, you need to be careful how you speak to me. You're making me erect, and I haven't felt that special in years. Your dirty talk is more than enough to pop my rocket, if you know what I mean."

Strike stared at him blankly, and Chris recognized that look as one he'd seen plenty of times. He had a way of appalling people beyond their wildest belief. It never got old.

"I appreciate your effort," he continued. "If that's what you call this. Most would just roll over and die, and that's no fun. You should make for a good show. You have quite the fan base, did you know? Some of your own stopped by earlier trying to negotiate on your behalf—they went behind the Road Runners' back and said they didn't agree with the decision to not trade Martin for you. I can't say I'm fond of that choice either."

"You lie!" Strike snarled.

"Heeeheee!" Chris giggled. "You should know I'd never lie, especially to your face. You see, Commander, this whole thing is bigger than the both of us. This isn't about you or me. This is about the war that no one has been able to make progress in. I'm not afraid to give credit where it's due. Your people have put up a hell of a fight. Your recruiting techniques appear flawless. Do you know how many times we tried to join your organization undercover?"

Strike stared at him blankly and shrugged her shoulders.

"At least five times a week for the past two years. You sniffed us out every single time, killing my poor soldiers dead on the spot."

"We have a very strict process. Maybe you should look at why your people are so willing to leave. Don't blame us for your own faults."

"Commander, I'm well aware that people will leave the Revolution. It's no secret that I rip apart lives to get people to agree to join me. I had my life torn to pieces for the same reason, and look at me now."

"Scum of the world. I'm sure your dead wife would be proud."

"There you go again," Chris said, tugging on his crotch. "Such a mouth on you, I could just kiss it."

"Come near me and I'll bite your fucking face off."

"Your words might as well be lingerie, Commander. Color me officially aroused." Chris smirked. "Anywho, I expect people to leave the Revolution, what I didn't expect was for them to join your side. I thought for sure, many would just flee to try and escape the fun. And you know, I'd leave them alone. Once I've caused them pain, I've already taken what I need. Aren't humans funny? So eager to split into two different sides. We don't have free thinkers in the world anymore."

Strike shook her head. "You're delusional. People flock to goodness and safety. No one wants to live under a man who demands pain from them. You pry on the weak and vulnerable, just like all of you dirtbags around the world. You're a coward—a pussy."

Chris leered as blood really did rush to his penis. "I suppose we should get you ready for the show, on that note." The guards who had brought her up remained by the door, and Chris nodded to them. "Gentlemen, please slide a chair over to the center of the room and tie the commander to it with her hands behind her back."

"Yes, sir," said a bear of a man, who took charge and stepped forward to start rearranging furniture.

Chris and Strike watched, standing beside each other while a strange hollowness filled the air. He wanted desperately to feast on Strike's fear, but there was none. Whatever she was radiating seemed closer to confidence, a much more sour flavor than fear or grief.

"What was the final meal of your life? Just curious?"

"I had a bowl of spaghetti with meatballs," she replied surprisingly quick.

"How lovely. Tell me, Commander, have you thought about death yet? Not the pain that's coming, but the darkness afterward? The fall into a pit of nothingness as you watch your entire life flash by."

Her stern expression softened, and Chris watched as her mind played through this exact scenario.

"Was it all worth it, Commander? Becoming this fierce leader for the Road Runners and trying to take me down? Surely you must have known this was a possibility for how it could all end."

"This isn't the end. They're going to come save me, and then we're going to kill you."

Chris grinned. "That's a nice daydream. You know, those people did show up with plans to take you out of here. And now their bodies are my front lawn decorations. Little gnomes, you could say. If anyone else comes this way, they'll have to navigate through a minefield of dead Road Runners."

Chris stopped talking and studied the commander's face, watching as hope gradually vanished from her eyes, her soul deflating like a balloon with an invisible leak. With that, the aroma oozing from her body changed from the bitterness of confidence, to the sweetness of fear. With a few words he managed to flip her emotions and spiral her thoughts out of control.

"Sir, everything is ready," a soldier announced.

A chair was set up in the middle of the floor, handcuffs and a thick rope lying on the floor next to a sanding table that held a pistol, various blades, pliers, a hammer, and the wires and control panel for the electroshock device.

"We're going to have so much fun, Commander. Shall we?"

Chris grabbed her arm and forced her to the chair, ensuring that her hands ran over the back, where they would remain handcuffed. He grabbed her head and pushed her down like a police officer guiding a suspect into the backseat of their patrol car.

The helpful soldier returned and tied the rope around Strike's body and the chair, pulling it snug enough to apply pressure on her liver, making her squirm in discomfort.

Chris squatted down to meet her eye level and checked his watch. "Ten minutes, Commander, and then we'll start the show."

16

Chapter 16

They landed in Aruba right on schedule. Time was unfrozen at the exact point Antonio had said, and he took control of the plane for their descent to the small island. During the latter half of the flight, once the shock of everything had worn off, Martin pondered many questions regarding this and future trips. Mainly, what was the plan? He understood they wanted to ease him back into the United States, but did that even matter at this point? Were they waiting for Strike to actually die before bringing him home, to ensure no one would try to pull off an exchange with Chris?

The scent of saltwater surrounded them when they stepped off the jet. The ocean waited a whole mile away from the small airport they had landed. With all the stress of the flight gone, Martin suddenly craved a plate of seafood. Lobster, crab legs, and shrimp jumped to the front of his thoughts as he followed his two guards out of the hangar.

"Commander Blair made arrangements for us, and likely will for all of our stops," Everett said while they each pulled a suitcase behind them. "No one knows we're here, so we can spend a couple of days on this island. We have a penthouse suite overlooking the ocean. We'll be staying together now—can't take any risks."

"I hope dinner is on the schedule," Martin said, feeling a comfort that reminded him of the first day he arrived at Crooked Island.

"Absolutely," Everett replied.

"One of the finest restaurants on the island is in our hotel," Antonio said. "You know we're going there, but we do need to wash up—I'm sure they have a dress code."

"The hotel is only five minutes from here," Everett said as they were walking toward nothing. "We're supposed to have a town car picking us up."

"It's coming," Antonio said, nodding in the direction of an approaching black car. "Remember, no speaking aloud of anything Road Runner-related. Not until we get to the suite."

The car pulled up and a local stepped out to greet them. His skin was dark, accent thick with the flavors of the tropics. They rode without conversation, their driver whistling along to the music playing on the radio. All the tension faded as they trusted the plan would work to ensure no one had a chance of finding Martin.

The "hotel" turned out to be a resort. It overlooked the beach, had its own swimming pool, casino, restaurants, night clubs, and golf course. It felt like they were pulling into another world as they entered the massive building. Martin hung back with Antonio while Everett checked them in and gathered the room keys.

He returned with a wide grin and a bottle of champagne. "Compliments of the hotel," he said. "For their special penthouse guests."

"You know we can't drink on the job," Antonio said, snatching the bottle away. "Martin, you can have this bottle, but we won't be joining you."

Martin grabbed it and examined the label as if he had been a lifelong connoisseur. "I won't tell anyone. One glass won't kill you. You guys work tirelessly."

"See, Tony? The future commander wants us to have a drink with him," Everett said. "What do you say?"

Antonio shrugged. "Maybe. Only after a perimeter check."

"Of course. I wouldn't have it any other way," Everett replied with a grin.

"Martin," Antonio said, returning to his stern self. "Some rules do apply while we're here. Even though we don't expect anyone to know you, we can't afford to play it safe. We'd like for you to stay in the suite the whole time, but understand that's unreasonable. One of us has to stay by your side the moment you walk out of our room. Is that clear?"

Martin nodded like a scolded child.

"I don't mind if you go to the beach, but I've got to urge you to not go into the ocean itself. There's just too much that can happen in open water."

"No worries on that front – I'm not one for swimming."

"Perfect. Now, let's go check out this suite and see if the pictures do it justice."

They followed Everett down a hallway toward an elevator, and rode it up to the sixth floor penthouse.

When they walked in, Martin's jaw nearly hit the floor. Crystal chandeliers hung from the ceiling. Wide, leather couches surrounded a tiger-hide rug. A fireplace crackled softly along the back wall, just below a TV that appeared to be no less than 100 inches wide. The kitchen sparkled, its countertops so shiny they could see their reflections on the granite.

Even with all the luxuries his new life as a time traveler provided, Martin still let himself be amazed with each new discovery. *There are real people who vacation to a place like this*, he thought. His trip to the Bahamas had been the only significant thing he'd done since coming into his fortune, aside from buying the big house for him, Sonya, and his mother to live in.

Sonya. What she'd give to come to a place like this.

He shook his head free of the thought, not wanting to let her consume his mind like she had done on so many lonely nights.

"Is this really where we're staying?" Martin asked.

"You know how we do things," Antonio said. "Nothing but the finest."

"I guess it's official, then. You guys have to have a drink with me in this place."

Everett cracked a grin while nodding. "Most certainly."

Antonio remained silent and walked across the living room, plopping down on the couch where he rubbed his temples.

"Something wrong?" Everett asked.

Antonio nodded slowly. "With all the commotion today, I completely forgot about tonight."

"Commander Strike?" Everett replied. "You don't think that's actually going to happen, do you? Why would he kill our commander? If anything, he's probably keeping her around to use for information."

"No." Antonio shook his head violently. "She's been with him long enough. He either has all the information he needs, or has given up trying to get it."

"But he can use her as leverage in negotiations."

"He tried—it didn't work. We wouldn't be here if it had."

"Well, thank God for small favors," Martin said with a chuckle.

"Thank the voters actually," Antonio said.

"The execution is supposed to start in an hour," Everett said while skimming his cell phone. "There's a report of a group of Road Runners who were killed on Chris's property. Sounds like they were there with the intent of breaking out Strike. They found their private jet at the hangar, dozens of boxes of ammunition waiting for them to use."

"Jesus Christ," Martin said, putting a hand over his lips. "How many?"

"Twelve. That's a clean sweep for Chris – not a single survivor."

"What are we going to do about it?" Martin asked.

"Not much we can do," Antonio said. "Those people went of their own free will."

A heavy silence hung over the room for a few seconds while they reflected on what had happened to their fellow Road Runners. Martin had a mental flashback to that godforsaken mansion. He could still feel the brisk coldness of the air, smell the snow in the clouds, and hear that crunching noise of walking on snow-packed ground. He pictured those dead bodies on the front lawn, lifeless blobs of flesh to remind anyone else what happened if you dared to approach the mansion.

"We're not going to actually watch this broadcast, are we?" Everett asked.

"I think we need to," Antonio said, matter-of-fact. "How else will we know if it's a bluff?"

"He doesn't bluff," Martin said sharply. "He just doesn't. If he already said she's going to die tonight, then consider her dead."

Antonio nodded. "Well, I'll be watching. You two are more than welcome to join me. How about for now we get settled into our bedrooms and you can think it over?"

They agreed and split their separate ways. Martin wasn't interested in setting up his bedroom, not for a two-day stay. He had no issue living out of his suitcase. This allowed him to kick off his shoes and splay across the king-sized bed. A ceiling fan hummed above and provided him with fresh air that he'd fall asleep to. Until they came to wake him up to watch Commander Strike get murdered on live television.

17

Chapter 17

Chris rummaged through his desk drawers, making final preparations for the live stream of his upcoming show.

"The time has arrived, Commander. Any final words before we turn on the broadcast?"

The camera that typically clung to the top of his computer had been turned around and moved closer, but was still out of range from any potential blood splatters. No one had time to wipe the lens clean.

Strike remained silent, tied to the chair. She looked around the room, and Chris wondered if she was having that moment where one's entire life flashes before their eyes, like a highlight reel of all the magnificent events that fall forgotten during the day-to-day grind of life.

"Very well, Commander. I'll take your silence as acceptance that you are indeed ready."

Chris had grown giddy with excitement as the time approached. This may have not been the outcome he wanted when he first snatched Commander Strike away from the Road Runners, but it was still titillating regardless.

Three soldiers stood around the perimeter of the room, out of the camera's view. They watched like statues, Chris having made it clear he wanted no intervention unless specifically asked.

He adjusted the camera once the preview came onto the screen, wiggling it to capture the area only around Commander Strike.

You're stalling, he thought. *Still wishing for someone to come knocking on the door with Martin on a silver platter? Push the damn button, and start the featured presentation.*

"Time to party, Commander," he said, and pushed the button to start the live feed overriding the Road Runners' network.

He stepped back and stood in front of Strike, but stayed to the side just enough for the viewers at home to see Strike tied to the chair. The green signal flashed on the screen to confirm the connection was live.

"Good evening, my Road Runner friends. I have to admit, I'm incredibly surprised by your decision to keep Mr. Briar and leave your precious commander here to die. I understand there is quite a rift among your population, and I'm siding with those who are angry about the decision. I want Briar, not this useless commander."

He paused, turned away, and punched Strike in the face. Her head jolted sideways as she let out a soft grunt that likely wasn't picked up in the audio feed.

Chris returned to the camera. "I'm not sure how many of you have heard, but a courageous group of Road Runners came to my house yesterday. They had that typical Road Runner ambition. You know, the kind where you all think you're better and smarter than me." Chris let out a giggle that seemed both accidental and genuine. "It's my understanding that they came behind your backs. See, they understood loyalty. They refused to sit on their hands while their leader is killed. These were my kind of people, and I was ready to welcome them back to the light of the Revolution, but they pressed on a little too hard for my liking. My only regret is that they are no longer here to witness this beautiful event today."

He paused again, and stepped in front of Commander Strike, her head hanging down to her chest. Chris reared his foot back and swung it forward with all of his might, kicking the commander square in her kneecaps, rocking the chair off its feet for half of a second. He then punched her once more before returning to the camera, a bright red mark appearing clearly on Strike's left cheek.

"The funny part is how one day you're going to look back and realize your decision was all for nothing. I'm still going to get Martin Briar if I have to chase him to the end of the world, and there's nothing you can do to stop me. I'll have Briar, and you'll have nothing." He stopped speaking and stepped closer to the camera, wanting to get in the Road Runners' virtual face. "Can you feel it yet? The end is coming. Pretty soon, you'll turn on each other. Once that happens, it's checkmate, and the Revolution wins once again. As you watch this show today, I want all of you who voted for this to ask yourselves one question: Was it worth it?"

Chris drew back, a wide grin stuck on his face, as he returned to Commander Strike. He grabbed her chair and swung it around so she was facing the camera straight on. "Say hi, everyone!" Chris cackled. "Hi, Commander. Any last words of advice before you leave your people behind?"

Strike raised her head and stared into the camera, her face

plastered with zero emotion, skin turning white with fear. "Burn this motherfucker to the ground."

Chris howled and started skipping around the chair in what looked like a half-assed attempt at dancing. "Commander, you never fail to bring a smile to my face. I really am going to miss you."

He leaned over and kissed Strike on top of the head. She remained silent, eyes glued to the camera as if someone might jump out of the lens and save her. But no one was coming. There was no way into this mansion, and certainly no way of negotiating with a psychopath. Doom and dread clung to every particle in the air.

"The show goes on," Chris barked. He moved to the table covered with all of the tools of torture he planned on using, studying them for a second, lifting a hammer and examining it like an ancient relic. He drummed it softly against his open palm, then did the same thing on Strike's head to get her full attention. "Now I can taste you, Commander. You'll be mine forever."

He knelt down next to Strike's feet, the rope snug around her ankles strapped to the chair legs. "We're going to start down here and work our way up," Chris explained to the camera, as nonchalant and cheery as Bob Ross explaining his next brushstroke.

He raised the hammer, its handle appearing not much wider than Chris's thin arm, and slammed it down on her right foot with an audible *THWACK!*

Strike shrieked and jolted within her chair, but Chris kept hammering away like he was crafting a wooden table.

THWACK! THWACK! THWACK! From the left foot to the right foot. Strike screeched in agony, especially after the final blow shattered her left foot bones into dozens of pieces. She writhed and wiggled, face flushed red as tears ran down her face.

"We're only getting started, folks," Chris said to the camera with his devilish grin. "Don't change the station quite yet." He returned the hammer to the table and returned empty-handed, starting to take his belt off his pants. "You've been a naughty little girl, Commander. All those Revolters you've killed. Now you get the belt so you can think about what you've done wrong."

Chris laughed as he snapped the belt in front of Strike's face, making her wince back and almost tip the chair all the way over.

"Relax, young lady. We're not moving to your face quite yet. This is a process. Think of it as art—it takes time for a finished product that you're proud of."

He stepped a foot back from her and focused his gaze on her shins. They had dressed her in shorts, leaving her legs bare. Chris pulled the belt back and whipped it forward, slapping Strike's legs with a horrendous *CRACK!*

A bright red mark instantly appeared across her pasty legs. Chris reared back and let the belt fly six more times, throwing all of his body weight behind each swing. Droplets of blood had formed where the flesh had turned to a dark shade of red, a couple of them dripping to her ankles.

Strike whimpered like a wounded animal, her head slung down once again. Chris could tell her will was gone, and that signaled that he must continue until she was no more than a fraction of herself. Until she stopped breathing.

He dropped the belt back onto the table and reached underneath the black cloth draped over it, pulling out a sledgehammer with blood caked across its handle.

"Now for the knees," he explained calmly to the camera. "Folks, please know that once I'm through with this phase, our dear commander will never be able to walk again. Never able to chase down a Revolter and end their life. Isn't that a pleasant thought?"

He returned to Strike, dragging the sledgehammer behind him, tugging the floor covering. "Now, I imagine you're all at home, watching in shock, gasping in horror," he said to the camera. "But rest assured, our event will be ending soon enough. Consider this your last call for drinks. I'd hate for any of you to get killed because you drove drunk." Chris threw his head to the ceiling and let out a howling laughter, then grunted as he lifted the sledgehammer. He lacked the physical strength of his prime, and figured he might only get two swings in before he had to stop. Fortunately, there were only two knees to hit.

He held the sledgehammer above his head, arms wavering from its weight, tongue pinched between his lips as he drew all of his concentration on landing the hammer's head squarely to the kneecap.

It steamrolled through the air and didn't miss, connecting like a crisp, home run swing by a baseball player. The sound wasn't much aside from the cracking of the bone, split down the middle like the Liberty Bell, but Strike had no chance of containing herself with this particular pain.

"MOTHERFUCKER!" she screamed. "PLEASE STOP! I CAN'T TAKE ANY MORE!"

Chris grinned before raising the sledgehammer one more time and connecting again with Strike's other knee. Her eyes rolled back into her head as it bobbed forward and backward. Both knees already turned purple, the area no longer hard, but appearing jiggly like a bowl of Jell-O.

"Just kill me already," she moaned, her words barely audible.

"Did you hear that, Road Runners?" Chris asked as he spun around to the camera. "Your dearest commander just begged to be killed. That doesn't sound courageous. That doesn't sound like something a brave little Road Runner would say. There are no martyrs in this war – you will all die when I decide it's time."

Strike's head was now leaning back, her throat stretched as she stared to the ceiling, surely praying for it all to end.

"I must say, your pleas are music to my ears," Chris said as he dragged the sledgehammer back to the table, shifting his attention to the electroshock device. He had to untangle the wires, but continued speaking as he did. "I don't know. Should we let the electricity be the final stage? Or shall we have it as an encore?" He turned to the camera and shrugged. "I think one more after will be fine. We should probably cook our Road Runner before we feast, right? Oh, and for you watching at home... if you haven't eaten dinner yet, my apologies! This next bit is sure to make you hungry."

Chris licked his lips before lugging the wires and box to Strike. He dropped the device on her lap, but she didn't so much as budge. Surely her entire lower body had turned numb by now. Chris lifted Strike's shirt enough to feed the wires underneath, pressing their adhesive ends against the flesh on her stomach, sides, and chest. "Don't worry, Commander, I'm not here to cop a feel. I'm a gentleman, don't you know?"

Strike mumbled something, but Chris would never know what she was trying to say. He didn't dwell on it and returned to the camera. "Electricity is a funny thing. At this point in time, we *need* it to live. But did you know if you have too much of it, it can cause some serious issues? I think we just might be able to turn Commander Strike braindead. Or is that taking it too far? I'm sure she always imagined a peaceful death, and not one where her mind felt like a California wildfire." He shrugged. "Well, let's just see what happens!"

He grabbed the control box and turned the dials without any further dramatics. A subtle grunt left Strike's mouth before her body tensed up as stiff as a board. Her hair stood up in a frazzled mess, her legs and bottom elevated from the chair as she looked like a tethered balloon caught in a windstorm. Her jaw was clenched so tightly the bone protruded crisply beneath the flesh on her face. Smoke started oozing from beneath her shirt, and this made Chris howl with joy. "Kentucky Fried Chickenshit!" he cried out.

Once he decided she had sizzled enough, he turned the electric current off and watched Strike's body fall back into the seat, limp and unconscious. Electricity was still flowing through her body as it kept twitching randomly, her head jolting back while her tongue flipped and flopped outside of her mouth like a fish out of water.

"It looks like she's still breathing," Chris said, pointing to her chest as it rose and fell. "Can you hear me in there, Commander?" He stuck out his bony fingers and snapped them in front of her face, only to receive no reaction. "She's on her last limb, folks. The end is near for our dear Commander Strike. Now, the real question is, how do we end this? How do we send her home for good?"

Chris approached the table and rubbed his hands together as he made this ultimate decision. He picked up and examined a pair of pliers, a screwdriver, and a chef's knife, promptly putting each back down as he frowned in disappointment and placed his hands on his hips.

"I know," he said, leaving the table and crossing the room to his desk that was outside of the camera's range. He returned into view a few seconds later with a plastic grocery bag. "Suffocation is beautiful," he said to the audience surely watching in disbelief. "It really allows the body to put up its final attempt at living, until it just gives up. You can literally watch a person lose their will to live."

He stepped up to Strike, her head cocked upward, eyes still open as they stared blankly at the ceiling.

"It has been an honor getting to know you over these past few days, Commander," Chris said in a tone as if he were delivering a eulogy. "We've gone after each other for the past year, and I'll admit, you gave me a scare when that Russian man shot me from the trees. What an incredible shot! I wish I had someone of his talent on my team." Chris turned and stared into the camera. "If you're out there, Mr. Russian Sharpshooter, give me a call. I can take much better care of you than these people."

Chris turned back to Strike after delivering his public service announcement. "I'm just sorry that it came to this, Commander. You had a good run, it's a shame your own people chose to let you die like a forgotten animal on the side of the road. I'll see you on the other side."

He whipped open the bag and worked it over Strike's head, tying the two handles into a bow beneath her chin, pulling them snug so no air could escape. "Your beautiful bonnet, my lady," Chris said, taking a step back and moving his hand to his chin.

Strike's head bucked forward, her arms flexing against the rope in a hopeless effort. Chris watched her struggle for another thirty seconds until her tied-up hands stopped moving and her head slumped forward, motionless.

He lowered his head and pressed his ear against her chest, a wide grin spreading across his face. "She's gone, ladies and gentlemen. That's all she wrote." He stood and straightened his shirt before facing the camera one final time. "The ball is in your court, my dear Road Runners. You forced this move. Let this serve as a reminder of what happens when you choose to dance with the Revolution. This war is just about over – it's been a pleasure dueling with you all."

Chris stepped closer to the camera, sticking his entire face in front of the lens so that his face filled the screen. "And Martin Briar, I know you're out there. If you're watching this, we know you're in Aruba. My team will not sleep until you are in my possession. Mark my words. Have a good night, everyone."

He stepped back and blew a kiss to the camera before circling behind his desk and cutting the feed, the final image that of Commander Strike sitting dead in her chair.

18

Chapter 18

"Let's get the fuck out of here, right now!" Antonio shouted moments after Chris called out Martin's location on the live broadcast.

"How did he know?" Everett asked, jumping over the couch to start running toward his bedroom.

"He knows everything. He's always shown up wherever I am. It's like he can see into my mind," Martin said.

The two guards dashed around their penthouse suite like mad zombies. Martin wasn't shaken up by Chris's direct message; he even half-expected it. Deep down, he knew there was no actual way to hide from Chris. The old man's death would be the only way to live in true peace.

Everett ran from room to room, cell phone to his ear as he made calls for a car, the plane, and arrangements for wherever they were going next. Martin also overheard a reference to Commander Blair and a decoy jet as he shuffled to his room to grab his suitcase that he hadn't even opened yet.

Within five minutes the two guards were ready, panting for breath as they dashed to the door with their suitcases rolling behind, loaded guns cocked and ready in their free hand.

"Martin, stay in the middle of us, same routine as earlier," Antonio commanded.

"You guys know I can work a gun," Martin said, smirking. "You don't have to treat me like some incapable princess. I passed my field test, just like you."

"We know that," Everett said, exasperation slipping into his voice. "We just have direct orders to not let you get involved in any sort of shootout. If bullets ever start flying, we just need you to get behind us and let us do our jobs."

"I appreciate that, guys, but I really don't think Chris is remotely interested in shooting me. He only wants me for my Warm Soul."

"We know that, but can't afford to risk anything. This is Chris, after all. He can change his mind in the blink of an eye and decide he wants to wipe you off the planet."

Martin hadn't considered this true fact, and after watching the torturous death of Commander Strike, had no interest in seeing what plans Chris had in store for him. They had watched the show in silence, cringing at each act of violence carried out by their enemy. Martin's blood boiled, his mouth pooling with saliva as he dreamed for the day of Chris's death.

Antonio pulled open the door and stepped into the hallway, pistol first, swinging it from the left to the right. "We're clear," he called over his shoulder, waving his arm before grabbing his suitcase and rolling it out.

Martin followed while Everett brought up the rear. They ran down the hallway, the gold and red patterns of the wallpaper zooming by in a blur while their feet rumbled over the carpet.

"Stairs!" Everett shouted from behind, and Antonio ran right past the elevator lobby and its shiny gold doors.

"We're on the sixth floor," Martin said.

"It's a precaution," Antonio said over his shoulder. "Elevators are a trap. Chris can cut off the power and leave us in the shaft for him to come feast."

They reached the end of the long hallway where Antonio kicked open the stairwell door. They ran down the six flights, each level feeling longer than the prior one for Martin. He still didn't feel anxious, no adrenaline rush, and wondered why they were so willing to have a knee-jerk reaction based on Chris's words. Martin believed the old man was just playing games. What if he was counting on them fleeing the hotel to return to the jet? Surely his people would be waiting there to intercept him and have an easy exit off the island. The more he thought about it, the more it seemed like a classic Chris maneuver, always a step ahead. Martin debated bringing it up to his guards, but trusted their decisions as they had little earpieces in communication with a private group of Road Runners monitoring the entire world.

They reached the ground level and burst through the exit door like a herd of rhinos. The humidity clung to their skin, bringing the sweat that had already started to form thanks to their sprint down six flights of stairs.

A black car sat idling, waiting for them, and Antonio barreled forward as the trunk opened and their same driver who had brought them jumped out and dashed to the back to help them.

"We need to get back to the hangar right now!" Antonio barked, the driver immediately sensing the urgency. They all tossed their bags into the trunk, Martin and Everett lunging into the backseat, while Antonio took shotgun. "Let's go!" he shouted, the driver wasting no time flooring the accelerator.

They drove in silence, the only sound that of their heavy

panting for breath. The driver kept them moving at a rapid pace for the next couple of minutes until Everett called out, "We're being followed!"

Martin looked over to see him staring out the back window.

"Are you sure?" Antonio asked, pulling his pistol out and cocking it, the driver's eyes bulging for a brief second as he took his eyes off the road.

"Who else would be driving this fast right behind us?" Everett replied, also pulling out his gun.

"Keep driving," Antonio instructed the driver. "Faster, faster!"

"Who the hell are you people?!" the driver shouted, driving faster as his own panic settled in.

"Just go, we can lose them!"

The engine roared as Martin looked out the back window. Headlights glared in the dark of the night, matching their exact pace as they sped toward the coast.

"I can't lose them!" the driver screamed, his eyes dashing from the rear view to the road like he was watching a ping pong match.

"Pull over!" Antonio shouted, his hand already moving toward the door's handle.

The car came to a screeching halt, sending Martin and Everett into the back of the front seats. Antonio dropped his shoulder into the door and tumbled out to the side of the road, stood up, and immediately started blasting at the car.

"Stay in the car, and stay down!" Everett snarled, jumping out to join Antonio.

The car didn't slow down one bit, its brake lights not even flickering on. The collision into the rear of their town car sounded more like an explosion. Glass and shards of metal exploded into every direction, sticking into Antonio's and Everett's arms as they shielded their heads.

The front end of the vehicle flattened like a soda can, making it impossible to see what kind of car it was. A man opened the driver side door and rolled onto the pavement, vomiting as he stumbled to his feet like a drunk. "LONG LIVE THE REVOLUTION!" he screamed to the sky, reaching into his waistband. He never had a chance of grabbing his pistol before Antonio and Everett each shot a slug through the man's chest.

They watched as his body collapsed to the ground, skull cracking on the road like an egg on a skillet.

Meanwhile, in the town car, Martin saw stars dancing around his vision that was already blurring in and out of focus.

"Martin!" Antonio shouted, lunging for the car.

Martin pushed himself back in a seated position, his head bobbing from side to side. "What happened?"

Antonio looked to the front seat and saw their driver slouched over the steering wheel, hands limp at his side. "He's still breathing," Antonio said. "He's not dead! How are you, Martin?"

A red mark had spread across Martin's forehead that he started to rub. "My head hurts, but I'm okay."

"Do you know where you are?" Antonio asked, getting in Martin's face.

"Aruba, heading for the jet to leave."

"And why are we leaving?"

Martin shrugged. "Because you guys are afraid of Chris."

The response caught Antonio off guard, causing him to step back.

Everett joined them after checking on the Revolter's car. "Let's get out of here before anyone else shows up."

"Help me move our driver over to the passenger seat," Antonio said. "He looks fine, just knocked out. I wish we could stay to help him, but we really need to get on that jet."

Martin waited in the backseat, still gathering his bearings while his two guards slid the driver to the next seat and fastened the seat belt over his shoulder.

Antonio dropped in the driver's seat and started the car. The collision had only smashed the trunk and their bags. The car ran with no issues, and they continued to the hangar where the jet waited to take them to their next destination.

19

Chapter 19

Road Runners from all around the continent fled to New York City, but didn't announce their presence. Instead, the Council watched from their underground offices as the map of their city showed an influx of Road Runners in the area.

"An increase of fifteen percent and climbing every day," Councilwoman Murray announced, reading from the latest updates, a new ritual that had started over the past week.

"Why?" Councilman Martinez asked.

"Hopefully a peaceful protest," Chief Councilman Uribe said. "We can't afford any other dramatics at this point, and this better not be exposed to the general public."

"Do we have a team ready to prevent that from happening?" Murray asked.

"Not exactly," Councilman Pierre said. "We've had to increase security at all of our offices around the country. After Strike's death, many of those opposed to the decision took to their local offices to protest. Some got a bit too rowdy and the Lead Runners made calls for additional support. We've had to move our soldiers all around to where the biggest threats were posed. Primarily in the cities where leadership and the population have differing opinions."

"This wasn't even decided by leadership," Martinez said. "It was strictly a vote."

"And that's what I fear," Uribe said. "Right now people are just upset and feel the urge to raise hell. Going to a local leadership office seems like a good place to start. Once this initial shock wears off, people will start taking the fight to each other. Opinions will be voiced, and it will eventually become clear on who voted for which side in this debacle. Once that knowledge is widespread, then we're looking at a major issue on our hands."

"A civil war," Councilwoman Thrasher stated.

"I don't think we'll get to that point," Uribe said. "Emotions and tensions are high right now, yes, but we have to get back to business. We have an election to run, and hopefully that will take everyone's minds off of the horrendous act we all witnessed."

"The people don't want an election—they want their commander back," Murray said sternly. "They especially don't want to vote for the man they feel responsible for Strike's death."

"First off, Chris is the only person responsible," Uribe snapped back. "Secondly, we have no involvement with the election aside from administrative duties. We don't pick the candidates, or run campaign commercials. We count the votes and make sure nothing questionable is happening."

A hurried knock rapped on the door that led to the hallway, and all heads turned to it.

"Come in!" Uribe barked, rubbing his forehead in frustration.

The door swung open and one of the aides stepped in, a young woman by the name of Amber Sandoval who had been a direct aide to Uribe for the last five years. She was a tall woman who walked with confidence in each step.

"We have an issue," Amber said, strolling in as she brushed back her wavy brown hair.

"Is this urgent, Amber?" Uribe asked, dropping his pen on his notepad and clasping his hands together.

"Yes, sir. We've been monitoring the increased Road Runner population this morning and it appears there are thousands headed here."

"Here? Goddammit!" Uribe snarled.

"That's not all, sir. There's been an incident at the Chicago office. We're still gathering details, but the entire office has been set on fire. There was a group of Road Runners who traveled from Iowa to Chicago, picking up more as they went. That group barged into the Chicago office with cannisters of gasoline and set the place ablaze."

"Our own people?!" Pierre gasped.

"Do we know who these people are? Do they have any connection to each other, or to the Revolution?" Uribe asked, raising a hand to the rest of his team to remain silent.

"That's what we're still trying to piece together. They tagged the wall with red ink before the building went up. It said 'Liberty is the future.' Any thoughts on what that means?"

Uribe looked to his Council for responses, but only received blank stares in return.

"No," Martinez finally said, defeated.

"We did a quick scan of the voting records from those we know were involved," Amber said. "At least thirty of them we could identify as having a part in setting the fire. All thirty voted to save Strike."

"Chicago is one of our biggest offices," Uribe said. "How many survived?"

"Correct," Amber replied. "There were seven hundred in the office today, going back to follow the tracking devices shows at least five hundred escaped before things got out of hand—we went back to check the footage from inside the office, but nothing came up."

"Someone cut off the security system?" Pierre asked, leaning forward in his seat.

"Yes," Amber said. "About five minutes before the fire began."

"I don't believe this," Thrasher said, standing up. "We need to leave."

"No one's leaving," Uribe snarled. "We need to sit down and figure out how to address this. We need to send reinforcements to Chicago. We need to launch the election. This is not the time to make a run for the hills – our organization needs us."

"You can sit here if you want," Thrasher said, packing up her bag and grabbing her purse. "Those people aren't coming here to have a discussion." She had her things and dashed for the door, brushing by Amber who had remained only a few steps inside their private chambers.

"Stop!" Uribe barked. "Get back here right now!"

Thrasher didn't so much as pause, keeping her head down as she charged out of the room.

"Goddammit!" Uribe cried. "Anyone else want to leave?"

Martinez and Councilwoman Lewis nodded while Murray crossed her arms. Pierre studied his phone, scrolling down the screen frantically in search of information. Uribe stared in his direction until the councilman looked up.

"I was just checking the disbursement of soldiers," Pierre said. "Even though this office is the second most protected, we can't withstand the amount of people coming this way. The safe decision is to leave. We don't know what these people want. I hope it's a peaceful protest, but after Chicago, why stick around to find out?"

"Well, someone needs to. We are the only Road Runners in power – we are here to serve the people."

"With all due respect, sir, that is not a wise decision. The Chicago attacks are only the beginning, I'm afraid. We have a rocky road ahead."

"Councilwoman Murray," Uribe said, turning to his left and ignoring Pierre. "Since when are you so silent? What are your thoughts?"

"Councilman Ryan hasn't said anything, either. Why are you singling me out?" Murray replied with a frown.

"I'm not asking about Councilman Ryan, I'm asking you."

"I have no issue staying here," Murray said confidently. "I'm not afraid of hypothetical situations like everyone else. Do we really think the people of our organization would travel across the country just to hurt us?"

"Amber," Uribe said, turning his attention to his aide. "Where are the people coming from? Have you had a chance to see?"

"Not for everyone, sir, but it appears to be random. We've only pulled a small sample size, but it appears to be along the same trend of Chicago—all people who voted to rescue Strike."

"Understood, thank you. Please let the rest of your team know to go home immediately. Thank you for your hard work today. We'll plan to be back to business as usual tomorrow morning."

"So you want all of us to leave?" Murray asked after Amber stepped out of the room.

"Might as well. We don't even have a full team here – what are we supposed to do?"

"We can stay and talk to these people coming," Murray said. "If anyone can come to a peaceful conclusion, surely it's you."

"The world is going mad, Councilwoman. It already was before this drama started. Ten years ago, maybe I'd stay. Back then I never had doubt about people's intentions. Today is a different story. It's hard to trust anyone, you know? Common sense and compassion are fading with every year that passes. And we're the ones who get left with the job of finding a way to keep pushing through it all. I don't know what our future holds. Sure you can jump ahead and see, but you know that stuff is never accurate.

"It only takes one event to change the course of everything. We lead in the present, looking back to the mistakes of those before us, hoping to shape a better world from it. But it feels to me, that no matter what we do, the world just keeps on going down a dark rabbit hole."

"It all stems from Chris," Martinez said. "He's the goddamn devil, tricking people, pitting them against each other. Don't ever forget that we all share this ability because of him and the Revolution. All time travelers come through the only funnel he has control over. I like to think we all have more in common than Chris would like us to believe."

"We're beyond that," Uribe said. "We should have killed Chris a long time ago."

"That's a job for a commander, not us," Murray said bluntly.

"We can bicker all night about our past, but I'm going home and getting to bed early while I have the chance. I'm sure my guards at home are just ecstatic to stay up all night sitting on my front porch." Uribe stood, and this prompted everyone else to follow suit, trailing his steps as he left the room.

Everyone left, except Councilwoman Murray. She remained at the table, offering a fake smile to each councilor as they passed. She had no intent on leaving. She'd be the one to stay and speak with those on their way.

20

Chapter 20

Despite what happened in Alaska, the Liberation grew, gathering new followers in every town they stopped on their way to New York. The Council worked out of the small town of Thornwood, just under an hour's drive north of Manhattan. They wanted to be near a busy city, but not *in* the city. Their front above ground was a strip mall, where every member of the Council entered through the mall's only restaurant, going through the back kitchen and down a secret flight of stairs that took them to an entire world of offices and private meeting chambers underground.

The place was deserted when the Liberation arrived, but they didn't care. They came to send a message, and dammit, that's what they intended to do. The parking lot was deserted as their caravan pulled into the mall, hundreds of cars lining the road and seeming to take over the town. They preferred to move at night, still wary of being caught by regular civilians.

Chicago was a close call, but they managed to slip out just in time. That had also been a warning shot of things to come, New York and the Council being the biggest targets for their destruction.

As far as the Liberation was concerned, the Council had the power—and the right—to make the decision and trade Briar for Strike. They failed to do their job and sat by while their sitting commander was killed in a most gruesome fashion on live television.

Stephen DeVito had been killed in the botched Alaska mission, and they were too new of a group to have procedures set in place for what to do in such a scenario. Instead, they allowed a new leader to naturally rise to the top. That ended up being a man by the name of Thaddeus Hamilton, a ruthless advocate for all matters opposed to Road Runner leadership.

Thaddy, as his closest friends called him, wasn't always this way. He was once a loyal Road Runner, grateful for the opportunities they had presented him, but after a mission they had authorized sent his brother—his only living relative—to his death, his opinions toward leadership quickly soured.

Thaddeus led the caravan and was the first to step out of his car as they stood in front the strip mall's restaurant, Pavilion. He flicked a cigarette butt into the distance, the lot's gravel crunching beneath his boots as he approached the building and popped a fresh cigarette between his lips. He stood one inch above six feet and always wore a flannel shirt with a black vest, and a pair of jeans. His face was pale, but weathered, partly due to the pack he smoked every day, but also thanks to his life as a farmer in northern California. Even with all of the riches he earned as a time traveler, he couldn't resist working with his hands every day, tending to a farm where he grew vegetables that he sold to local markets at an unbelievably generous price. He wasn't in it for the money, and felt he could make the world a better place by contributing this way.

He was a man tied to his beliefs that everyone should have the freedom to do as they please as long as their actions didn't put others at risk. Thaddeus was by no means unreasonable, believing that structure had to exist to ensure chaos didn't run rampant, but when the Road Runners made laws regarding when and where you could travel, he gathered his like-minded friends and protested at the office in Sacramento, pleading with local leadership to do what they could to prevent such laws from passing.

If someone wanted to travel into the 2070's and put their life at risk, they had the right to do that just as much as the people who traveled back in time to enjoy a Sinatra concert. These matters bothered him, but never to the point of raising hell over it. People tried to rule the world by enforcing restrictions on what others could and couldn't do, a fact as old as time.

"Why is no one here?" Thaddeus asked, more to himself, as he stood and faced the building with his hands on his hips.

"I just got off the phone with Councilwoman Murray," a young man said, running up to stand beside Thaddeus. "She said they all left. She tried to keep them in the building, but one of their aides barged into their meeting and told them we were coming."

Thaddeus didn't respond, and simply took a long drag from his cigarette, blowing the smoke out of his nose. "That's unfortunate for us, but good for them. Oh well, we came here to send a message, and we still can. Is Councilwoman Murray still inside?"

"Yes, sir."

Thaddeus started for the building, the parking lot now filled to its capacity with cars and people. The whole reason for bringing thousands of people across the continent, and hundreds to this particular location, was to wipe out any resistance. He looked over his shoulder to find the roughly three hundred Liberators waiting for his next command. With no one to put up a fight, this mission could have only taken two people to complete.

"I want you all to wait here," Thaddeus shouted to his anxious group. On the surface they appeared peaceful, perhaps a regular crowd visiting the already closed mall. But beneath, they all had a burning rage toward the Road Runners for what they had done to Commander Strike. Deep down, they were ready to burn this building to a pile of rubble.

He turned and started for the building, entering through the restaurant's front doors that had been unlocked thanks to Councilwoman Murray. The lights were off, minus a glowing lamp in the parking lot. The restaurant had its chairs placed on top of the tables, every inch of the place freshly wiped down with cleaning chemicals before another day of business arrived in the morning.

Except they won't be open, Thaddeus thought. *Unless you want your toast extra burnt.*

He continued down the dark hallway, cutting past the dining room and slipping into the kitchen as he wove between stoves and ovens, beyond the freezer and to the furthest back corner where a narrow door stood in the wall, tiled to match the rest of the kitchen and blend in. Every Road Runner office was essentially the same type of setup, and they had already visited three different locations during their journey to the Northeast. All the hype for the Council's office was the heightened security detail, but with multiple attacks around the continent, resources were spread thin, and they now had the building to themselves.

Thaddeus pressed on the door and it clicked as it popped open, the slightest of creaks escaping its hinges, revealing a dimly lit stairway. He stepped down, a clear sense of abandonment in the entire building as his boots clopped and echoed with each step.

When he reached the floor below, motion lights flickered on and illuminated the entire space, which was nothing but a long hallway with dozens of doors. He started down the hall, passing the doors of Council members with their names etched onto golden plates.

"Councilwoman Murray?" he called out, his voice bouncing back like a boomerang.

A door opened and splashed brighter light into the hallway, and out stepped Murray, a wide grin on her face as she raced down the hall to meet Thaddeus.

"It's so great to see you," she said, opening her arms to embrace him. He planted a kiss on her cheek.

"And it's great having you in our corner. I know all of us with the Liberation are excited for what we can achieve together."

"As am I. I'm sorry about tonight. You know how tight our security is. It was worth a shot, but it sounds like they've had eyes on all of you since this morning."

"It's okay, totally out of your control. We appreciate you trying to get your colleagues to stay. If only we had an easy way of removing these damn tracking devices."

"I know it. That will be one of my main focuses. If we can lose the trackers, the possibilities truly become endless."

"Now that's the kind of world I want to live in."

They shared a chuckle followed by a momentary silence as Thaddeus looked around.

"Do you want to see our chambers?" Murray asked.

"Absolutely. Do you think that's the best place to start?"

"It's our main meeting area. We spend hours in there bickering about what to do." She led them three doors down the hallway where she pushed open the door to show their grand chambers, complete with a glimmering round table, white boards, and its own kitchen area.

"So this is where the decision was made to let the people vote on Strike's death?" he asked, crossing his arms as he admired the room.

"Don't remind me of that horrible day. I still can't believe how everything has played out since."

"Neither can we. That's why we work tirelessly to find a way to take control of our beloved organization back from all of those who have lost touch with common sense. What do you know about this Martin Briar, anyway?"

"Well, he's the only Warm Soul in North America, and the plan is for him to use that ability to finally bring down Chris. He received permission from Strike to go into the future to obtain a special medicine for his mother suffering from Alzheimer's. I don't know why she decided he could go—she had rejected similar requests hundreds of times during her year in office. He must have made a compelling case, or she owed him."

"Wasn't he the one in Sonya's house when Strike ordered the hit on Chris?"

"Yes he was. Sent there to kill Sonya and ended up getting seriously wounded himself. I'll admit, we shouldn't have much to dislike about the guy. From what I've heard, he's a hard-working man who cares about the organization."

"We'll see about that. The others still want to endorse him?"

He was referring to the other commanders around the world. Their endorsement, even from a different continent, carried major weight in an election. Typically, when they endorsed a candidate, that person went on to win the election.

"Very much so. Commander Blair is a huge advocate, as is Quang. I'm not sure about the others, but they all usually come to an agreement."

"It should be interesting to see how Briar responds to that new role. We've seen plenty of others before him lose touch with themselves and fall into that dirty trap of politics."

"Always possible, yes, but from what I've heard he's a man of his word. Did you know he managed to get the medicine he went into the future for? I'm not sure how he ended up with it, but when he brought it back home he found his mother slaughtered to death. Chris left a note claiming responsibility."

Thaddeus shook his head. "I don't know if the Road Runners should hand over the organization to a man surely dealing with some troubling emotions."

Murray shrugged. "He's only been a Road Runner for a few months. I think they're looking to get someone with fresh blood and ideas into the position. Someone not conditioned to our ways."

"Don't say 'our' ways, Councilwoman. You're a member of the Liberation now."

"Yes, of course. You know what I mean. I still have appearances to keep up—I am a Council member."

"The purest Council member," Thaddeus said with a smirk. "We have no chance of taking over without an insider like you."

"I know that. You just make sure my name stays out of the news. The second any of this leaks, they'll vote me out of the Council."

"I'd like to see them try—we're growing an army."

"You're numbers are strong, but still no match for the Road

Runners if it comes to it."

"We'll be there in time. For now, we attack in the night, limit our confrontations, and make our way, city to city."

"They were on to you today, so you must be more careful. Next time you might not be as lucky."

"Thank you, Councilwoman. We really do appreciate your help. It's too bad your colleagues aren't in the building, but shall we proceed with wiping this place off the map?"

"Yes, but wait five minutes before you start, so I can get my things together. And stay in touch. I don't want to hear about what you're up to from the news. Okay?"

"Yes ma'am, you have my word."

Murray gave a final hug to Thaddeus before turning and leaving the Council's offices for the final time.

21

Chapter 21

Martin and his two guards were back on American soil, hiding out in the bustling city of Miami. There were over 10,000 Road Runners in the city alone, a factor in their decision to hide somewhere with a higher population than the remote islands they had originally planned to bounce around.

Commander Blair again froze time to allow them to travel in peace, and offered to send two of his own soldiers for added protection after hearing of the sneak attack the Revolters tried to carry out in Aruba. Antonio declined, insisting they had matters under control. Plans were also moving forward with the election, and Martin was expected to formally announce his candidacy back in Denver in exactly three days.

The campaign and election night loomed, but were currently the least of their worries. For now they bounced around different Miami hotels every night, but what troubled Martin was seeing Antonio and Everett wandering off to the corner of their hotel rooms, or even stepping outside, to have hushed conversations in private. Martin sensed something was wrong that they didn't want him to hear about.

That all changed tonight, when Antonio urged them to gather around the TV after he connected his computer for the live Road Runners network feed.

Chip Halsey, the Road Runners' longest tenured broadcaster, filled the screen with his gray hair slicked sideways, and his deep, green eyes staring into the souls of Road Runners across the nation.

"I wish I could open our show tonight with a simple greeting of 'Good evening, Road Runners', but I cannot." He spoke in a smooth, deep tone that had lulled viewers for decades. "As an organization we are ill, plagued by the poison that has been fed to us over time. We were supposed to be a better group than this, a level above the average human being, but we have fallen into the same traps of division and hate—even when we're all on the same team.

"Ladies and gentlemen, Chris Speidel is our enemy, a fact that has always been and always will be true. There is no reason for a Road Runner to ever fight another Road Runner, let alone kill one another. We have reached the tipping point of our existence. Maybe this should have been discussed earlier—the signs were certainly present—but it's too late. This is where we are now. The damage has been done, but we are still hanging on by a thread. We must work together and unite against our enemy. Chris Speidel is responsible for the division we are experiencing. He has turned us against each other, and is sitting in his mansion laughing. He's a sick man and thinks this is all a game.

"I beg you all to take a long look in the mirror tonight and think about the ugly road we're headed down. We're a couple of bad decisions away from becoming no different than the Revolution. Is that the kind of world you want your kids and grandkids, your loved ones, to grow up in? For the moment, we have no commander. And as of tonight, our last resort of leadership, the Council, is in hiding. Roll the tape, please."

The screen cut away from Chip and showed an image of a familiar strip mall, the home of the Council. It was dark, so it was hard to see at first the many people standing several feet away from the building. The words 'Liberate or die!' were written across the facade in several places. For a moment it seemed the footage was showing a protest, until the mall exploded.

A bright orange flashed through the windows of the restaurant, a ball of fire bursting out of the building, sending debris barreling into the night sky. The people—mere silhouettes in this footage—jumped and cheered like they were watching a planned fireworks show.

The feed cut back to Chip, his expression stern while he shook his head. "That was the destruction of our Council's chambers. Our only leadership no longer has a place to convene, nor do they have reason to feel safe anywhere they might try to meet. It appears Councilwoman Murray was present in the building tonight, but she did make it out in time. Once all Council members were confirmed safe, our security team decided to turn off their tracking devices for security reasons. Council members, if you're watching, please know that we support you through these difficult times.

"Ladies and gentlemen, we are under attack. From ourselves. Our team has done research on the group responsible for this and the recent attacks. There is a new group of Road Runners who call themselves the Liberation. These are people who fell so out of touch with reality after the decision to spare Martin Briar's life that they've resorted to violence and corruption.

In a sense, they have aligned themselves with the Revolution. They kill Road Runners, blow up our buildings, and are working toward further division and mistrust. We must resist. This time will pass, hopefully sooner than later. We don't know their numbers, but it was enough for Chief Councilman Uribe to send everyone home tonight, including the security detail that protects their offices.

"These people are dangerous. If you find yourself in a situation where they have gathered, run. Don't waste time trying to figure out what they're doing. Put your head down and run for your life. Their arson tonight on official property is a high crime—these people have no limits on the damage they can do.

"As I sign off tonight, I regret to inform you that I, too, will be going dark. Now that I have exposed the Liberation for what they are, my safety is most certainly in jeopardy. Until we can right this ship as an organization, I'll remain offline. Vote in our upcoming election like your life depends on it . . . because it does. Good night, and stay safe, my fellow Road Runners."

The screen cut to black and Martin's mouth hung open. "What the hell is going on? I don't understand why we don't just wipe them all out—we certainly have more numbers than them."

"It's not a matter of numbers," Antonio said flatly. "We have no way of knowing for sure who is part of this Liberation group. Keep in mind these are Road Runners who have turned against us. Unless we catch them in the act, we don't know who is partaking in their activities."

"And how exactly am I expected to run this campaign now?" Martin asked, his voice wavering at the thought of a constant target on his back.

"It's not going to be a normal campaign. You'll have to deliver many messages from remote locations via a live feed. We can't afford for you to make public appearances."

"Doesn't sound like much of a campaign."

"It wasn't going to be, anyway. We're looking at a three-week campaign window, whereas normally you get three months. Every candidate will be getting creative in trying to get their message out to as many people as possible. There's no time to tour the entire continent like past elections."

"Is someone going to help me through this process?" Martin asked. "I literally know nothing."

"Yes. Commander Blair is sending over his campaign team for you. They're expected in Denver on Monday, where you'll make the announcement."

They sat around for a moment of silence. Everett had been on the opposite couch, but kept to himself as he typed away on his cell phone. Antonio checked his phone for any recent alerts, but saw nothing.

"Do we know if this Liberation has a leader?" Martin asked, not quite ready to end the discussion regarding his immediate future. If these people weren't afraid to burn down a sacred building, what would they do to the man they viewed as the direct link to Strike's death?

"We have a handful of suspects that we're watching," Everett said. "For now, it appears Denver is safe. This group originated in the Midwest and moved toward the east coast. We suspect they recruited during their trip, meaning anywhere west of Iowa has likely not been contaminated with the Liberators."

"We can only hope," Antonio added. "We don't actually know that. No attacks have been carried out in the west, but that doesn't mean they're not preparing to do so, or recruiting."

"I think once you show your face," Everett said, "we're going to be on the run until we can get this matter under control. We're arranging to increase your security detail during the campaign and afterward, should you get elected."

"And if I don't win? I'm just on my own?" Martin asked.

"Of course not. You'll still have safety as long as these people remain a threat. But, if you do become commander, you can expect to go everywhere with at least fifteen guards surrounding you."

"A virtual wall covering your every angle," Antonio added. "This change has been in discussion since Strike was kidnapped. We can't afford to ever have that happen again."

Martin nodded, a twisting knot wringing his guts like an old rag. His life as an innocent time traveler looking to carve out a new beginning seemed decades away—like Izzy. He still hadn't convinced himself that he wanted to run for the commandership, feeling very much a newbie to the organization, but this whole thing was moving forward beyond his control.

For the rest of the evening, they all tried to direct the conversation away from the gloomy announcement Chip had made during his final time on air. They flipped through the regular channels, settling on a random tennis match taking place on the other side of the world. No one wanted to speak of the dark days that lay ahead.

II

The Rise of Chris Speidel

22

Chapter 22

Chris wasn't one to reminisce about the past. That wasn't a straightforward task for him, as it was for regular humans. His past was complicated, time non-linear, as he often lost track of the current year. However, the recent happenings—his progress in this seemingly never-ending war—had him thinking back to his earliest days as the Keeper of Time, a title that carried so much weight and power that only a strong-minded individual could be trusted with it.

He had been forty-two years old when he came into his position as leader of North America. The year was 1962, ten years after he had killed his wife in her sleep and rolled her body into a river where she floated away like a stray leaf in autumn.

That was perhaps the only event he looked back to from his past life. The night that changed everything and set him on a crash course with his destiny as the Keeper of Time. The Road Runners didn't come into existence until 1974, leaving Chris with a whole twelve years of peace and free reign without anyone trying to overthrow him or shoot him dead in the street.

He had plenty to celebrate in the present time. He had recently become the longest tenured Keeper, with fifty-seven years in his position. Those before him typically served terms of ten to fifteen years in real time, and spent hundreds of other years floating around the void of time while their bodies aged only ten minutes per trip.

Chris entered his role with ambition and vision never before seen by the Revolution. Before him, Keepers of Time had no real sense of guidance, making decisions on a whim. They only had a handful of rules in place, a big no-no in the eyes of Chris, and one of the first tasks he sought to address after taking the reins of the organization.

Before him, there were no guidelines regarding what kind of people should have the Juice, let alone the secret of time travel. It had always been an unwritten rule to use your best judgment when inviting people into the group, resulting in many families populating the Revolution. Back then, one had to bring their invited guest to meet the Keeper of Time, where a blood sample was drawn to help create that individual's bottle of Juice. It was a tedious process that inevitably hindered the growth of the Revolution.

Chris wanted to explode their numbers. They were the unofficial police of the world and time, and with a couple thousand members, it felt like they had no chance of achieving anything substantial. They had plenty of research missions into the past and future with the goal of manipulating the world as time progressed. Many Revolters also continued their regular lives after obtaining the Juice, dragging themselves to their day jobs and grinding their way through life.

Chris had been recruited on the promise of a lifetime of wealth and unlimited resources. He was surprised to learn, after joining, that a majority of the population was left in the dark to struggle financially, an archaic rule in place that any money earned on a time travel trip had to be reported to the Revolution, who typically took an eighty percent cut to cover "administrative fees."

Having come from a grueling life himself, Chris abolished this rule, which created his first wave of enemies from those who lived life above everyone else.

"There is no reason for anyone in our group to live in poverty," Chris said at his very first public address to the Revolution, a small gathering at a high school gym where 800 members crammed in. "The possibilities are endless with time travel. I'm not saying we need to pay our members for the work they do, but if they earn money on a trip, they have the right to keep that money. We can become a powerful organization through our own missions. We can create missions with the sole purpose of bringing back money.

"Look at all of the great things that have been invented in the last ten years. We've seen Mr. Potato Head, the Hula Hoop, and even the pacemaker. Imagine how much more will be created in the *next* ten years. We can travel ahead, learn of the new advances, and make them our own today to reap the financial benefits. We can turn not only our organization, but all of our members, into the wealthiest members of society. Imagine a world where we are the hidden superpowers, creating, advancing our planet toward a bright future. We'll have so much wealth thanks to our knowledge of the future. We can bring our less fortunate neighbors to join us at our new level of excellence. People talk about ending poverty and world hunger all the time, but we could actually make that a reality."

Half of the crowd remained silent while the other half cheered for Chris and his promises. A divide started that very day. The ultra-rich felt entitled to their wealth, as if anyone else who might rise to their level somehow made them less wealthy.

Little did Chris know when he stepped into the role, that those same wealthy members were the ones running the organization all along. They made generous upfront offers to new recruits, just like Chris, but hoarded all of the wealth for themselves. Their goal had been to run a sort of slave ring, giving people the gift of time travel, but using it to earn themselves more money off their labor from assigned missions.

This particular speech came before Chris had formally gone through the process to become the Keeper of Time. They didn't have elections—the current Keeper decided who they wanted to hand their power over to—but they did like to take any potential candidates around the continent to deliver speeches and see how the crowds responded.

Chris rose to power thanks to a perfect storm. Had it been any other Keeper of Time, they wouldn't have so much as looked in Chris's direction for the powerful role. But the sitting Keeper felt the urge to shake things up and stray from the status quo. He wanted fresh blood, and someone in it for the long haul. Someone with youth and ambition.

The Keeper of Time, Chester Mayfield, joined Chris at a local diner after his speech.

"That's quite the show you put on back there," he said, sipping from a steaming cup of black coffee. Chester, like every other Keeper before him, was an older man, hair well beyond gray, wrinkles and bags plentiful across his face, and a raspy voice that buried years of shit beneath it. Seeing as they were the only existing organization with access to time travel, it had become a sort of unwritten rule that the Keeper be at least sixty years of age when they assumed their role—Chester had to have been at least ninety at this particular moment in time. Surely giving the power to anyone younger was an irresponsible move. Only experience and wisdom were allowed for such a title.

"Thank you," Chris said, a slow drip of adrenaline finding its way into his veins. His fingertips throbbed with excitement as he picked up his own coffee mug. He hadn't ever thought about the position of Keeper, knowing it wouldn't even be realistic for another two decades. But here he was, rubbing elbows with Chester, after being picked out for a brief tour around the country. "I don't know what to say. I feel very passionate about our abilities and what we can do with them. We can have such a major influence on the world."

Chester nodded, intensely gazing across the table at Chris with his heavy, brown eyes. "You know how to work a crowd, that's for sure. But I want to learn more about you, Chris. Relating to the people is honestly a minor aspect of this role. You'll be involved with high-level decision-making on a daily basis. Can you actually turn your words into action?"

"I absolutely can. I haven't come this far in life to be nothing but a cheap politician making empty promises. I believe in every word that comes out of my mouth. I'm honest to a fault, and don't give a damn what anyone thinks of me. To me, those are great qualities in a leader."

"Indeed they are. Tell me, if you were to become Keeper, what would you do on your first day?"

Chris nodded as if he expected this question. He had actually imagined this scenario numerous times since he received the initial letter in the mail stating Chester's interest in him. "The first thing I would do—that *needs* to be done—is set some ground rules for recruitment. We can't keep relying on ourselves to recruit our families and friends—there's no true growth that way because everyone more or less thinks the same way. We need to set the bar higher, find people who are smart and capable of change. Quite frankly, we should be looking to recruit people who would be natural fits into positions of power within the Revolution. Imagine a group full of potential Keepers. Obviously not everyone can become that, but you're only as good as the people you surround yourself with."

Chester nodded, clearly pleased with this response. "Are you suggesting implementing more leadership positions? The Keeper has always been a solo type of role, held in check by no one. Above the law, if you will."

"I wouldn't say leadership positions exactly, but we will need some help. If we can recruit at the rate I'm envisioning, it will be impossible for one man to overlook the entire organization. We'll need to break into regions or chapters, and have a smaller leadership look over those. More like delegating the work, since I—the Keeper—can't be everywhere at once."

Chester nodded again and rubbed a finger around the rim of his mug. "Right now we have three candidates: yourself and two others who are . . . closer to my age, we'll say. You're a major underdog in the eyes of the public, an unknown. But I know the work you've done, the sacrifices you've made . . ." He trailed off and left Chris waiting on the edge of his seat.

"What are you getting at, sir?" Chris asked in his most patient voice.

"This is a difficult ship to change course. As open-minded as you'd think time travelers would be, they're not. These people are so set in their ways. What I'm getting to is that you would be a highly controversial choice. You'd be the youngest Keeper ever to assume control, by far. I think the youngest we've had was a fresh sixty-one-year-old on his first day in the role."

"With all due respect, sir, I think the age thing is complete bullshit."

Chester cracked a grin, surprising Chris, and waved a hand. "Go on."

"Age is irrelevant in this life. I can travel back in time two hundred years, live there for that long, come back, and still be forty-two. I can live for *two hundred years* and get credit for none of it when it comes to this. It's absurd."

Chester nodded. "I couldn't agree more. But this is one of those things where people are set in their ways. You'd have to come out and *show* this experience. How many years have you lived since joining?"

Chris shrugged. "I can't even say. My first year with the Revolution was wild. I went on a mission every two days, many of them were five year trips or longer. If I had to guess, probably somewhere close to 1,000 years with all the missions I've done."

Chester's eyebrows shot up to his receding hairline. "Impressive. And my point exactly. That's probably more experience than some of the past Keepers."

"What can I do to give myself a real shot?" Chris asked, scooting back in his seat.

Chester pursed his lips and stared at his mug while he thought. "My friend, you *do* have a real shot. I just want to get more of a feel for how you'll handle the . . . adversity of being the youngest Keeper."

"Surely there will be some members who support the change. Let's make them my unofficial bodyguards."

"Of course there will be. But will they want to do something like that? That's the real question."

"I take care of those who take care of me. Like I said, I'm a man of my word."

"What if I told you it all works out?"

Chris furrowed his brows as he stared at the Revolution's leader. "What do you mean?"

"I've already taken the liberty of taking a peek. I traveled to the year 1990 and spent a day there—the future honestly bores me and any longer would be torture. But, I did find a local hangout of Revolters, and it was quite the scene."

"How so?" Chris returned to the edge of the chair.

"Well, for starters, you're still the Keeper at that time. The Revolution's membership was almost to two million, according the gentleman I spoke with. And the people absolutely adore you."

Chris couldn't help but smile at these words. Receiving praise for a job he didn't even have yet? Only in the Revolution.

"Now," Chester continued. "It wasn't all 'far out', as kids today like to say. It appears there is some resistance in the future—a whole group of people who hate you and want you removed from power."

"Removed? That's never been done before."

"I know. I tried to prod for more information, but no one could give me a concrete answer as to *why* these people were so pissed. It almost seemed petty from what I could gather. Perhaps you just being in power for so long made people sick of you, I don't know. It didn't sound too serious."

"I suppose I can worry about that when the time comes.

Probably just need to find common ground with the newer generations of time travelers. Perhaps I can spend some time in the future, just to get acquainted. I understand why no one likes traveling forward, but it really doesn't bother me."

"Well, that would be another first," Chester said with a chuckle.

Chris returned a polite grin as he watched Chester finish the rest of his coffee.

"When I came into my role," Chester said. "I wanted to be sure I left a mark when the time came to hand over the power. I think choosing you would be the ultimate legacy. I haven't done much but keep us a well-functioning group of people who love to travel to the past and write the history books. And that's fine. I can leave this role right now and I'd go down in history with no negative marks next to my name."

"And there's nothing wrong with that. You've done a great job."

"Nothing wrong at all. But isn't it boring? I'll just be another name on a long list of Keepers who did nothing of significance. Or I can be the one who took a gamble on a young man who wanted to change the world for the better."

"And if I fail, what would that mean for you?"

Chester shrugged. "I don't know, and quite frankly, I don't care. But let's be honest, if you're still running the group well in 1990 like I witnessed, that's far from a failure, wouldn't you say?"

"That's true." Chris couldn't contain his excitement. His leg bounced out of control below the table, and he had to place a hand on his knee to make it stop. When he woke up this morning he thought he'd deliver a speech for pleasantries and nothing more. Surely Chester had wanted cheap entertainment.

But the day flipped after his speech. He didn't know how Chester was leaning before the speech, but it was now clear that he wanted Chris to take control of the Revolution and guide it into a new era.

He had put in tireless work since sacrificing his own wife for a chance at a better life. Sure, his daughter was now in college and wanted nothing to do with him, but she'd come around some day. Especially now that her father was about to become the most powerful person in North America.

"I can't formally make an announcement on my decision until it's addressed to the public," Chester said. "I'm planning that final speech in two days back in Austin. Let's just say you need to make sure you're there, okay?"

Chris grinned, and had to make a conscious effort to not leap out of his seat and start jumping around the diner like an exuberant child. "Yes, sir, I'll be there."

They finished their dinner with further discussion about Chris's plans for the future. Chris would return home that night unable to sleep, the weight of the world settling onto his soul as his destiny loomed.

23

Chapter 23

Chris caught the first flight in the morning to Austin and spent the day on Sixth Street, enjoying live music while he dined and drank the day away. The next day was the scheduled event where Chester would announce his selection for the next Keeper of Time, and Chris couldn't contain his anticipation. He wanted to climb to the rooftops and scream to the world.

While it was the peak of his life as a Revolter, the upcoming announcement also made him feel lonely. He wanted his little girl by his side, cheering him on as he elevated his career to its highest potential. She was a legacy Revolter, had been since the day Chris joined and recruited her by default. He didn't know how much she kept up with the happenings of the organization, but hoped she'd hear the news and come back into his life.

He knew she was safe at her college in California, but his heart still ached whenever he thought of her, which was quite often. He had done this for her sake, as well. In their prior life, they were going nowhere fast, stuck in the rut of lower-class society with no hope for the future. It had pained Chris to come home from a long day of work, his body aching, his mind exhausted, knowing that no matter how hard he worked at his factory job, it would never be enough to provide his little girl with a brighter future.

If they had stayed the course, would she still be at Stanford today? Maybe she could have earned a scholarship, but not likely. She was in elementary school when Chris killed her mother, an event she didn't quite understand until she was a teenager and asked questions every day.

"I didn't murder your mother," Chris explained to her one night. "Murder is when you *want* to remove someone from existence because you hate them. I didn't hate your mother. In fact, I still love her. What I did was called a sacrifice. I exchanged her for this new life that we have."

She always nodded and wandered off after Chris explained this, and continued doing so until she wandered right off to college and never phoned home. Chris knew their relationship would never fully mend. She had good reason to hate him, but watching her flourish in life and not have to struggle the way he did made it worth it. And things would only become greater once he became the Keeper.

Not a day passed where Chris didn't think of that fateful morning when his wife tumbled down the hill like a boulder. He had lived in constant paranoia for the following month, worried someone would find her body and spark an investigation that led back to him. He had momentary flashes of an angry judge sentencing him to life in prison, or worse. He imagined those long days in a prison cell, staring at the walls and waiting for death to free him.

Today, he tried to keep his focus on what lay ahead, but ran into plenty of difficulties since he was in a college town and continually saw girls that reminded him of his daughter.

After wasting the day, Chris tumbled back to his hotel and cried himself to sleep.

* * *

The event was scheduled for noon, leaving Chris the morning to laze around and fight off the minor hangover that throbbed in his head. He caught himself nervously pacing around the hotel room, chain-smoking without a care in the world. Nerves rattled his arms and chattered his teeth at random moments. The time was coming where he'd have to lean on his ten years of experience as a Revolter, and guide his fellow people into the future. The idea of still running things in 1990 was both comforting and overwhelming. This was his life now, the ultimate goal that had been achieved through years of busting his ass. All the missions, late night meetings, and strategy sessions led him to this moment.

He would've still been happy if this had never happened, continuing the bustle of life as a time traveler, seeing the world and living history one mission at a time. What did 'Keeper of Time' really mean? With no one to report to, couldn't he still do as he pleased? The organization was already self-governed for the most part, so how much work did he really have to do as Keeper?

When eleven o'clock struck, he raced out of the hotel and to the restaurant on Sixth Street that Chester had rented out for a private event. He liked to offer these business owners so much money that they kept their staff out and let his own people handle matters for the day. He paid for the privacy, as that was all that mattered. They didn't go to these places to actually eat lunch and order rounds of beers; they needed a meeting place and it came down to where could host the number of expected guests.

For this grand announcement they expected a crowd of at least 1,000 people, with camera crews on site to film the speech and take home to their local meetings. Since they hadn't dabbled much in the future yet, the Revolution still lacked knowledge on hosting their own private broadcasts.

The venue chosen was Rolling Smoke BBQ, the biggest restaurant downtown, with a dining capacity of 500. They had moved all tables aside, making it a standing-room-only event where Chester would speak from the back of the restaurant to the jam-packed crowd.

Chris was welcomed into the restaurant with warm smiles and handshakes as he made his way to Chester, who was waiting with a microphone. The space was primarily filled with the elite members of the Revolution, the ones who could drop what they were doing and fly across the country. Chris had chosen to wear an all-black suit to the event, a choice that would stick with him for the rest of eternity.

Everyone else, though, sported flashy jewelry, poignant cologne, and the finest of suits. Not a single woman was present in the room, a fact that didn't change until Chris later assumed power.

The chatter of hundreds of people in a tight space made it sound like everyone was yelling at each other. Chester employed a fellow Revolter to man the bar. Glasses clinked while people loaded up on the open tab. This was a celebration, after all, a passing of the torch that only happened every generation. Little did any of those in the audience know that they wouldn't get the chance to celebrate this particular occasion again for a very long time.

Chester remained stuck in a conversation with faces Chris recognized, but couldn't put a thumb on their names. His two fellow candidates were chatting with each other a few feet behind them, lost in the background of the busy area. Chester locked eyes with Chris and grinned, waving him over.

"Hello, sir!" he said. "Glad to see you here. Are you ready for the big day?"

Chris stuck out a firm hand to shake. "Absolutely. I've never been more ready for anything in my life."

"That's what I like to hear. Have you met Randall Stone?" Chester asked, gesturing to the man he had been speaking with.

"Not yet. It's a pleasure to meet you."

Randall Stone, a bored-looking man who appeared the same age as Chester, offered a grin with his handshake. "The pleasure is all mine, Mr. Speidel." He leaned in and whispered. "Chester has told me all about you and your vision. Don't worry, you're not alone in the things you want to achieve." Randall stood up straight again and winked.

"Mr. Stone is a great resource," Chester said, placing a hand on Randall's shoulder. "One thing about this role is the need for a sounding board. While you are the sole person in control and can do as you please, it's never bad to bounce some ideas off of a trusted person. Randall has been that for me during my entire time as the Keeper."

"Someone has to keep the power from going to this old bastard's head," Randall said, prompting a hoarse chuckle from both of them.

"Do you have any close friends within the Revolution?" Chester asked Chris. "Someone who could maybe fill that type of role?"

Chris nodded. "Do you know Duane Betts? From Albuquerque."

Chester nodded. "The name sounds very familiar."

"He's my best friend in the Revolution. No idea if he'd be interested in doing that sort of thing, though."

"Well, it's not an official role," Chester explained. "Just something to consider."

"Chester, we need to get started," Randall said.

"Ah, yes, of course!" Chester dropped back from the crowd and stood behind a microphone stand that had been set up. "Chris, please join the other candidates back here, please."

Chris obliged and joined the two older men who were bickering about the weather. They both locked eyes with Chris, but offered no greeting. Surely they were a couple of the old-timers who thought Chris had no business being in the running for Keeper.

Chester tapped the microphone with his finger and cleared his throat. "Good afternoon, Revolution. How are you all doing today?"

The chatter gave way to applause before the room fell silent. Too silent, considering how many people were in there.

"This is always an exciting event for our organization, and I'm proud to be a part of our long-standing tradition of passing on the responsibility of Keeper of Time. I remember my announcement gathering a whole twenty-two years ago, but that's a story for another day. Today is about looking to the future. We have three strong candidates that have made the last week of my life hell by having to narrow it down to one winner. Behind me, please give a warm welcome to Chris Speidel, Joseph Delacroix, and Oliver Adams."

The crowd broke into a new wave of cheers and whistles.

"You may have seen all three of these outstanding gentlemen deliver speeches over the past few weeks, and hopefully you've gotten an idea of what they stand for and what direction they want to take our beautiful organization. All three of these men possess the raw skills to make a great leader, but as I've discussed with each of them, there's more to it than that. Anyone can learn and develop leadership skills. What has always stuck out about past Keepers has been intangible attributes like vision, determination, and willpower. These are things, I believe, that cannot be taught, but rather are ingrained within men from the time they are born. You either have it, or you don't.

"For those of you who might not be familiar, the nomination process starts with each state or province mailing in their suggestion for the best candidate they can offer. From there, the list of about ninety candidates is reviewed by myself and a team made up of those I trust, and any former Keepers who want to get involved in the process. This part of the process normally takes two weeks, as we give our due diligence to researching each candidate's past and look for what they have done in their mission work and how relatable they are to the rest of the population.

"We have friendly arguments, whittling that pool down to the three finalists who are standing before us today. At that point, the decision rests solely on me to make. I go with each candidate for a one-week tour around the continent where they deliver speeches to other Revolters. We spend every waking second together so I can get a complete understanding of who each of these fine men are. The beauty of this is that there are no *bad* choices. I can choose any of these three men and know our organization will be in good hands for years to come. Unfortunately, there is only room for one person, and the thought process is all about who is the *best* fit for our future.

"Let me tell you, this has been the hardest decision of my tenure as your Keeper. I suppose that's a good thing. Now, after more than two decades of learning this organization inside and out, and meeting all of the phenomenal people who make us great, I've made my decision. And my decision is one based on potential. Not potential of the man I'm choosing today, but of the organization's potential. Things are going great for the Revolution – never better, in fact. But we can do so much more. And the candidate I've chosen has the best vision for taking us to the next level. He is ambitious and ready to get to work. Since becoming a Revolter he has grown into a key figure among his peers. Gentlemen, it is my distinct pleasure to introduce your next Keeper of Time: Chris Speidel!"

Chris heard a few shocked gasps before applause drowned them out. He watched as some people turned and looked to each other with confused expressions, others outright refusing to clap and standing with their arms crossed below their smug expressions.

Chester turned around and waved him over.

Chris smirked as he started for the microphone, waving to the crowd who started to fall silent again. He shook Chester's hand before taking the microphone.

"Good afternoon, Revolution," Chris said, his arms trembling in what would be one of his final moments of feeling nervous. "I want to thank Chester, first and foremost, not only for choosing me, but for doing incredible work over these past twenty-two years. I'd say you've made this an easy transition for me. Let's give him a round of applause."

The crowd obliged and Chester took a bow before them, a wide grin stuck on his face throughout the rest of the speech.

"I'm not going to stand here and lie to you," Chris continued. "I know I wasn't the popular choice. We had two other phenomenal candidates that I'm sure would have done an excellent job. Trust me when I say I'm just as shocked as you all. From the onset I thought Chester was just pulling me along as some sort of joke. But I have been called to this role. As he mentioned, I have plans for a bright future for our organization. We already do so much great for the world, but we can do even more. I'll cover this in a more formal speech. I look forward to getting to know you all as we continue to make this organization thrive. Thank you!"

The crowd gave one more round of cheers as Chester returned to the microphone. "Thank you all for attending our announcement ceremony today. We have the restaurant booked all day and night, so feel free to stay and mingle, have some drinks, and find Chris to congratulate him. Thank you."

The crowd returned to its loud chatter. Chris stayed in the back where the two other candidates had already disappeared into the sea of people. A natural observer of the world, he watched the room, studying the people and trying to figure out what they were thinking. Many kept looking over their shoulders to see him, whispering with each other, and surely gossiping about what they believed was a botched decision by Chester.

But none of that mattered now. Chris was chosen as the new leader, and he'd never look back.

24

Chapter 24

Chris had no idea what he was getting himself into, physically speaking. Since he'd never taken his candidacy seriously, he hadn't asked what exactly the process of becoming the Keeper of Time entailed.

Chester invited him to his hotel suite the following afternoon, suggesting a time of noon so they could enjoy lunch before jumping into the transfer of powers. Revolters had always been told that the Keepers were invincible, but no one actually believed it. The conspiracy theory was that every Keeper was someone from the future, sent back in time where they never aged to ensure they could lead for long amounts of time.

"That's a lie," Chester said. He had ordered them a room service lunch of steak and lobster, with a bottle of scotch to share. "You'll find that there are many lies that get spread about the Keeper of Time. It's part of the job."

"So you really are invincible?" Chris asked as he swallowed a bite of tender steak.

"Yes, sir. You can shoot me in the head and my body will heal itself. It's quite fascinating."

"So is it some sort of magic that I'll get access to?"

"Magic is the wrong word—at least, I believe so. Magic—which is real, by the way—is something that one has to channel to use. It takes effort and concentration. Our gift is more a special ability. It takes no effort to, say, read someone's mind. It's more a matter of focus, like trying to listen to a friend across a loud room. I can focus on your mind right now and hear your exact thoughts. Do you want to give it a try?"

Chris couldn't recall having ever received such an absurd question in his life. "Okay?"

"Great. Think anything you want."

This steak is delicious, but I don't like lobster. I've never been one for seafood.

Chester giggled. "Well, Chris, you should have said you don't like seafood, but I'm happy to take that lobster off your hands." He reached across the table and grabbed the lobster right from Chris's plate.

"How the hell did you do that?"

"I told you. Focus. That is just one of the many abilities you'll get to enjoy."

"What else?"

"Well, that's a big one, as is the invincibility. But you'll be able to do things like close your eyes and enter someone's mind. You can't control them, but you can watch the world from their point of view. Find out where they are and what they're doing. Also, your brain becomes a walking encyclopedia. You just . . . know things."

"Is there anything you can't do?"

Chester pursed his lips and looked to the ceiling in deep thought. "No. I'd say fly, but wait until you see the jets they have in the future. The world moves so fast, the transportation has to keep up."

They shared a laugh, and Chris tipped back the final remains of scotch in his glass.

"Now, it is great, but do know there are some things that . . . change."

"Such as?"

"For starters, enjoy that scotch. I'm not saying you can't have it anymore, but you'll no longer have a *need* to eat. In essence, your body sort of dies. It no longer needs food, water, or sleep. But you still function as normal."

"No sleep? So what do I do at night?"

"At first, you're probably going to go on more adventures. Why not, right? You'll have an extra eight hours a day. But over time, it becomes lonely. The whole world is sleeping while you're the only one awake. After a couple years, I just started going to sleep again, more to pass the time than anything."

"But you don't actually need to?"

"No. My mind is just as sharp on zero hours of sleep compared to ten. I'm never tired, therefore I never wake up with that groggy feeling in the mornings. It's more like a blackout in time than a recharge of your brain."

Chris scratched his head in confusion.

"I know it's a lot to take in, and even more to adjust to, but you'll pick it up in time."

"Okay, so how does the process work? How do I obtain these abilities?"

"Well, that's what we're going to do today, and why I brought you here for a nice meal. The process itself is a quick injection, but the recovery and aftermath will be excruciating for you over the next forty-eight hours."

"What hurts so bad if it's just an injection?"

"Are you ready to start?"

Chris recoiled as if Chester had pulled a gun on him. "Uhh, I suppose." He looked down with hopes of there being more food to stall, but he had already cleared the final bites.

"Perfect. Just so you know, after I inject you, this will be your room. I'll be heading back home."

"What?!" Chris gasped. "You're going to leave me in pain by myself?"

Chester raised a hand. "You're going to be fine. Yes, you'll be in pain, but that's the beauty of your transformation—you won't actually need anything. You just gotta roll with the punches."

Chris squirmed as he stood from his seat, suddenly nauseous, the room off-balance. He crossed toward the bed and sat on the foot of it, fidgeting with the comforter. "What's this going to feel like? I gotta know, Chester."

"The best way to put it, I suppose, is an intense weakness. And your veins will feel like they've been filled with fire. It'll burn at first, but will eventually turn to a numb, throbbing sensation that consumes your entire body. It lasts forty-eight hours, and once that time has passed, you'll be your new, enhanced self. I've instructed the hotel staff to not disturb this room until you check out. You'll be stuck in bed, unable to get up – not that you need to. Your new abilities will set in as soon as I inject you, so no more need for food or water, or even using the bathroom."

"Understood," Chris said, wondering what the hell he had gotten himself into.

"Lie down, get comfortable, and let me grab the syringe from my briefcase."

Chester left Chris alone, disappearing into a bedroom for a

couple of minutes before returning with a syringe filled with red liquid.

"What's in it?" Chris asked.

Chester studied it as if having never seen it before, placing it on the nightstand next to the bed. "It's the blood of all the past Keepers of Time, dating back to the Greek god of time, Chronos."

"Greek god? We don't originate that far back."

The Revolution was only a few hundred years old, nowhere near the time of Greek mythology.

"That is correct, but that doesn't mean the blood of Chronos wasn't preserved. That's how the Revolution was born – we found it in a cave in Greece three hundred years ago. Do you know the story?"

Chris shook his head. "I should, but can't say I've ever been told the history of our origins."

"Our founder, a gentleman named Igor Ivanov, was a Russian explorer who went on a trip to Greece with hopes of discovering a rare rock in their caves. He never found the rock, but came across a vial of liquid and two stone tablets carved in ancient Greek. After some research and translation, he discovered that the liquid was indeed blood that belonged to Chronos. To this day, we don't know *why* the blood was stored in the cave. The tablets offered no explanation aside from what the liquid was."

"So Igor decided to start a group of people who studied time after this?"

"Not quite. On a whim, he drank half of it. He claims that the vial was speaking to him to do that. Others thought the discovery of something so significant drove him mad. Why else would someone drink unconfirmed blood? But he drank it, and fell sick to the point where everyone around him thought he was dying. After a couple of days he jumped right out of bed and continued with his business. From there, he slowly discovered the new abilities that we still enjoy today. And the rest is history, as they like to say."

"Wow," Chris said, his jaw hanging. He was not one to be easily impressed, but the story was overwhelming. "So we still have the vial of blood?"

"We don't. The vial remained with Igor. He kept it hidden for fear of what could happen if the world found out about his prized possession, let alone his abilities. That's why the Revolution was started. He let his closest friends in on the secret and made them swear to a life of secrecy. They wrote the very first rules of our organization, but they were more of terms on what to do should someone learn of the secret they all shared. Word got to the wrong person, and a Greek historian who believed the story threatened Igor to turn over the vial. If it really was from Chronos, then it belonged in Greece. Igor refused and was killed later that night in his sleep. We all know it was the historian, but he was never seen again, and the location of the vial remained a secret with him."

"Unbelievable. So someone else might stumble across this vial of blood?"

Chester shrugged. "I suppose they could. We have constantly had a team searching for this vial. We want it on our possession—can't trust anyone else with that, as you can imagine. But it's a nearly impossible task. The historian could have hidden it in any location, in any year. We've rummaged through his home and possessions and have never found a clue. It could be hidden under an old dinosaur nest for all we know. Hell, we don't even know for sure if it still exists. We believe it's hidden, but what if he became overwhelmed with the secret and dumped it down the drain? We'll never know. It's just one of those mysterious wonders of the world."

"I can't believe I've never heard this story. Why doesn't every Revolter get told about this when they join?"

"Well, we can't possibly do that. If we shared this secret, then everyone would be after the blood. And what if someone actually found it? They'd find themselves in the same danger that Igor did. It's a secret passed down from Keeper to Keeper, and they can each decide who they would like to tell. Even if we find it one day, we're not going to tell anyone. The very existence of this vial will remain a secret."

"Should I continue the search for it?"

Chester chuckled. "No one's even found a clue in the entirety of our existence. I suggest you don't spend too much time on this particular issue—especially with everything you're trying to achieve."

"I understand that, but I'll probably assign a small team to keep the search going in the background."

"I expect nothing less. Now, can we get started with your transformation? I don't mean to be pushy, but I do need to get back home tonight."

"Okay, yes, sorry."

"I know you have lots of questions, but do know that you and I will have a sort of orientation, you could say, to get you up to speed with your new abilities and role. We don't give too much information before the transformation, just in case you were to back out at the last second. Once it's complete, you'll know everything you need."

Chris nodded. "Okay, fair enough. Let's do this."

Chester grinned and picked up the syringe from the nightstand. "Lie in the center of the bed."

Chris did as instructed, scooting from the foot of the bed, kicking off his shoes, and allowing himself to sink into the exact middle of the queen-sized bed. He lay with his hands crossed on top of his stomach.

Chester got on his knees and crawled toward Chris. "Let me have your arm, please."

Chris stuck out his left arm, mind running rampant as his life was on the verge of changing forever. He fought away the tremble that tried to creep into his limbs, focusing on his breathing and closing his eyes.

"Perfect," Chester said, grabbing Chris's arm. "Okay, just a little poke like any shot. Three . . . two . . ."

Chris felt the syringe bite through his flesh, his brain wincing at the sharp pain, while his body remained composed. Chester emptied the fluid into the vein, and the process was finished as soon as it started.

"Easy as pie," Chester said with a grin as he admired the empty syringe. "I'm going to wait with you about ten minutes—that's how long until you'll start feeling the symptoms. Once those kick in, I'll know the job has been done successfully. Now, we just wait. In the meantime, I'm going to make sure my bags are packed and dispose of this needle."

"Okay, thanks," Chris said, his eyes still closed. He was scared to open them, fearful of what waited on the other side of the injection, anxious for the pending pain to come his way in just a few precious minutes. His heart raced and he didn't know if it was a side effect, or just his own panic. Perhaps a little of both.

Breathe, he told himself. *Don't panic. This is the life you've worked so hard for. Man up and deal with your transformation, because it's going to be worth it. More than anything else you've done up to this point.*

His brief pep talk helped his nerves settle and he opened his eyes to stare at the white ceiling. His body locked, leaving him unable to move, but he didn't *feel* paralyzed. His mind was still sharp, and he could do things like wiggle his toes and fingers.

"How are you feeling?" Chester asked as he stepped back to the bedside.

"I think it's starting – I can't move."

Chester grinned. "Yes, that is the start. Okay, mentally brace yourself. It's going to feel like a tingle at first, and then it will burn."

"I feel the tingle," Chris cried. His body gradually tingled across its every inch, the sensation of his foot falling asleep and having to shake it to get the blood flowing again.

"Okay, ease into it. Welcome it. This is literally the blood of gods working its way into your system."

"Oh, fuck!" Chris screamed through gritted teeth. His face turned bright red, veins bulging from his forehead and neck as he looked like someone trying to lift something far too heavy. "It burns! It burns!"

The inside of his body felt engulfed in flames. From his toes to his fingertips, his entire body raged with the fiery blood of Chronos and past Keepers.

"Okay, Chris. It sounds like everything is working as planned. Remember, forty-eight hours and it's all over. When you feel normal again, you'll officially be our new Keeper of Time. I'm going to head back home now – I'll be sure to check in with you as soon as you're feeling well again."

Chester's words fell on deaf ears. Chris heard him, but had no mental capacity to actually listen. Besides, his ears rang with a subtle burning sound of their own, much like they do after a night out at a loud concert.

The burning crept into his stomach and planted itself there like a stubborn weed, making him curl into a fetal position as he rocked from side to side. He clenched his entire face: jaw locked shut, eyes squeezed tight like he was walking through a sandstorm. He never saw Chester leave because of this – he simply heard the man's voice fade away until it was no more.

With all sense of time gone, Chris writhed around on the bed like a crippled insect, begging to be put out of his misery, hoping the other side would be worth it.

25

Chapter 25

Despite becoming the new Keeper of Time, Chris never had a true appreciation for time itself. Sure, he'd been on missions to the past where he'd spent decades, only to return home to find ten minutes pass in real life. Perhaps that made him take time for granted. How could one truly enjoy their precious moments on Earth if life dragged along slower than a snail in molasses?

But he now learned the value of forty-eight hours. Two entire days of being essentially chained to his bed, head on the verge of exploding, body feeling like it had a kidney stone trying to pass through its entirety. Nausea and sweat. Hot flashes, chills, and furious coughing attacks all complemented a trembling so intense he believed he had suffered through multiple seizures.

And Chester hadn't lied. The hotel staff never so much as knocked on his door while he was in there looking death straight in the face. Thinking back, that was obviously for the best. Anyone who might have entered and found him would have surely called an ambulance, and who knows what they would have done or discovered in his blood tests.

He kept waiting for the pain to dwindle, but it never did. It remained elevated and steady, a steady climbing of sorts, until Wednesday afternoon when the pain simply vanished. Chris lay in bed, his muscles sore from two days of flexing and clenching through the bouts of pain, the sheets cool against his skin from the buckets of sweat they had absorbed. He hardly noticed these nuances as relief flooded his mind. Relief it was over. Relief his new life was ready to begin.

He hadn't slept for those entire two days, an impossible task considering the level of pain, yet he didn't feel an ounce of fatigue as he rolled over and jumped out of bed. He expected his legs to be weak, but they caught him and his balance with no issue. He expected hunger, but felt full.

Chris shuffled to the bathroom, anxious for a look in the mirror to see how raggedy and beat-up he looked, but he appeared completely normal with his usual skin tone and bright blue eyes. He even looked a bit younger, the dark circles under his eyes no longer there.

"Impressive," he said to himself, smiling to check his teeth.

The room's telephone blared, causing Chris to jump and gasp as he ran toward the nightstand, knowing it had to be Chester.

"Hello?"

"Chris!" Chester cried out. "I'm glad to hear your voice. How are you feeling?"

"Well, I just became better not too long ago—that was the worst time of my life."

Chester chuckled. "It's awful, but worth it. Now you have the rest of your life ahead. Invincible and ready to lead the world into the future."

Just hearing those words made the last two days seem like a

distant memory. Almost. "I hope so. What am I supposed to do now?"

"I love how eager you are. Most people take the day off to relax and gather themselves, but you're ready to go. I knew I made the right choice. I've got a jet waiting to fly you to my house in Portland. Whenever you're ready—and please do take your time—there is a driver waiting for you outside. He's in a black Camaro and is getting paid by the hour to sit there, so the longer you take, the happier he'll be. When you land, there will be another driver waiting to bring you to my house. Once you arrive, we can begin your official initiation as the Keeper of Time."

"Okay, that should work. Is there anything I need to do?"

"Not at all, just bring yourself and your usual insatiable curiosity. Today's Wednesday—in case your brain is so rattled that you forgot. I have all day Thursday and Friday planned for you on my calendar to get you all caught up. Remember, we don't have to sleep or take breaks. Be prepared to learn for forty-eight straight hours."

Hearing 'forty-eight hours' spoken aloud made his stomach do a flip. "Great. I look forward to it. I'm definitely ready to get out of this room, so I'll be heading down to that car in a few minutes."

"Perfect. I'll see you later this evening."

They hung up and Chris packed his few items before heading downstairs.

* * *

The flight took a little over four hours, leaving Chris with all the time he really needed to mentally recover from the trauma of the past two days. He wanted to sleep, as he normally did on long flights, but his mind was too excited for what awaited when he landed. The invincibility must have settled in because he felt like he could do no wrong.

The jet was lavish, from the tables and furniture, to the sparkling dishes and silverware. A waitress served him a gourmet burger and glass of champagne to celebrate. Chris still wasn't hungry, but devoured the lunch just the same.

After he landed, the drive was about twenty minutes from the airport, away from the city and into the woods of Oregon where tall trees hid a covert Tudor home. The brick house stood two levels tall with massive windows, long white curtains drawn for privacy. A cobblestone pathway split the bright green front lawn. Thick bushes ran along the sides of the home, leading to a backyard out of sight.

Chris stood on the front pathway, birds chirping their evening tunes while the sun cast an orange glow across the front lawn. The steel double doors swung inward, and out stepped Chester, his grin wide, hands on his hips. "Come on in!" he shouted.

Chris walked up the pathway, his suitcase rattling along the stones. "This is quite the place you've got."

Chester looked up the massive house behind him and shrugged. "It'll do. You'll get to create a house of your own, or buy one if you'd really like, but we'll get into those details later. Come in."

Chester stepped aside and held out an arm to guide Chris into his not-so-humble abode. They entered to a pristine foyer, complete with a rack for shoes and jackets. Hardwood flooring glistened under the bright lights as Chris gawked around. Portraits hung on the walls of Chester with famous figures from President Kennedy, the entire Rat Pack, and even a shot with Marilyn Monroe.

"You'll get your own collection of these over time," Chester remarked, continuing down the hallway and toward the living room that waited with two cups of steaming coffee.

Chris hurried to follow him, kicking off his shoes as he slid along the floor in his socks.

"We have to jump right into things, I hope you don't mind. But there is a ton for us to cover," Chester said, sitting down on a plush couch. A coffee table stood centered between that couch and another across the way, where Chris sat.

"Not a problem."

"Perfect. First question: how are you feeling?"

"I can't lie, I feel incredible."

Chester nodded as if expecting this response. "Glad to hear it. And the beauty is that it never fades. You will feel this way all the time. You no longer will hunger for food, but rather emotions. We believe that either Igor or Chronos were depressed men – maybe both of them were – but it seems the only emotions that satisfy our hunger are sadness and anger. Fear is also a delicious treat—more of a dessert. This will be what you consume now."

"I don't understand."

"That's the best part, there's not much to understand. You'll know when you're hungry—it will feel like your chest is hollow, sort of like the sensation when you lose a loved one. When this happens, you need to find somewhere with people experiencing either sadness or anger. I'll usually stop by a funeral or cemetery, where the grief is so high. Once there, you'll be able to physically see these emotions present in the air, floating around like pixie dust from the bodies of those experiencing the emotions. You just breathe it in, and that's how you feed yourself."

Chris scrunched his face in disbelief. "Okay. How often does this need to happen?"

"About once a month. But the great thing is you can store a surplus. Your soul will feel satisfied, but you can keep on breathing in those emotions and stock up. Sometimes I'll travel back to the Depression and just walk around the streets. There's so much sadness and anger there, I once made it three whole months off of one feeding." This was the most absurd shit Chris had heard, but he nodded his way through the conversation. "Tonight I'll be taking a vial of your blood now that you are the newest Keeper. We store this in case something ever happens to you, we'll have the most recent blood for a successor."

"I thought I'm invincible?"

"You are, which brings me to my next point. The invincibility lies within your blood. So technically, if someone were to drain your body of all its blood, you would die. Something we have started doing is injecting a single drop of blood into a trusted person's body. A single drop isn't enough to give them any of your abilities, but that lone drop is that much of your blood residing somewhere besides your own body. Think of it as an insurance policy, so make a decision before Monday on who you would like that lucky host to be. As long as your host is living and well, you can guarantee there is no chance of you dying."

"I'll inject it into my daughter. I think I can convince her."

"I thought you two had a rocky relationship? We don't advise giving it to someone who might hold it over your head. If she decides to turn on you one day, you're out of luck."

"She hasn't forgiven me for killing her mother—I don't blame her. But I think she's starting to see the light out of that whole mess. My new position will be even more cause for her to want to help. I can now pretty much guarantee her a life of whatever she wants."

"It's a grand feeling, isn't it?" Chester said with a grin. "My best memories as Keeper are definitely taking care of my family and close friends. I had two sons—they had no interest in joining the Revolution despite my numerous recruitment attempts. I still sent them on the most lavish of trips around the world."

"Where are they now?"

"They both passed away. One was in a nasty car accident, and the other caught a pneumonia bug that took him."

Chris shook his head, unable to imagine such a tragedy happening to his daughter. "I'm sorry to hear that."

"It's no worry. I sometimes go back in time to when they were little and just watch them run around the yard without a care in the world. One of the luxuries of this lifestyle, I suppose. But back to you. We know who you're giving blood to, and that's great. Have you thought about where you'd like to set up your main living quarters? That's what I love about the Revolution, they let the Keeper choose where he would like to lead from. You can choose anywhere in North America."

"On the beach in Costa Rica?"

"If that's your thing, yes."

Chris laughed. "Not really, I just wanted to know your response."

"The world is your oyster – well, the continent."

"I'll have to think about it. Am I stuck with where I choose?"

"Absolutely not. You can do whatever you want. There's not a single person in the world who can tell you otherwise. We've had some Keepers change their locations during their reign, that's completely fine."

"Good to know."

Chester reached under the coffee table and dropped a heavy three-ring binder on top. "Those are the big picture matters I wanted to discuss up front. More will come up, but let's dive in—we have a long two days."

Chris's eyes bulged at the sight of the binder that was at least four inches thick, papers and tabs bulging out of the sides. The work seemed daunting up front, but by next week, he'd have total control and abilities he'd never dreamed of.

26

Chapter 26

When Monday morning arrived, Chris woke in his own bed in Colorado Springs, a sense of purpose consuming him. The past week had vanished in a blur. They had indeed completed the full orientation program at Chester's home by late Friday night, and Chris spent all day Saturday mentally relaxing in Chester's massive backyard where a hammock stretched between two oak trees.

On Sunday they had flown to Chris's hometown together on Chester's private jet. They chatted about the overall state of the Revolution, the type of information that wasn't necessarily pertinent to their orientation, but still needed to be discussed before Chester officially handed over the reins.

Overall, at least in Chris's opinion, he was entering a fairly easy time for the Revolution. There were no fires to put out, no drama to settle, and only the future to worry about.

They had rented out the biggest hotel in Colorado Springs, the Broadmoor, a resort complete with a golf course and hundreds of rooms for their guests from all over the continent, but more importantly, it had a row of ballrooms that they opened up to host 3,000 guests.

"Be ready for the biggest show of your life," Chester had said. "We call it the 'Transition', and there will be thousands of people there to support you—and oppose. Quite different from the little gathering we had in Austin."

"Oppose? I haven't even done anything yet."

"I know. We try to stay away from politics, but people still get stuck in their ways and refuse to support anyone who wasn't their candidate of choice. It's childish, but it's life, I suppose. Don't dwell on it. People come around in time if they like what you're doing."

"Didn't you say no one wants change?"

Chester grinned. "You listen well. And yes, there is a majority who are going to resist the changes you want to bring, but they'll have no choice. They either need to adapt or leave the organization. And trust me, not a soul on Earth is planning to do that."

Chris reflected on these words as he dressed in the morning, slipping on what would become his signature all-black suit. *You're in charge now,* he thought as he looked into the mirror. *No matter what happens, these people are dedicated to their lives as time travelers. That will never change.*

Once dressed and mentally ready for the day, he remained in front of the mirror a moment longer, considering both the minor and major events that led him to this day. His hair was black, with only a couple of gray streaks starting to run from his forehead. His face was still tight, only the slightest of bags hanging below his eyes, and overall he had a new glow that he'd never seen before. "You handsome devil," he said, and winked before turning to grab his coat and leave for the event.

Chester had stayed the night at the Broadmoor while Chris

remained in the comforts of his home. For living his entire life in Colorado Springs, he'd never actually stepped foot inside the city's grandest hotel, and brimmed with excitement at the thought of doing so.

During the drive over—in a limousine, no less—Chris thought of how proud his parents would be to see where he was going on this special day. They had worked hard during Chris's childhood, scraping together just enough money to survive on a weekly basis. Chris never saw his father take a day off or fall too ill to work. His mother maintained their home and juggled an evening job at a local restaurant. Their dedication and work ethic surely helped shape who he was today, and he kept them close in his heart as he started this new journey.

The hotel was a short ten-minute drive, and when they pulled into the front loop that led to the entrance, Chris gazed out the window as they passed the front lawn that was an immaculate green: shrubs groomed to perfection, and a four-level stone fountain spewing water into the clear day.

Once they reached the entrance, it felt like they had entered a whole new world. Thick, towering spruce trees surrounded the property, cutting them off from the rest of civilization. The driver pulled up to the portico decorated with a row of multiple Colorado and United States flags. A gentleman in an impressive suit trotted to the car and opened the back door where Chris waited, welcoming him with a warm smile.

"Good evening, sir," the man said. "Are you staying with us or just here for a visit?"

"I believe I have a room here tonight, but I can't say for sure."

"No worries, sir. May I have your name, please?"

Chris scooted out of the car and soaked in the grand hotel in front of him. "Chris Speidel."

"Oh," the man gasped. "Yes, sir, you certainly are staying the night. You are our guest of honor in the presidential suite for the next two nights."

Chris couldn't help but grin, a new wave of ecstasy filling his soul. The man guided him inside the hotel, opening the doors to a lobby with polished tile floors and a crystal chandelier hanging from a stained-glass ceiling.

"And you're here for the clocksmith summit?" the man asked.

The question caught Chris off guard. "Uhhh, yes. I'm a clocksmith." He hoped there wasn't another gathering in the hotel on this particular day, and figured the Revolution would use a wise cover-up about a clockmaker convention.

"Delightful," the man said. "Our main ballroom, where your conference will be, is down that hallway to the left." He pointed in the direction ahead of them and Chris saw a line of signs directing traffic anyway.

"Thank you."

They crossed the lobby where the man took him to the reception counter. "Enjoy your stay, sir."

"Wait," Chris nearly gasped. "I had a bag in the trunk of the car. I hope he's still here."

"We've already taken care of it, sir. The bag is on its way to your suite."

"Oh, well thank you." The man waited for a moment awkwardly, and Chris assumed he wanted a tip. He had no cash, didn't even have his wallet, in fact, as it was in his bag. "Have a good day, and thanks for your help."

The man's plastered grin wavered into a momentary frown

before he scurried away. Chris was surely the first presidential suite guest to not tip the bellman.

He shifted his focus to the reception desk, where an older woman greeted him with an envelope, pushing it across the counter. "Welcome, Mr. Speidel. Everything for your stay has been covered and you are all set. Your bag should be in your room by now. Is there anything we can do for you to start your stay with us?"

"No, thank you very much."

"Great, your key is in the envelope. Just take the elevator up to the fifth floor and your suite will be at the end of the hallway."

Chris grabbed the envelope and offered a polite nod to the woman before turning away. The lobby filled with more people, many of them staring at Chris as if he were a celebrity. They didn't make their gawking obvious; a few hid behind books or newspapers as they sat in the lobby's lounge chairs. Others leaned against the walls across the lobby, pretending to be in conversations with each other as their eyes followed Chris.

Are these the protesters or supporters? Chris wondered as he made his way toward the elevators. No one physically followed him, a great relief as paranoia had started to flood his mind. He took the elevator to his floor and entered the presidential suite to another jaw-dropping scene.

The suite appeared larger than his house and was covered in gold carpets, drapes, and furniture, all in different shades of the luxurious color. From the doorway he saw a ten-foot long sofa surrounding a coffee table with three loveseats on the opposite side, a full kitchen, dining room, and living room complete with a bookshelf and television. The day's newspaper sat on top of the coffee table.

"Am I staying here by myself?" he asked as he stepped all the way in and closed the door behind him. He glided toward the open door on the other side of the living room, the suite's bedroom.

A king-sized bed devoured most of the room, but left plenty of space for him to walk through and soak in the breathtaking view overlooking the mountains to the west. His bag rested atop the foot of the bed, delivered unscathed.

Chris checked his watch to find it was noon, leaving him an hour until his big speech. He debated heading down to the bar for a quick bite before the ceremony, but decided to stay in his room, unsure what people might do if they saw him.

Instead, he'd stew in his room for the next forty-five minutes, fighting off the final nerves he'd ever feel for the rest of his life.

* * *

At 12:45, Chris left his room and took the elevator back to the main level. It was a quick ride that felt like forever, dragged out by the anticipation of his life about to change for good. Chester had left him with no instruction aside from the ceremony's start time. He didn't know where he was supposed to go, or if there was someone he needed to speak with upon entering the ballroom.

When he reached the main level, the hallway leading to the ballroom was jam-packed with people inching their way toward the doors. It made his stomach drop at first, but as he started weaseling his way through the crowd, it became apparent that the flooded hallway helped him blend right in. Everyone was too consumed with trying to get into the venue to pay him any attention.

The line moved much quicker than it appeared, and Chris found himself in the ballroom within five minutes. The space opened up, with a long stage at the front of the room, and well over one thousand chairs lined up from wall to wall. Chester had said to expect 3,000 in attendance, and it might very well have been more crammed into the ballroom.

He saw Chester on the stage, sitting in a chair behind the podium with a crowd of people chatting around him. Chris dashed down the aisle toward the front, a walk that seemed to take longer with each step.

Chester noticed him and immediately stood up and dismissed those he was speaking with. "Hello, Mr. Keeper. How do you like this hotel?"

Chris shook his hand with a wide grin. "I can't lie – this is a childhood dream come true. I've never been here."

"Well, that is what we do here at the Revolution: make dreams come true." Chester looked to the crowded room and raised his eyebrows. "It looks like we're about ready—are you?"

Chris looked around, not seeing an empty seat, and the chatter rising to a level where it made it almost impossible to hear. Men in suits sat in the chairs, picking up conversation with those around. "Yes, let's do this."

Chester smirked and made his way to the microphone, tapping on it with a steady finger as he cleared his throat. "Testing, testing... can you all hear me?"

The noise dropped to a murmur before completely fading to silence.

"Thank you for joining us here today for this delightful occasion of our annual clocksmith convention."

The crowd responded with laughter, but Chester needed to protect their identity from any eavesdropping hotel staff. He had even gone as far as having signs made and hung, welcoming the guests of Clocksmiths of America. He never overlooked a detail.

"Today will be the official Transition of our Keeper of Time. As you may know, Mr. Chris Speidel has been chosen to succeed me in that role."

A mixture of applause and booing burst out, and this caught Chris's attention. He couldn't recall a time he'd ever been booed in his life, but he supposed there was a first for everything. A line of people standing against the back wall held up signs of protest. *Too young to lead. Chris is NOT our choice. We don't want more Revolters!* were just a few of the messages being waved around. His stomach sank at the sight of people already opposed to his plans.

"We had our official announcement last week in Austin, where I also performed the first step of our Transition ritual. Keeper blood now flows through his veins, and he is ready to lead us into a bright future where we can shine brighter than ever. Gentlemen, it is my distinct pleasure and honor to introduce your new Keeper of Time, Chris Speidel!"

In that instant, as the applause broke out once more, drowning out any boos, Chris experienced the first wave of extreme confidence in himself. Any remaining nerves vanished. The room was his, and he knew it. He stepped up to Chester, shook his hand, and grabbed the microphone with determination.

The applause continued for another minute, many of the Revolters standing while Chris waved with his free hand, the microphone clenched tightly in the other. Once the room fell silent and everyone sat down, he began his speech.

"Thank you, everyone. And thank you to Chester. I've had the pleasure of working alongside Chester for the past week, learning the ins and outs of being the Keeper, and I'm forever grateful for all the knowledge you've shared with me."

A small round of applause went around the room, prompting Chris to look over his shoulder and give a nod to Chester.

"I'll admit, I was just as surprised as you all probably were upon hearing of my nomination. I'm too young, I thought. I don't have anywhere near the experience of those I was going up against. I was only known here in Colorado Springs. Even with all of these factors stacked against me, I decided to go along for the ride.

"Through it all, I learned so much from Chester and from my fellow candidates. There is so much knowledge and intelligence within our community, and I couldn't be any prouder of my decision to leave my old life behind and dedicate my new life to the Revolution. We have such unique opportunities, and it's my hope to keep it that way and make it even better for each and every one of us.

"Even for those in the back with the signs protesting, I look forward to the challenge of winning your respect. Whatever your reason for protesting, I'd love to work with you and learn what it is you want out of the Revolution. This is an organization for all of us, and my vision to is to enable those who are interested in making a better life for yourselves.

"The way I see it, there is no reason for a Revolter to have to work at a job. We sit on untapped earnings for each and every member, earnings that we do not need to take a cut from as an organization. We can come up with better ways to earn for the

Revolution that do not include detracting from our members' hard work.

"Imagine going into the future for the sake of gaining knowledge of that future world. Now, imagine coming back to today, with that same knowledge, and inventing something you saw. Or investing in a business that you know will do well. We can print our own money, in a sense. This will be my main priority as we move forward, and I welcome any suggestions on how we can best achieve this *and* make sure we're not all chasing after the same things in the future."

The crowd gave him a moment to catch his breath with a wave of applause. He took the opportunity to gulp a glass of water that Chester handed him.

"To conclude my speech today, I know I'm not the ideal candidate for Keeper of Time. I don't look like any past Keepers, I'm not the same generation of Keepers that we've come to expect, and my ideas might seem a bit progressive from the norm. But you can rest assured, everything I do is for the betterment of this organization. I love the Revolution, and have fully dedicated my life to it. It is my last, true love. My love drives me to make it something we can all love and feel the way I do. Don't be afraid of change, welcome it. Don't be afraid of success, bask in it. And don't fear the future, for we will be visiting it a lot more to learn how to make ourselves better.

"Thank you, and long live the Revolution!"

The crowd immediately rose to their feet and showered applause for the next two minutes. Chris heard no more boos, and couldn't see the signs in the back, thanks to the entire ballroom now standing. He waved and grinned, soaking in the moment, one he would always look back on as the moment he became *the* Chris Speidel.

"Incredible," Chester shouted from behind, the only way to make his voice heard. He stepped up to Chris and put his lips a couple inches from his ear. "You just won over this entire room. And I'm sure our broadcast around the world is all feeling the same way right now. You're the future. Our future."

Chester patted Chris on the back before he stepped back to let the newest Keeper of Time have his moment. The night ahead would bring constant celebration as Chris would shake hands with nearly all those in attendance. He had already forgotten about the grueling process he had endured to reach this point, and for the first time in his life, Chris Speidel felt like he was on top of the world.

27

Chapter 27

Over the first decade in his role as the Keeper of Time, Chris did as promised in his early speeches as an unknown candidate. By 1974, the Revolution's population had jumped from 200,000 to well over two million. Member dues to the organization were halted, as a team of savvy financial investors developed a plan for the Revolution to earn its own money—billions of dollars—without burdening its members. These same methods trickled down into the membership, turning them from a group of stagnant history aficionados into the upper one percent of society, quietly running the continent from the background.

In December of 1974, the world of time travel officially changed forever. They had already known there were members of the Revolution leaving the organization to join another called the Road Runners. These were upset Revolters fed up with Chris and his antics, that felt the need to form an alliance with one another.

Initially, word of this secret exodus angered Chris, but after further investigation—and introspection, for that matter—he found no one to blame but himself.

After years of driving intense recruitment efforts, the Revolution reached a point where they were flooded with great minds and hard-working individuals. Gone were the days of members being satisfied with missions only into the past to play and study. Chris had recruited people just like him: curious, urgent, and borderline reckless in their time travel work.

Keepers of the past had been traumatizing new recruits for decades as a sort of initiation into the Revolution, but none of those recruits had the knowledge or desire to really look into those tragedies that seemed so random. Even Chris had to live through the hell of killing his own wife, and in his initial years with the organization, had never considered looking deeper into the purpose of that murder. Had he, he might have found out that it was his initial test for one day becoming the Keeper of Time. Chester had eyes on him since day one, and made sure to get the result he wanted.

The Revolution's newest members, recruited under the strict instruction of Chris, had no issue digging into the issues of their own lives, and those who left had found Chris behind every tragedy.

He had been caught, and even though it was explained to new members that they would endure the pain, it didn't stop them from turning their backs on the man who had blessed them with the gift of time travel in the first place.

This discovery was the turning point for not only Chris, but the entire Revolution. The time of peace that they had enjoyed since their inception was now over. On this cold night, Chris lay in his bed in their New York headquarters, a full-sized facility that housed over one hundred Revolters, whether on a permanent basis, or for those traveling and needing a place to stay for a couple of nights.

Everyone knew he was invincible, yet no one had put that theory to test until this particular night. Little did Chris know the floodgates his attempted murder would open. He'd be dodging bullets and death threats for the rest of his life. Somewhere along the line of great men who had served as Keeper of Time, they arrived at the conclusion that it was best to store blood within another person to guarantee that invincibility.

This saved him when the traitor known as Maxwell Hart tossed a hand grenade into his bedroom in the middle of the night. Chris had acclimated like Chester said, opting to spend many nights sleeping in bed, even though his body didn't need to. Why be awake past midnight if no one else was? Especially with so many taking on roles that he had delegated, freeing up time to focus on bigger matters, like people leaving the Revolution in droves.

He was sleeping on his back, and the grenade landed on his belly, feeling like someone had tossed a baseball and he missed the catch. The room was pitch-black, so he never saw what it was until it banged and flashed in unison, like lightning had just struck.

His skin immediately stung all over. Shards of metal wedged into his flesh, smoke filling the room that made him cough with each inhale. He felt so dazed that it took a few moments for him to realize the massive hole in his stomach, cratered like a meteor had struck it. His fingers flailed around, feeling the warmth of blood and the smooth, almost silky, surface of his body's insides.

Footsteps thundered down the hallway and approached his

room, the door already open from whoever had tossed the grenade.

"Sir, are you okay?" a man barked, and Chris couldn't make out who it was through the thick cloud of black smoke consuming his entire room. "Sir, are you in here?"

Bulky arms swung through the air, clearing miniature lines of vision as the smoke grew thicker with each passing second, oozing out of the spent grenade, out of his gut.

"Oh my God!" the man gasped, and Chris briefly locked eyes with his head of building security, Dominic West, a meathead who dedicated his every free moment to lifting weights and shooting guns. "WE NEED HELP!" he screamed over his shoulder. "RIGHT NOW!"

His voice boomed, but sounded like a whisper to Chris, his head still ringing from the explosion. Dominic's bearlike arms slid under Chris, hoisting his body into the air, and carried him out of the room like an oversized package.

"Mr. Speidel, can you hear me?!" Dominic shouted into his face once they reached the hallway where fresh air welcomed them both.

Chris stared blankly into Dominic's panicked, brown eyes, reading his lips, but certainly not hearing him. Despite not needing sleep or food, Chris had never quite understood the functionality of the rest of his organs. Did his heart still beat? Sometimes he felt it drumming away in his ribcage. But other times, he'd hold his hand steady and feel nothing but cold flesh.

Dominic shook his body, jolting Chris's head backward. Two other Revolters appeared at the far end of the hallway and broke into a mad sprint toward their leader.

"Is the building secure?" Dominic snarled. "Do we know

who did this?"

"Footage shows it was Maxwell Hart, sir," said one of the men, his face trembling with fear as he gawked at Chris falling in and out of consciousness.

"Hart?" Dominic asked. "Can't be."

"It was. We need to get him out of here."

Dominic nodded. "Bring a gurney—I can't carry him the whole way. Let's go to the basement."

"Is that the best—"

"To the basement!"

Chris had taken plenty of ventures into the future and decided to build underground fortresses for every new Revolution building. The New York offices were one of the first to have one, a requirement since Chris lived there full time.

The two men ran back in the direction they had come, leaving Dominic with Chris in his arms. Being a power lifter, Chris was by no means a burden for him to hold, but the length of time doing so started to cause a slight burn in his biceps. The smoke oozed into the hallway, where it finally dissipated for good.

"How are you doing, Mr. Speidel?" he asked, meeting the blue eyes that stared blankly at the ceiling.

Chris nodded, unable to speak. His body felt like it was being smashed by a hydraulic press machine, yet it somehow didn't *hurt*. He flailed a weak hand toward his stomach and insisted the hole in his gut had already shrunk in size.

My body is healing itself, he thought. He hadn't had so much as a paper cut since taking over as Keeper of Time, at least from what he could remember in this flustered moment. His body presumably had this ability to heal itself this whole time, but he'd never had a chance to put it to the test.

Until now.

"I think I'm okay," he managed to say, his voice strong and practically its normal self.

The men returned at the end of the hall, one pushing the gurney toward Dominic and Chris.

"Put me down," Chris said.

"Sir, with all due respect, I don't think that's the best thing right now. We need to make sure you're okay."

"Dominic, I'm fine. Put me down—that's an order."

Chris spoke with a bit more authority, and Dominic lowered him as carefully as a toddler learning to swim into a pool.

Chris remained hunched over like he had a deformed spine, but that was simply caused by the hole in his stomach. The men reached Chris with the gurney and halted in their tracks.

"Won't be needing that, gentlemen," Chris said. "But thank you. This was Maxwell Hart, you said?"

The man clenching the gurney nodded, eyes fixated on Chris and his stomach, where the hole had already shrunk to half of its original size.

Chris plucked a shard of glass from his shoulder and flicked it away like an annoying bug.

"Sir," Dominic said. "Is this normal?" He nodded toward the gut hole, that had reduced even more.

"Completely normal. Now, we have business to tend to. We're under attack, and I won't stand by while it happens. Find everything you can on Maxwell Hart. Let's get eyes on him around the clock. I want to know every time he so much as sneezes. If he's working with the Road Runners, then it's an easy next move for us."

Chris stood up straight for the first time since the explosion and patted his stomach, now solid again, no sign of an explosive device ever having detonated on his body. His flesh had pushed the shards of metal out, leaving him completely back to normal, aside from the debris that remained in his hair.

Not only was the wound sealed up, Chris felt his normal self. Apparently, the healing that his body went through put his mind in a sort of fog, a minor nuance considering what he had just survived. But now his brain was sharp again, ready to scheme and get revenge.

"Stop staring at me like I'm the second coming of Jesus," he said to the three men gawking in amazement. "Meet me in my basement office in fifteen minutes. I want information and plans for next steps."

He strolled away like he was on a leisurely walk through the park, whistling down the hallway where he disappeared into the darkness. Up until this point, Chris had been a humble, peaceful man. But his limits had been stretched, and not to his knowledge, a new Chris Speidel was born out of this tragedy. A Chris Speidel driven by paranoia and rage, desperate to rule the world.

28

Chapter 28

There had already been widespread panic throughout the Revolution, thanks to the sudden emergence of the Road Runners. No one knew who to trust. The monthly meetings around the country saw drastic dips in attendance, members both worried of being seen as a stronghold in the Revolution, others suspicious that undercover Road Runners attended with hopes of relaying the Revolution's secrets back to their new organization.

Chris found himself at a crossroads for the first time since taking over as Keeper, and he leaned on a trusted resource, one who had promised to stay away and blend into the background of society unless called upon. The time had come, and Chris needed him.

He was surprised to learn that Chester had moved out of his Oregon mansion, heading south to Puerto Vallarta in a beachfront condo for the rest of his life. Chester agreed to meet in person, the matters too sensitive to discuss via any other means, but he was in failing health, and Chris would need to make the flight south of the border if he truly wanted his old leader's wisdom.

So he did just that, clearing his schedule and hopping on his private jet to arrive in Mexico five hours later. Chris was surprised to find the condo smaller than imagined. Surely a former Keeper didn't allow himself to live in a shack, but it appeared that's exactly what Chester had opted to do. After an adventurous cab ride from the airport, complete with Spanish cursing, honking horns, and a definitive middle finger out the window, Chris arrived to Chester's complex and immediately felt the cool ocean breeze brush across his face and ruffle his hair. The temperature flirted with ninety degrees, while the humidity made it feel like everything was sticking to Chris as he strolled down the stone pathway toward Chester's unit.

When Chris heard the phrase 'beachfront condo', he imagined something that looked a bit more like a resort. Instead, he arrived to a complex with faded exterior walls, cracked windows, and clunky air conditioning units that whined as they attempted to cool off the residents. A small courtyard was to the side of the walkway, a group of ten little boys chasing around a soccer ball and trying to kick it through the goalposts they had created with two trash cans.

Chester's unit was on ground level, and Chris approached the door with a slight shake in his fist as he knocked. He wasn't nervous, but rather anxious as to why someone who had been so adored by the Revolution was living in a dump like this. Had he lost his powers? Run out of money with no way of getting it back?

Chris stood on the other side of the door, running through these thoughts, until Chester opened it and revealed what looked like a skeletal version of his former self. The old Keeper hunched over, his limbs nothing but a thin layer of skin stretched over the bones. Chester's lips sunk inward, as if he forgot to put in dentures, and what hair remained was as white as a fresh blanket of snow.

"Chris Speidel," Chester said, his voice still healthy and strong. "I never thought we'd meet again. How are you, my friend?"

Chris had to make a conscious effort to not let his jaw hang open, his eyes glued to Chester's body as he looked up and down, refusing to believe what his eyes saw.

"Uhhhh, hi, Chester."

Chester grinned, revealing a handful of teeth. "This is what you have to look forward to. You might be immortal, but that doesn't stop your body from aging. Live long enough, and this is what will happen."

"I'm sorry, Chester," Chris said in a tone he might have used when offering condolences to someone who lost a loved one.

"It's funny you called when you did. I was in the middle of planning my death, but figured I should at least wait until after we met. Your call has kept me alive a few more days."

"Death?! How? Why?"

That old grin returned, more gums than teeth behind those parted lips. "Look, Chris, what do you think happens to us old Keepers? You don't actually think we still have men living from hundreds of years ago."

"Well, no. I guess I don't know what to think. I've never heard of a Keeper dying. I guess I figured you all lived somewhere far away from civilization."

"That we do, as you can tell by my humble abode here. But no, we don't live forever. My blood's host actually passed away three months ago, and ever since then I've figured it's time to pull the plug on my own life. See, our souls can live forever, but our bodies cannot. My body is 106 years old. My mind may be sharp, and I still feel no pain, but I can't move around like I used to—my body doesn't react to the same speed as my mind."

"So how do you plan your death? Can't you just wait until your heart stops beating? Surely it can't last much longer after your host died."

"That would be nice, wouldn't it? See, there is still much power flowing in my blood. Even though I'm mortal again, my body won't die of any natural causes. I have to force it."

106 years old? Chris thought, still stuck on that number. He knew his body kept aging throughout his life as a Revolter, but never once considered that the end of the road looked like this sad sight in front of him.

"I'm so rude," Chester said, taking a step back into his condo and holding his bone of an arm out. "Please, come in."

Chris obliged and entered the room that smelled like stale cigar smoke. To his surprise, the inside was much nicer than the exterior, well-kept with clean countertops and no clutter or messes. The backside of the condo had a walkout balcony that housed two seats facing the ocean. Chester had the balcony door open, allowing the breeze to blow through his living quarters.

"You like living here?" Chris asked, unable to imagine that he'd ever move out of the country to live in a tiny place like this.

"I know it seems a bit crazy, especially considering the resources available. But after two decades of the constant hustle and bustle, the flashy events, gaudy tuxedos and dinners, this suits me just fine. You'll find that after being Keeper, all you want to do is nothing. I wake up without a single care in the world. I still don't need to eat or sleep, but I do just to have some sort of routine. After breakfast I'll grab a book and head out to the beach. I read for a couple hours then I head back in for a quick lunch when I'll usually watch TV. Then I go back to the beach and spend the day there until the sun goes down."

"That actually sounds like a marvelous life. So do you keep up with the Revolution at all? Do you know what's going on?"

"There is a local chapter here that meets every month, but I haven't been in at least six months. People treat me like a celebrity and it's too much. I understand their excitement, but I'd rather stay home and have no worries. So that's what I do."

"You've never heard the term 'Road Runner', then?"

Chester frowned. "I'm not sure what you mean. I know what a road runner is, both the animal and the cartoon."

Chris grinned. "Well, it means something else quite different within the Revolution. We have people leaving us to join this other group of time travelers called the Road Runners. All of their members are Revolters who have decided to defect because they're upset about one thing or another."

"Ahhh, the war," Chester said. "This must be who it's with."

"Excuse me?" Chris asked. He didn't mention anything about a war, and hoped this old man wasn't losing whatever remained of his brains.

"One thing every Keeper has to do before finalizing their successor is take a peek into the future and make sure the world hasn't gone to shit under your reign. I made a few stops for you, checking the 1980's, 1990's, and late 2000's. Three different decades and the world is still the same—perhaps a little crazier, but the same. I did come across the fact that the Revolution was at war during all three of these decades. It sounds like it escalates into quite the battle. The struggles you face today will only get worse."

"Well, that's why I came to meet you. I don't know what to do, and was hoping you might have some guidance."

Chester crossed his skeletal arms while his lips pursed together in thought. "I can't say I have any direct advice regarding this matter. I oversaw a time of peace, and thinking back, we've always been at peace."

"So this is all my fault."

"No. These are called growing pains. Like I mentioned way back when, no Keeper has ever taken a chance on anything. The ones who ever thought of shaking things up always consulted with the future, and ended up not liking what they saw. That's where you came in and made a difference. You didn't make a trip to the future to see how your decisions affect the world, you just went for it. And honestly, that's the way it should be done. I've always thought the whole peeking into the future was a bunch of nonsense. There are millions of factors that can change on a whim that alter the future, many well out of your control. Don't beat yourself up over this—learn how to make it a positive for you and the organization."

"But you saw a war in the future. Surely something like that has multiple ways of coming to fruition."

Chester nodded. "Sure, but you can make a decision today that ends any chance of a war. Maybe you do nothing and it goes away on its own. Or maybe you make a bold announcement to shake up these Road Runners. You obviously have more knowledge on the matter, so you'll need to decide what's best. If it were me, I'd seek common ground and kill any chance of a war from actually breaking out. No matter how people feel, we can't afford to let our secret slip into the general public—that's bad news for all of us."

Chris considered this. "I'll have to get with my team and consult on what the numbers look like. I've authorized them to take a deep look and see what we can find out. Our initial reports suggest that the Road Runners are nothing but a fraction of angry Revolters. They have no numbers compared to us."

"Then why did you come here?" Chester asked. "Sorry to be so blunt—and I'm glad to see you—but if this isn't that big of a deal, then what triggered you feeling that we needed to speak?"

"They tried to kill me," Chris said sharply. "Tossed a grenade on my lap while I was sleeping at night—don't think I'll be sleeping any time soon."

Chester raised his eyebrows. "Wow. I definitely haven't heard of an attempted murder on a Keeper—threats, sure, but never anything concrete. I take it your body absorbed this grenade?"

"Yes. I had a hole in my stomach, and it healed within thirty minutes. It was mind-blowing and overwhelming while it happened."

"Well, that's why we do everything we do before you officially step into the role. Glad to see it all pay off for someone."

"Look, I know I'm safe from harm, but I'm not trying to deal with people wanting to kill me for the rest of my life. I want this attack to stop right where it did. How can I get these people off my back? Surely you dealt with some clingy opponents in the past."

"More than you know. The best approach, Chris, is to show your muscle. I don't advise making the first move, but if someone throws a grenade at you, then you should throw two right back to them. You are the leader of the most powerful organization in the world – don't be afraid to remind anyone of that fact."

"Well, I certainly plan on getting them back, but to what extent? Do I just eliminate all of these people? Or give them a chance to return? I like to think these Road Runners are just lost and need to find their way home."

"That's a nice thought, and perhaps it's true for some people, but I wouldn't bet any money on that. I'd say that entire group became traitors the second that grenade was tossed in your room. You can't trust any of them, unfortunately."

"You said you looked into the future... did you ever see an end of this war?"

Chester looked down before meeting Chris's intense gaze. Chris could see the truth swimming behind the old man's eyes, that he had indeed seen the end results. "I can't say for sure if it was a definitive end, but it was an end. You need to take care of this before it spirals out of control."

Chester's tone sent a chill throughout Chris. It was threatening, yet hid a disturbing truth that would never be spoken.

"Thank you, Chester. I'll make sure these Road Runners never see the light of day again."

"Come in and have some tea with me," Chester said, softening his tone. "It'll make us both feel like normal people again."

"I wish, but I really need to get back home. I've got a team working on this issue, and I'm ready to make the next move."

Chris stuck out a hand to shake, grabbing the fragile bones that belonged to the former most powerful man in the world. He'd never see Chester again, his old leader slipping quietly into his self-induced death without an announcement. A sense of rage brimmed within his chest as he walked away from the rundown condo, a burning fire that would make a permanent home in his soul for the rest of his life.

29

Chapter 29

The meeting with Chester sparked a wave of changes for the Revolution the day after Chris arrived back in New York. Before, they had a security team of five that patrolled offices. Now, Chris started assembling an army of Revolters to protect the entire organization. They were under attack, regardless of how small the Road Runners were.

"A threat is a threat," Chris said on the phone to his longtime friend, Duane Betts. Chris had done as Chester advised all those years ago, and used Duane to bounce ideas off and stay grounded in this chaotic life of time travel. But now he was asking him to step into a much more important role for the organization.

"You want me to form a military, is what it sounds like," Duane said, his voice flat and uninterested, never fazed by anything Chris said.

"No, don't be absurd. We don't need an entire military . . . just an army."

"Why me? I have zero experience. Surely you can find someone who does."

"It's not about experience, it's about trust. I'm talking about someone to not just form and lead this army, but someone who will be working with me every day and ensuring that things run smoothly. There's simply no one else I can ask."

"Do I have to move to New York?"

"Not initially. I do want us in the same location eventually, but for the start of this you're going to need to travel the continent. I want groups of soldiers trained and ready to fight in every city. This will be a very long process, but one that takes us to the next level and kills any hope these Road Runners might have. Did I mention you'll be doing a ton of traveling?"

Duane chuckled in a rare show of emotion. "Yes, you did."

Duane craved traveling, and Chris knew it. He had visited all seven continents, each in different eras of time to gain an understanding of the world. His assigned missions from the Revolution always included trips across the country, sometimes even across the ocean. After becoming friends in their early years as Revolters, Chris had watched as Duane became the smartest person he'd ever known. Choosing anyone else to lead this special project would be a disservice to the Revolution.

"You can count me in, but I want you to know I have no interest in moving to New York."

"Don't worry, it would only be temporary. I'm looking into a new location for our headquarters, and it's going to be somewhere very remote. I need it to be impossible for anyone to stroll into my bedroom and toss a bomb like we're playing hot potato. If someone wants to find me, they'll need to go out of their way to do so."

"That's probably a good idea. The more remote, the better. You have a target on your back. What is our total population?"

"Last time we counted, just over two million."

"Okay, great. If we can recruit even one percent of that, we'll have 20,000 soldiers across the continent. What do you think?"

"I think we need two percent, at least to start. And we'll keep recruiting new members with this in mind. I'm going to send some teams out to canvass army soldiers and marines right here in the U.S. Imagine if we can recruit actual soldiers."

"If I'm heading up this army, then you really need to focus your time and resources into studying the Road Runners. What if we recruit 20,000 soldiers only to find that the Road Runners have 30,000?"

Chris let out a childish laugh. "Please, Duane, their entire population can't be more than 10,000."

"We were once 10,000 strong. Look at us now."

Chris sighed. "It's not the same. They don't have access like we do to recruit people from the street. They can only recruit *from* us. Having soldiers in place will help stop that. I can see it already, dead Road Runners caught trying recruit people away from the Revolution. Like they're so much better than us. I gave these people their ability to time travel, and I'll be damned if they turn their backs on me!"

Chris slammed a fist on his desk, rattling some pencils and paperclips. Just talking about Road Runners set him off. He wanted nothing more than to remove them completely from the equation. They threw a wrench into the day-to-day life of the Revolution, ending their once peaceful existence. All because a few people were upset with the terms Chris provided in exchange for their Juice.

"I'm sorry," Chris said, Duane having remained silent on the other end of the line. "I'm frustrated. This wasn't supposed to be part of the job, you know? This was supposed to be a good time, and it's being bogged down by these Road Runners. Please tell me you'll help."

"Chris, you know I love this organization more than anything. I'm willing to help as needed—even leading this army. But I have to encourage you to look at other options first. It seems to me that this is a generational matter. You and I come from the same times. We understood the risks of doing what we did. We both got hurt and went through some emotional trauma, but we knew what we were getting ourselves into. This new generation . . . they don't listen. They're entitled, think they can have it all, the best of both worlds. Eliminating these people won't solve your problems. As long as you're recruiting for the Revolution—which I know you will—this issue will keep repeating itself."

Chris nodded as he held the phone between his ear and shoulder. "You see, Duane, this is why I chose you to be my number two. No one else would tell me this. People act like they're walking on eggshells around me and never tell the truth. But you always offer a fresh perspective."

"Well, we go back far enough that I know you're not a scary person. You may have everyone fooled, but I know the clown that you really are."

Duane spoke in his same, flat tone, offering bits of sarcasm that made Chris howl with laughter. He understood his good friend's desert-dry humor, and appreciated it as much as his brutal honesty.

"I must say, revenge sounds a bit more forceful. We need to make a fast statement, not coddle our enemies."

"So you see these people as your enemies already?"

"They tossed a grenade on my lap – they're not exactly my friends."

"There are two types of leaders all throughout history. Leaders of compassion, and leaders driven by hate. You need to decide which you want to be."

"I have no issue showing compassion, but I don't exactly have the luxury of time to heal people of their hatred for me."

"Aren't you the Keeper of Time?"

Chris smirked, shaking his head. "That doesn't mean much in this matter."

"It means everything. You have all the time in the world. Clearly you can't die, so what if you catch a few more grenades or bullets. You can afford to be patient right now. Retaliation will only escalate matters, and in the long run, that's not the best play. You need to be making the best choices for the long term."

"I'm always looking ahead, but I have to consider the present as well. What if these attacks start spreading to others? Then that's innocent blood on *my* hands for doing nothing to stop this right away. I can hear it already: 'How many Revolters have to die before Chris does something?' I need to make a move yesterday."

Even though he couldn't see Duane, he knew his friend was likely standing in his kitchen, face blank as he gazed out the window with focused eyes.

"I'm merely here for a different perspective," Duane said after a few moments of silence. "You're obviously more involved in the happenings of the organization than me, so if you feel something needs to be done sooner, then so be it. But I'll always discuss what's best for the Revolution's health, not necessarily your own."

"Thank you. That's all I want." Chris couldn't help but smile as he sat at his desk and brushed a finger along its grainy wood.

It really was all he wanted from Duane. A breath of fresh air among the clouds of smoke everyone else tried to blow up his ass.

"Are we done with this conversation?" Duane asked. "I'm ready to get to work on forming this army."

"Yes, sir," Chris said. "Give me a call in a week and let me know how things are going. In the meantime, I'm going to reach out and see what kind of resources we have available right now. I think bombing one of the Road Runners' hideouts is the best way to go. A bomb for a bomb."

"I'll call you then," Duane said, and hung up.

30

Chapter 30

When the sun broke the horizon the next morning, Chris was already awake. He refused to sleep the night before, and wouldn't attempt the useless act for another fifteen years. Why sleep if you didn't need to? And why sleep if you might wake up to your own guts splattered across the walls?

While his security team scrambled to figure out what exactly went wrong that night and worked to ensure it could never happen again, Chris authorized a bombing of the Road Runners' Los Angeles office, a hideout in the basement of an office supply store that they had owned and operated as a front for their shady dealings.

It didn't take his team long to find the location, especially since they already had eyes on the place for a couple of months. The man who had thrown the grenade into Chris's bedroom was confirmed as Maxwell Hart, a former Revolter who had turned sour toward Chris and wanted revenge. Maxwell was on the run, spotted on occasion by teams of Revolters spread across the country and throughout time. They'd catch him eventually, and Chris would bring him to surefire justice.

What Chris never realized was his own devious transformation. Perhaps the thirst for revenge clouded his vision. He grew obsessed with the Road Runners, dedicating an absurd amount of the Revolution's resources to studying them, finding them, and killing them.

The killing didn't start off intentionally. It wasn't until a Road Runner pulled out a revolver and showered bullets at the unsuspecting Revolters hiding in the distance. That was the final straw for Chris, promptly authorizing deadly force against any and all Road Runners. "Shoot them dead in the street if you have to," he said in a meeting with his security team. "They're an infection to our way of life. The sooner we get rid of them, the sooner we can return to peace and prosperity."

While these matters waited in the future, Chris reflected on the prior night. Early news reports showed an office fire in Los Angeles that killed more than forty people who had been gathered in the basement. They speculated on why so many people were there at such a late hour, landing on a logical explanation that they were having some sort of company party. It sounded plausible, and no one questioned it. The police dug for more information on the place, but the entire building ended up a pile of ashes.

"Our boys did good," Chris said to the TV with a hearty chuckle. He watched as the newscasters tried to piece together their fabricated story. Clearly no one had a clue about the Revolution or Road Runners, the fire still being investigated and presumed to be a gas leak.

"Today is a great day for the Revolution," Chris said to his empty office. He wanted to call Duane and share the news of over forty dead Road Runners—and counting—but knew his good friend despised interruptions during his work. Soon enough, they'd have an army and could destroy all Road Runners on the planet if they wanted. *It'll be worth the wait,* Chris had to remind himself.

He planned to spend the day following updates on the fire, needing to ensure that nothing of their existence somehow leaked. There were certain parameters in place should such a thing occur, and it wasn't a pretty sight for the general public.

He was too giddy to sit still, pacing the room as thoughts ran rampant. The urge to keep killing Road Runners had swelled into borderline lunacy, and at times he had to remind himself that he was no murderer. He acted out of revenge, and to send a clear message to whoever was trying to attack his great organization. Chris Speidel never threw the first punch, and only responded with violence when cornered.

He wanted more, the thought of additional dead Road Runners gnawing in his stomach like physical hunger, so he snapped the phone off his desk and dialed their Los Angeles office who had successfully committed arson the night before.

"Hello?" a man's voice answered, exhausted and a bit dazed. It was three hours earlier on the west coast, as compared to Chris watching the news at 8 A.M. in New York.

"Bobby, is that you?" Chris asked, voice packed with excited energy.

"Yeah, who's this?" the groggy voice asked.

"Your fearless leader," Chris replied with a grin.

"Chris? Good morning, how can I help you?" Bobby's voice woke up like someone had splashed water on his face.

"Two things. I want to congratulate you on last night. I've been watching the news, and it sounds like everything went as planned."

"Thank you, sir."

"Secondly, I'm curious if we might have enough resources left over to do another couple of these stunts. Perhaps tonight?"

"Tonight?!" Bobby gasped, unable to hide the shock in his voice. He sounded like a man who desperately wanted to go to sleep, but kept facing never-ending interruptions.

"Yes. Why stop where we did? Sure, it sent a message, but people tend to not listen. I want the Road Runners' complete and full attention. Can we make this happen?"

"You want us to send the materials to another city, or what exactly?"

Chris giggled. "Of course not. You and your team are now the expert arsonists for the Revolution. I want you and your team to carry out this process. You made no mistakes, and that's precisely what we need."

"I'm happy to get my team on it again, Chris, but it doesn't work like this. We don't just show up to a place and burn it down. We need at least two days to scout the place and learn it inside out. That's why no mistakes were made."

"I'm sure that's true and all, but your team is on fire, no pun intended. You just pulled off the perfect crime without leaving a trace. I'd say you're locked in and can carry that momentum into the next city."

"Chris, my men are exhausted. It's been two days of long hours preparing for last night. Then we had to deal with last night, of course. They need some rest if we expect them to operate at the same level."

"Momentum, Bobby!" Chris snarled. "Do you know what that word means?"

"Yes, sir."

"Good. Now ride your momentum into Seattle tonight. And tomorrow night we'll do Chicago. Are there any questions?"

"No, sir." Bobby's voice came out deflated.

"Thank you, I'll make sure your flights and hotels are arranged. Someone will call you to confirm."

"Yes, sir."

"Oh, and Bobby. Don't fuck this up. The future of the Revolution depends on it."

Chris hung up and stroked his chin as he sat back in his office chair.

By the end of the night, another Road Runner hideout would go up in flames, but it was the response from his enemies that slipped under his radar.

The Road Runners had a much higher number of members than Chris believed, many still not publicly straying from the Revolution, but having plenty of closed door discussions about the Road Runners and their goals to overthrow Chris. In fact, the Road Runners were ahead of the game in regards to an army. Theirs was already formed and ready to fight. Every single person they recruited had a strong interest in removing Chris Speidel from the world, and because of that, volunteered to take lessons in fighting, shooting guns, detonating explosives, and survival skills.

They were a determined bunch who believed they had the proper strategy and will to achieve what they desperately wanted. The Road Runners worked twenty-four-seven in their many locations around the continent, and were now creating decoy offices as a response to Chris sending one of their biggest hubs up in flames.

The war was brewing, and little did either side know the mess they were getting into. A war with no clear end in sight and a death toll in the hundreds of thousands over the course of the next several decades.

With one swift decision, Chris had set the Revolution and Road Runners on a collision course. Neither side would ever surrender, each continuing to recruit and multiply their army.

Time travel was now a vehicle for strategists to find a way to end the war and take more lives. More smoke and fire would fill the skies, chaos and madness looming on the horizon. Chris Speidel had wanted to go in the history books as the Keeper of Time who changed the world and the organization forever, and was getting exactly what he wanted.

III

The New Candidate

31

Chapter 31

Back in 2019, Road Runners were in hiding and Martin had returned to Denver. A busy week waited, primarily with Martin needing to announce his candidacy, and meeting with Commander Blair's campaign team on a strategy for winning the election.

The Road Runners had indeed disappeared from the public eye. Upon returning to Denver, Martin and his team ventured through the downtown office to check in, only to find the place deserted, lights out and a cool draft—even for a basement—as if no one had been there in months.

The Road Runners were still at work, though, many from the comfort of their homes or meeting at spontaneous locations throughout the week. Every one of their offices across the country had been abandoned for the moment, with the exception of the main hub in Barrow, Alaska. There was simply nowhere for them to go nearby, and they needed to remain close to Chris's mansion. Still, they scaled back the amount of staff working in that location from the typical fifty Road Runners to a mere twenty.

With the Council's chambers going up in flames, they decided no office where Road Runners gathered should be occupied until further notice. Communication remained through email and the private network. The cyber security team revamped their protection so that Chris wouldn't be able to manipulate their television network, and so far ran into no issues.

Their broadcast had taken more of an infomercial type of showing, with many of the candidates running commercials and broadcasting speeches. Occasionally, Chief Councilman Uribe hopped on for a few minutes to discuss the happenings of the organization.

Martin's security team had no information regarding the nationwide blackout, so after poking around the empty office, they headed for Martin's Littleton home in an awkward car ride. Even though their world as Road Runners had come a standstill, the rest of society continued on without a worry. Downtown Denver was nearly abandoned on Sunday night, and the highways were wide open as they sped out of the city.

They rode in silence, pulling off the highway twenty-five minutes later, and arrived to Martin's house.

"Expecting company, Briar?" Antonio asked as he killed the headlights. Everett dropped his cell phone and replaced it with a pistol.

Martin's stomach sunk to his knees as he craned for a view of his house, one black car in the driveway that he had never seen before.

"Do you know this vehicle?" Everett asked over his shoulder.

"No," Martin replied, his voice cracking.

A man in a suit stepped out of the front door, his hands held in the air. Antonio parked on the curb, a safe distance of about

100 feet to the entrance. The moon provided just enough light to see the man on the front steps.

"An ambush?" Everett asked. "He could be trying to play cute and have all kinds of people inside ready to attack us. We wouldn't stand a chance."

"Possible, but I don't know. Why would he expose himself? They could just as easily have parked far away and hidden inside to wait for us."

Antonio rolled down Everett's window, prompting his partner to cock the pistol.

"Excuse me, sir!" Everett barked toward the man. "Please state your business at this residence." His voice came out sounding like an intimidating police officer, and Martin was glad he didn't have to arrive home by himself to these circumstances. He certainly would have assumed the worst and spent the night driving as far away as possible.

"Easy, mate!" the man shouted back, his accent heavily British. "We're from Commander Blair's team."

Everett looked to Antonio, who was frowning in deep thought.

"Please walk slowly toward our vehicle and keep your hands up!" Everett yelled back, lowering his gun, but keeping it pointed in the man's direction.

They watched as he made his way down the front steps, his hands stuck in the air. Martin's heart battered against his rib cage, but he didn't feel it, adrenaline taking over all sensation in his body.

"Is he legit?" Everett asked.

"We have a few seconds to decide," Antonio replied gravely. "If it's really them, they're early. They weren't supposed to arrive until tomorrow morning at the downtown office."

The man kept a slow, steady pace until he reached the car, stopping at Everett's window that was halfway down.

"What's your name?" Everett demanded.

"Tony Jenkins," the man replied, his voice swimming with terror.

"Stay right there and don't move," Everett snapped back.

Antonio was already on his cell phone, finding the email with the list of names they were expecting to meet tomorrow morning. "It says he's the head of the campaign team," he whispered to Everett.

"Why are you here? When did you arrive?" Everett asked out the window, sure to keep his tone stern.

"We landed early this afternoon. Our jet became available sooner than we planned, so we took advantage and wanted to see around the city. Our plan was to stay in the office overnight, but no one told us that was a bad idea right now. We phoned Commander Blair and he suggested we sweep Mr. Briar's house for any security concerns, then stay the night here."

"It would have been nice for someone to tell *us* that plan. I could have put a slug through your head," Everett said, softening his voice.

"Sorry, mate, we haven't received any of your information yet, and I dunno if Blair told anyone of significance. It's been plenty difficult to reach anyone in America these last few days."

"Yeah, we're a bit occupied," Everett said while shaking his head.

"Well, that's what we're here for. Help your election and get the group back on track."

"Show us some identification and we can get to work," Antonio said over Everett.

The man kept one hand in the air while the other reached

into his pants pocket, pulling out a wallet that he whipped open as he approached the vehicle, sliding it into the open window for Everett to grab.

Everett didn't take it, but craned his neck for a clear view. "It's him."

Antonio killed the engine and hopped out of the car, prompting Martin and Everett to follow suit.

"Good to formally meet you," Antonio said, sticking a hand out to their British counterpart. "My name's Antonio, you've met my partner, Everett, and this is Mr. Martin Briar, the next commander of North America."

They had gathered on the passenger side of the car and huddled like a group of kids at recess.

"Pleasure to meet you all. I'm Tony Jenkins, and the rest of the team is inside. Only four of us in total, but we run an intense campaign. No mistakes. No rubbish. Just a clean path to the commandership. Shall we head inside?"

"Yes," Martin said, his stomach flipping cartwheels. He hadn't been back home since finding his mother mutilated to pieces. And he certainly wasn't expecting to return so soon.

They started toward the house that no longer felt like a home to Martin, and even less so when they stepped inside. The team of four had wires and computers spread all throughout the main level, kitchen included. One man and two women sat on his living room couch, glasses of water in hand, the lights on, but dim.

"Martin Briar?!" one of the ladies gasped, jumping to her feet and slamming her glass down on the coffee table. "It's such a pleasure to meet you. I'm Lila Lawson, and I've been studying your life for the past month."

Martin scrunched his face in confusion, not sure how exactly to respond to such an outlandish statement. "Thank you? I'm sorry for what you had to learn about my boring life."

"Not at all," she replied, her accent growing thicker as she returned to her normal voice. "Your life is one of the most fascinating I've ever seen." Martin towered over Lila and her tiny frame. She lacked any wrinkles or gray hair, but seemed much older than her appearance.

"May I ask what you've all seen?"

"All of it," she replied flatly, tucking her blond hair behind her ears as she pulled out a cell phone and showed it to Martin. "Look, these are all the notes I've taken, starting from your birth."

On her screen were blocks of text that ran on forever as she scrolled with a skinny finger.

"Wow, what *don't* you know about me?"

"Nothing. My job is to learn about the candidate, study their life, and figure out how to translate all of your pain and experience into a strong campaign."

"She's the best publicist in the world," Tony said from behind, he and the two guards hanging back in the kitchen. "It's perhaps the most crucial role on any campaign team. Not only does the publicist learn your life better than you could, they have to find any potential issues that may arise from opponents. And when you receive an endorsement like you're going to, expect nothing but negative campaigns run against you—it's their only hope to sway voters because they know there's nothing they can actually say that beats the endorsement."

"Please," Lila said with a blush. "I just do my work, nothing to it."

The other two who were sitting on the couch had joined

together behind Lila.

"I'm so sorry," Lila said once she felt their presence. "I was so struck to finally meet you. Let me introduce you to the rest of the team. This is Madison Barker and Dylan Phillips."

The man stepped forward and gave Martin a stern handshake. "Pleasure, Mr. Briar. I'm Dylan and I work on anything technology-related. Keep our computers running, put together the commercials for TV, all that good stuff."

"Nice to meet you," Martin said before turning his attention to the other woman.

"Hello, I'm Madison, and I work closely with Tony on general campaign strategy, filling in all the holes that fall outside of Lila and Dylan's scope."

Martin was at first struck by Madison's beauty, her red hair silky and flowing down her back, her hand soft like a pillow as he shook it. She reminded him of a supermodel, her beauty both intense and intimidating.

"Great to meet you all," Martin said, gathering his composure. He was back in his house, and back in control, his guards happy to stand in the background while he met his new campaign team. "So what are our plans?"

Tony cleared his throat and stepped forward, joining the rest of his team. "We didn't want to waste time, especially being in your house, so we got to work right away, preparing the next four weeks of your life and working out the logistics for travel during this dark time in North America."

"We're not going to use an efficient route for your tour," Madison said. "Normally, we start in the north and work our way south by going east to west until we reach Panama. Understanding that Chris may have plans, we're not going to do anything predictable. Could be Seattle in the morning,

New York in the evening, and then Costa Rica the next day. We will not announce your appearances until we actually arrive in a city. We don't want to give the Revolution any sort of opportunity to crash the party."

"That's fair," Martin said.

"We understand the target that is on your back, and we've been hard at work trying to spin that into a positive for your campaign," Madison explained.

"It's really not that hard," Tony cut in. "I don't think anyone has ever seen Chris so obsessed with a single person. He's afraid of you, and that's the narrative we're going to run with. I can't lie, when Commander Blair asked us to lead your campaign, I was hesitant about doing it for an unknown candidate. But the more we've dug into the matter—and your history—this has become maybe one of the easiest campaigns I've ever worked on."

"I'm curious what your team costs," Martin said. "Surely you know your worth and can ask for anything."

"We normally charge five million up front, and another two if you actually win. And that's just our fee—not counting any travel or expenses."

Martin's eyes bulged. "And who exactly is paying for that? I didn't agree to any of this."

Tony raised his hand. "Calm down. Commander Blair is covering all of our expenses, and we've agreed to take on your campaign for no fee."

"Why on Earth would you do that?"

"For the survival of our organization," Tony replied flatly. "We can see the big picture from across the pond. North America and Europe are the two biggest populations of Road Runners. If one of those collapses, it's only a matter of time before Revolters slowly take over the entire world. This particular election is bigger than all of us—it's about survival."

"And you still think I'm the best person for the job?" Martin asked, eyebrows raised to his forehead. "Of all the people who have been Road Runners, *I'm* the one?"

Tony nodded. "For starters, it's not my job to decide that – it's my job to make the voters believe that. But yes, after our meeting with Commander Blair, I do believe you are the best option, for the lone reason of being a Warm Soul. We've reached a point in time where we either fight to end Chris once and for all, or we fall prey to the Revolution. There is no longer a gray area. Our existence is going to swing one of two ways, and we need to make sure it's the correct way."

Martin's palms slickened with a thin a layer of sweat. Sure, he expected this job to be stressful and high-pressure, but not so high-stakes. If they wanted to use his gift to try and murder Chris, then he'd have no issue with that. But why make him run for commander when he clearly wasn't cut out for such a role?

Once again, the thought of running away from of it all crept back into his mind and planted itself there like a toddler demanding attention. It would remain a thought, nothing more. He couldn't even take a piss without someone having eyes on him. He was in this too deep, and the only way out was to deliver what they wanted.

"How exactly am I supposed to kill Chris?"

32

Chapter 32

Chris had mulled over his past as he sat in his office. The barricades still surrounded the mansion, and he thought about lowering them to test the waters. How closely were the Road Runners watching him? How many more bombs did they have? Was it worth sacrificing all of his brainwashed soldiers for the simple matter of learning this information? Not to mention the hassle of needing to find shelter elsewhere.

No, it's not, he thought. *I'm so close to ending this thing, now's not the time to give them any hope.*

How he wished Duane was there to offer his no-bullshit advice. On the surface it seemed he was one knockout punch away from sending his enemies to sleep, but who was this other group that burned down one of the Road Runners' offices? His plan to spark division within their organization had worked flawlessly, only he didn't expect a new group to rise from the rubble. They were now a wildcard, and Chris needed to know what they sought. It was possible they hated both the Road Runners and the Revolution and wanted to overthrow both. They surely didn't have the numbers to seriously entertain the thought, but movements like this could spread like wildfire once started.

He'd have someone on his team reach out to the Liberation's leader and call for a meeting. But for now, he wanted to focus on that knockout punch. He had debated where to strike next, a difficult task seeing as the Road Runners had all gone into hiding, leaving their offices abandoned. He was thinking too big, wanting to attack them in a city like Chicago or Miami. But the answer became so clear, and was right in his backyard.

"They'll never abandon this Alaska location."

Why would they leave the location closest to his mansion? They watched and studied him, like a hawk waiting to swoop down and snatch its prey. And that's exactly what they'd do if he lowered the barricades without a reason. That Alaskan office was the only thing currently separating Chris from true freedom to roam his own property. He could bounce around different times and wiggle his way out, but he suspected they had Road Runners waiting at every period in time to find him.

All this time he thought he had the upper hand in the war, but he was the one trapped. It wasn't even him who had directly sent the Road Runners into hiding, but rather the Liberation. A strong message needed to be sent courtesy of the Revolution.

He picked up the phone to call Duane and immediately slammed it down. *No. You are in charge, always have been, always will be. Duane is at home dealing with matters. You're here with all the time in the world. Do as you please.*

Chris smirked as he opened the security software and buzzed the intercom at the same time. "I need all Revolters to my office right now," he announced, sitting back and waiting.

It only took a couple minutes for all dozen Revolters in the mansion to work their way to the office. They entered in silence, standing in a line in front of Chris's desk, arms at their sides, eyes glued on their leader as they awaited instruction. None of them even looked at each other, as you might expect people who worked and lived together to do. Chris had whipped their minds into a subservient state of blind loyalty, a process that took years, but now paid off impressively.

"Good evening, gentlemen," Chris said, standing with his hands crossed behind his back. "I wanted to gather you here to let you know that I am leaving. I'll be lowering the barricade and slipping out into the world. I need one of you to raise the barricade back up as soon as I'm outside. I don't know how closely our friends are watching us at the moment, but it's best if we keep appearances that I'm still in the mansion. I'm going to recruit more members for our team and we're going to end the Road Runners one city at a time. Any questions?"

"When can we expect your return, sir?" one of the men asked, his voice confident and demanding, just the way Chris liked.

"I'd say within a couple days, possibly sooner. Just keep an eye on the cameras and drop that barricade as soon as you see me. Now if you all wouldn't mind, I really do need to be going."

Chris sat back down and typed on his computer, the humming of the barricade's motors starting within seconds as they lowered. He opened his desk drawer, pulled out the pistol, and shoved it into his waistband before leaving the room with a quick nod to all of his soldiers.

* * *

"Thaddeus Hamilton?" Chris asked on his cell phone. He had indeed called Duane and apologized profusely for interrupting him during his leave. But he had no one else to trust with a sensitive matter like tracking down the leader of the Liberation, and certainly no one who could gather the requested information within five minutes. "Why does that name sound so familiar?"

"We recruited him four years ago," Duane said. "He converted to the Road Runners after one year, and is now the leader of the Liberation. I had a preliminary discussion with him about moving to Alaska to serve in the mansion. Shortly after, he abandoned us."

"Lovely. All can be forgiven when I meet with him."

"I found his address – I'll message it over to you."

"Thanks as always, Duane. Even when you're not working you're still a lifesaver. Take care of that mother of yours, and we'll see you soon."

They hung up and Chris instructed his pilot to take him to Sacramento where Thaddeus lived. He had grown accustomed to long flights, a given since he basically lived in the North Pole. The trip to northern California would be on the shorter end of seven hours in the air, six if his pilot wanted to press the matter.

He fell into his jet's recliner and let his mind wander ahead, preparing for what he was going to say to the leader of the Liberation.

* * *

They landed six hours later, thanks to the pilot making record time. The afternoon was mild as the sun fought through clouds to provide flashes of warmth between random gusts of wind.

Chris felt his legs turn numb after bouncing them for the last hour of the flight. Now was the time to strike a deal, and hopefully, turn this war on its axis. During the flight, Chris looked into the Revolution's database of every recruit they'd ever had, tracking down Thaddeus Hamilton to his current address on Pinedale Avenue on the northern outskirts of California's capital.

The hangar they had flown into was not too far from this location, a quick five-minute drive into the peaceful neighborhood with manicured lawns in front of the two-story homes that lined the block. Chris had been to plenty of middle-class suburban neighborhoods, and this one appeared no different.

The car stopped in front of the house, and Chris stepped out to catch a breeze ruffling his frosty hair. He didn't know if Thaddeus was even home. If not, he'd camp out all day and wait. Surely the potential end to the war against the Road Runners was worth a few hours of waiting after brewing for nearly fifty years.

Chris walked up the pathway and knocked a stern fist on the door, a solid oak with no windows to see inside, and no peephole from what he could tell. He crossed his hands in front of his crotch and swayed side to side as he waited.

The door's lock started to jiggle and click, the chunk of oak swinging inward to reveal a tall man whose bulging eyes met Chris's gaze. "What the—" Thaddeus cried out and slammed the door shut.

Chris smirked, understanding the poor man's surprise of seeing the Keeper of Time at his front door, and knocked again.

"Mr. Hamilton, I assure you I'm here in peace. I need a word, if you don't mind."

He stared at the door that returned silence. Thaddeus may have sprinted to his basement to start loading up his guns, but surely he knew that would have no effect on Chris. He raised his fist and banged on the door, rattling the hinges as tiny clouds of dust puffed from the edges. "Mr. Hamilton, please don't make me use force to break down this door! I just want a peaceful conversation."

The door rattled once more, and slowly creaked open, the barrel of a shotgun sticking out through the crack. "What are you doing here?" Thaddeus shouted.

Chris rolled his eyes. "I said I need to speak with you. I'm not here to hurt you. My God, does everyone really have this many trust issues with me?"

"You're pure evil," Thaddeus barked back. "You have nothing to speak of to me."

"That's where you're wrong. I heard the little barbecue you had at the Road Runners' New York office was all your doing. I applaud what you accomplished. You've struck more fear into them than I ever have. I've never seen them go into hiding."

"That has nothing to do with you!"

"Look, Thaddy—that's what they call you, right?—I know it has nothing to do with the Revolution, but you have to understand that I am the Keeper of Time. It's my duty to know what is going on with those of us who time travel. I hold nothing against you for leaving us for the Road Runners—you're hardly the first or last—but I am intrigued by this new movement you've started. Will you agree to let me come in and talk? You can frisk me if it puts your mind at ease."

Chris raised his hands to show that he was indeed not here

to start any problems.

"You can talk to me just like this. What do you want?"

Chris sighed. "I know that's not really what you want to do. It's my understanding you used to own a farm. Did you move to this nice suburban neighborhood to not be so isolated? Surely when you started to run an organization whose mission is to destroy the Road Runners, you understood the great risk of staying in such a solitary location and moved here where you know no one will cause a ruckus. Do you think I won't make a scene in front of all your neighbors? I can have this entire block engulfed in flames with a quick phone call, if you'd prefer."

The shotgun wavered before disappearing into the cracked open door. "Come in with your hands up," Thaddeus said, defeated, the door opening all the way.

Chris smirked and entered the house as instructed, meeting a scared Thaddeus who still had the shotgun aimed square at his forehead.

"You know if you shoot me in the head it does nothing, right? It just pisses me off, and then I have to kill you. For appearances, of course."

"Please don't speak until I say so." Thaddeus spoke in a voice mixed with fear and authority, an odd combination that Chris hadn't ever heard directed toward him. "If you try anything, I promise I'll blow your head off. Surely you can't piece yourself back together before I throw your skull fragments in the fireplace."

"I love that kind of talk," Chris replied with a grin.

Thaddeus lowered the shotgun and jab-stepped toward Chris, quickly patting his legs and arms, as if he were being forced to touch some slimy goo for a high school science experiment.

"Wow, you really are clear, who would've thought?" Thaddeus remarked.

"I'm not as evil as you all like to think—only when I need to be. I left my pistol in the car just so you'd talk."

"Come sit down," Thaddeus said, turning toward the living room across the way, shotgun back in his two-handed grip. He had two couches facing each other with a coffee table in the center, cleared of clutter with the exception of a potted plant that caught the direct rays shining through the window. Chris shuffled over and sat opposite Thaddeus, crossing one leg over the other and leaning back as if this had been his hundredth visit to an old friend's house. "What is it you want, Chris?"

"I'm not going to waste your time. I want to join forces and wipe out the Road Runners. We've got them dazed, just need to go for the knockout punch to send them to sleep."

Thaddeus frowned as he sat with his large hands planted on his knees, leaning forward. "Why on Earth would I do such a thing? I don't trust you, and neither does anyone else in my group."

"That's your first problem," Chris said, raising his bony finger in the air. "You only see yourself as a group of people trying to do good. You're an organization, and the sooner you start treating yourself as such, the further you'll go with your work. I have the experience of running the biggest and baddest organization in our world of time travel. I can offer resources that would take you decades to build—and we don't have time to spare. The Road Runners will retaliate. They always do."

"We're not worried about the Road Runners. They don't even truly know who we are. And like you said, many think it was you who burned their building down, and I don't mind letting them think that. It keeps their attention away from us."

"So you must be planning on doing more. If not, you would just claim responsibility for the fire. You like the thought of flying under their radar so you can do more work. And you know what, I'll help you. I'll play along. I'll even make a statement that the Revolution did this."

"You'd love to take the credit."

"Stop playing games. We both want the same thing—I wish you could see that. Take your blinders off, and see that we can wipe the Road Runners off the face of the planet if we just work together."

"You sound desperate, Chris. My group only has one thousand members across the country. We're less than one percent the size of both the Revolution or the Road Runners. Either of you could eliminate us if you decided."

"You may be small, but you have a monstrous movement behind you. The Road Runners shot themselves in the foot by letting Strike die. You can roll with that, especially once they elect Briar as their next commander—that's only going to spark a fresh wave of outrage for your base to recruit more members. I've seen this play out before – it's no different than the rise of the Road Runners, and look at them now."

Thaddeus considered this, brushing his fingers over his chin as he frowned in deep thought. He gazed into the distance, beyond Chris and toward the kitchen behind the old man. "What are your thoughts, exactly? How would this work?"

Got him, Chris thought, fighting off a new grin.

"I've already told you that I'm open to publicly taking responsibility for your attack. Let me help you by doing just that. You can keep working behind the scenes while all the attention is on me, and strike again. And if you need any additional resources, just let me know."

"And what's in it for you?" Thaddeus studied Chris like a poker player trying to figure out his opponent, burning a gaze into his very soul.

"The end of the Road Runners. That's all I've ever wanted. Then the Revolution can return to its peaceful ways before everyone decided they hated me."

"There's always something in it for you, though. That's *why* people hate you. Just tell me what you want."

Chris shrugged and tossed his hands in the air. "I've told you what I want, and that's why I came here today. You do realize I've been trapped in my house for several weeks now? I made a run for it and hoped for the best—it really was a good time, considering all the Road Runners are hiding. Before they vanished like the cowards they are, I couldn't step foot outside without someone wanting to snatch me away like a piece of property. The stars have aligned fatefully for us to meet today, and we can both get what we want."

Thaddeus looked down to the hardwood floor beneath his feet, and Chris watched as the man fought every instinct to trust Chris.

"Look," Chris said. "If you agree to join forces with me, I'll endorse the Liberation as a legitimate time travel organization. You can all live in peace without fear of the Revolution becoming territorial over you, and you can still operate under your own sets of rules and leadership. Zero interference."

"Answer one question for me," Thaddeus said sternly. "Why haven't you been able to beat the Road Runners on your own?"

Chris folded his hands on his lap before answering. "They have people within the Revolution, and it's been impossible to catch everyone who is living this lie. We plan things, but the Road Runners are always ready for it. Keep in mind, *they* departed from *us.* And that's why I want your assistance, because *you* have departed from *them*, and I assume you still have people on the inside."

Thaddeus nodded. "That we do."

Chris watched, knowing he was reeling Thaddeus into an agreement. "Well, what do you think?"

"I *think* I'm making a mistake, but I'm intrigued. Your support will help speed up our plans an entire three years. I'd be stupid to not accept this offer. Put it in writing, and you have a deal."

"Consider it done," Chris said, rising to his feet and extending a hand. "Let's get rid of these Road Runners once and for all."

Chris immediately made a phone call to get a formal document drafted and delivered to Thaddeus within the hour. Both men now had what they wanted: a clear path to executing the Road Runners.

33

Chapter 33

"I look out my window and don't see the world that I grew up in anymore," Martin said into his cell phone. When he woke in the morning after a late night of strategic discussions with his campaign team, he had the urge to speak with his closest friend and confidant, Gerald, who lived in the horrific future. They hadn't spoken since Martin's trip to 2064 for his mother's medicine, but they picked up as if they hadn't missed a beat. "And I'm not even talking about the state of the Road Runners—which is total shit right now—just the world in general. Violence is everywhere, everyone has become selfish and only worried about themselves, no one knows what exactly to trust. I just don't see how the world changes for the better."

"Well," Gerald said in his usual baritone, "The world doesn't change, as you saw from the future. It *does* get worse, and there's not much anyone can do about it."

"But what if we can? I'm announcing my candidacy for commander this afternoon."

"So I've heard. It's a big day the Road Runners will look back on, and I'm not sure how it will go down in history."

"What do you mean?"

"There's a split happening, Martin, and it's been in motion—slowly—until we all had to watch Commander Strike's murder. Just like when people left the Revolution to start the Road Runners, we're seeing the same thing happen to us. I suppose it's human nature for people to become dissatisfied with the status quo and take matters into their own hands. I can't say I'm surprised by the movement, but I am shocked at how quickly it has grown in just a few days."

"I don't know what I'm supposed to say to bring confidence back to all of these Road Runners."

"There's nothing you can say. I lived through this same thing in the future. In time, people will decide that their lives are best spent not hiding in their basement, and they'll find their way back to civilization. What you need to focus on is Chris and this Liberation group. I suspect they'll both be coming at you aggressively. When Chris smells blood in the water, he strikes. And right now, we are spouting blood as an organization."

Martin had taken the call in his second-floor bedroom, pacing around nervously. He had no desire to eat breakfast, but knew it was just nerves for his big speech later that afternoon.

"I need help, Gerald. I don't know anything about war or those types of matters. Would you be my number two if I actually win this election?" Silence poured out of the phone, but Martin could still hear the distant white noise of Gerald's breathing. "Gerald? Take your time if you need. The election is still a few weeks away—"

"I'll do it."

"Oh . . . okay?"

"I had every intent on helping the cause, I just wasn't sure in what capacity, exactly. But this is a great opportunity."

"Yes, I need your experience. I'll be leaning on you for just about everything."

"I understand, Martin, but I'll still follow your lead. You'll be the commander, not me."

"Will you be able to fly out here before my speech? It would be nice to have you present so I can announce you as my running mate."

Martin pulled the cell phone away from his ear to check the time, finding it was only eight o'clock. His speech wasn't scheduled until three in the afternoon.

"Yes, I should be able to make it."

"Perfect. I'll send you the address for where to meet. See you then."

They hung up and Martin had to stop himself from pacing. A weight had been lifted off his shoulders, knowing Gerald would be by his side during his commandership. He brought a militaristic approach to life and would serve honorably as the Road Runners' lieutenant commander.

With an extra bounce in his step, Martin returned downstairs where his campaign team huddled around the kitchen table, laptops open, sheets of paper sprawled across the table in chaos. They couldn't have had more than five hours of sleep, but worked and spoke with an energy Martin hoped he could match.

"Good morning, all," Martin said as he strolled in.

Tony sat in the center of his team and was the only one to look up and acknowledge Martin. "Morning, Mr. Briar. Are you ready for the big day?"

"I suppose I am," Martin said as he stepped all the way into the kitchen. Everyone else on the team was writing furiously, as if they might never get the chance to write again. "I spoke with Gerald this morning, and he's agreed to be my number two."

Tony's face lit up with joy. "Excellent. That's fantastic news. We can discuss that in a bit, but right now we're working on finishing up the first draft of your speech so you can read it over and let us know your thoughts."

"I didn't realize you were going to write my speech. I was planning on giving it on the fly."

Tony chuckled as he shook his head. "There are few people in the world who can pull off an impromptu speech and have its message truly resonate with their audience. Speech writing is a frustrating art, but necessary. We're not just writing words, although that's how it starts. But we have to mold those words to fit your voice, your flow, your timing. There are so many factors at play. The way you say a phrase may differ from the way I'd say the same thing, and that can lead to the message being received differently by the audience. We each focus on a different aspect of this process and polish the speech until it's perfect. We'll have you read it aloud to us to make sure you understand everything in it—we even write in when you should pause, when you should make eye contact, and even when to take a sip of water."

"I had no idea so much went into this."

"It's a grueling process, but we nearly have it down to a science. It's more a matter of making it sound like you. Remember, today will be many people's first impression of you, so it has to be strong but not aggressive, compassionate but not soft. It's a fine line we're walking here, but I like how it's coming along. Are you comfortable with public speaking?"

Martin shrugged. "I suppose. It doesn't make me nervous, like most people."

"That's ninety percent of the battle, glad to hear. If you can give us about twenty more minutes we should be all wrapped up."

Tony's voice came out dismissive, the rest of his team still not looking up as they were swimming in their work. Martin took the hint and vanished from the kitchen. His team had a lot to do, but he did not, leaving him anxious as the morning dragged. He went back to his bedroom to lie down and let his mind run circles, thinking of the days ahead.

Once he delivered the speech his life would change forever. That seemed to happen more often than not since he first took the Juice from Chris. He wondered if everyone who had joined the world of time travel had experienced so many drastic shifts in their lives. It had felt like he was falling down one rabbit hole after another. Surely there was someone with the pleasure of enjoying life as a time traveler and not having to worry about saving the world or fighting off bad guys.

For Martin Briar, though, he'd never have a chance to settle down, thanks to the target on his back. He wished he wasn't a Warm Soul, the lone reason he was thrust into the middle of this war. He wished he had never taken his mother to the Wealth of Time antique store. Sure, he might have lived out his life never knowing the truth about his daughter, but he had ways of coping with that pain. Life had been simple and straight-forward, and he missed that basic structure. Now, every day felt like a battle for survival, hoping to not catch a bullet to the head any time he stepped outside, praying Chris wouldn't slip into his house in the middle of the night and shred his body like he had done his mother's.

"Your old life is gone," Martin said to himself. "This is your life now."

He thought back on his life like a slideshow of memories, tears streaming down his face as he braced for the unknown future.

34

Chapter 34

Chris had returned to Alaska with the agreement he wanted from the Liberation. He foresaw a bright future with his new friends, and vowed to send an immediate message to assure the Liberation that he meant business. Plus, it was always a joy to destroy anything related to the Road Runners.

He felt confident, leaving the barricades down and daring the Road Runners to make a move on the mansion. His soldiers had grown a bit panicked at the prospect, but the Road Runners had no resources, having gone into hibernation after watching their own Council run for the hills.

That didn't mean Chris still couldn't have some fun. He had rounded up his soldiers in the mansion's living room and asked for one volunteer for a mission that would certainly end in death, but also leave a lasting legacy for the Revolution.

"Figure it out among yourselves, and have the chosen patriot come to my office."

Chris had spoken these words an hour earlier and now sat across from Bobby Francis.

Bobby had long twigs for fingers that rapped on the chair's

armrest. The rest of his body was equally skinny, showing a bulging Adam's apple as he gulped.

"Are you nervous, Bobby?" Chris asked. "You don't even know what the mission is."

Bobby's light green eyes seemed to tremble in his sockets as he returned a stare to Chris. His grip on the armrest tightened, turning his knuckles white as they stretched his pale skin to its limits.

"Of course I'm nervous, sir," Bobby said in a cracking voice. "Everyone said goodbye to me like I'm for sure not coming back."

"It would be a miracle if you returned," Chris said sternly. "Did you not understand the cost of this mission?"

"I understood that my life would be at great risk."

Chris shook his head. His soldiers weren't exactly Ivy League graduates, making them much easier to brainwash. He could have chosen anyone for the mission and they'd oblige, but he decided to let them choose. *Poor Bobby. Never saw it coming.*

"Unfortunately, there's only one way to pull off what we need to accomplish tonight. And it does involve you sacrificing your own life." Chris stood up and circled to the front of the desk, leaning on it as he spoke mere inches from Bobby. "You're doing an honorable act today, and the Revolution will forever be indebted to you."

"Thank you, sir."

Nice and robotic. Perfect.

"This might be long overdue," Chris continued. "But what better time than the present? We're going to blow up the little hideout the Road Runners have across the way. They've been camped out there, watching me for years like I'm some sort of zoo animal. But now they're hiding. And scared. And, oh, how

I just want them all dead!"

He threw his head back and howled like a loon.

"And my job is to go in there and kill them all?" Bobby asked, bracing himself for the obvious answer.

"Yes, but it's so much more than that," Chris said, unable to wipe the smirk off his face. "We can kill Road Runners whenever we want—that's not the issue. What we've never had the chance to do is kick them while they're down. Partly because they've never been down—not like this, at least. They consider this Alaska location as their main headquarters, even more important than the building that went up in flames in New York. Bobby, you're going to send them into a total frenzy, and you have my word that we will not waste the opportunity."

Bobby still trembled in his seat, yet Chris sensed a calm swarm over his dedicated soldier. *Let's go, young man.*

"I appreciate the explanation," Bobby said. "So what exactly will I be doing?"

Chris grinned hungrily. "Let me tell you."

* * *

Bobby rode in the backseat of their van, two soldiers in front, while two in the middle hung out of the rolled down windows with assault rifles sticking out to the world.

"Expect some company," Chris had told them before they departed. "Just because they're hiding doesn't mean they won't defend their ground."

He didn't actually know who was still residing in the underground fortress. There could be an entire army waiting to swallow up whoever might come knocking. But when no one arrived after having the barricades down for an entire day and night, he trusted his gut instinct that his enemies were indeed short-handed.

They rumbled over the uneven terrain, turning off the main road and creeping through the stand of trees that shrouded the Road Runners' hideout. The sun had settled on the horizon, casting an orange and purple glow across the sky. Bobby sat in the back seat, his heavy breathing compressed by the vest strapped around his torso, suffocating him with its weight. Sweat made his undershirt cling to his chest like he had just been caught in a water balloon fight.

"We're here," the driver called out, the van's headlights focusing on a wooden structure no bigger than a Porta-Potty.

The door burst open, three people barging out with guns pointed at the van.

"Shit!" the driver screamed, the rest of the Revolters already cocking their weapons and kicking open their doors.

Bobby sat in the backseat, frozen with shock. He was ordered to do so, instructed only to enter the fortress after any outside activity was cleared up by the rest of his crew. Gunfire rang out, echoing in the open air. The *clink!* of bullets hitting the van made Bobby duck down, hands clasped over the back of his skull while a stick of dynamite dug into his chin.

"Please don't let me die in here," he whimpered. "Not like this."

The gunfire had either lasted ten seconds or ten minutes—Bobby would never know—but when it ceased he peeked and found his team still standing, and not a Road Runner in sight. One soldier had opened the door to the wooden shack and stuck his head in.

"Francis!" he shouted. "It's all yours!"

Bobby gulped and felt a fresh wave of sweat bead his forehead. Instinctively, his right hand shot into his pocket where the remote waited for him to push the button that would detonate the dozen sticks of dynamite strapped to his vest. His heart drummed against his ribs as his fingertips pulsed.

Deep down he had hoped this mission would somehow be aborted due to complications, but here they were, three dead Road Runners on the ground and a clear path into their fortress where death waited.

The van's back doors swung open, letting in a gust of cold air that relieved his hot flash. His fellow soldier stood there with an arm extended to help him scoot out of the van. "We're proud of you, Francis," the soldier said as they clasped hands. It was Rudy, one of the longer tenured soldiers who had been at Chris's side for at least a decade. The soldiers all conversed, but none considered each other friends, not that there was time for friendship.

While Bobby trudged toward the shack, the soldiers parting into two lines to let him pass, he wondered why they had never been allowed to develop relationships that went beyond colleagues. It seemed any time a conversation steered toward personal matters or about their past lives, Chris redirected it to business. He didn't understand the pull Chris had on everyone, even though he experienced it himself. The thought of dashing into the woods and running away from this life hadn't been as tempting as it was at this current moment with a suicide vest around his body. Yet it would remain only a dream because the thought of abandoning Chris made him sick to his stomach. Was that fear or loyalty? It didn't matter, because he was going into this fortress to kill everything in sight.

Before he realized, Bobby reached the door and pulled it open, looking back one final time to the world and his fellow soldiers who would go back to the mansion and carry on their lives like nothing had happened. Meanwhile, Bobby drew a deep breath and braced himself for an imminent death. He nodded before stepping into the shack where darkness and silence swallowed him.

A flashlight was one of the handful of items found on a Revolter soldier's utility belt, so he rummaged for his, clicking it on. The room was empty, not a single item in sight aside from a control panel on the wall that had eight different buttons. Bobby stepped toward this to examine it, and determined the buttons to all be decoys with the exception of the two basic ones this structure needed: up and down.

Okay, this is it. He tried to psych himself up, but couldn't ignore the growing nausea that made him want to collapse to his knees and vomit his brains out. He reached back into his pocket and pulled out the detonator, clutching it tightly as his thumb avoided the trigger button. *One quick push and we all go up. How ironic if I went back outside and blew up all of us Revolters. What would Chris do then?*

He shook his head free of these dark thoughts. It was like Chris was camped out in his mind—all of their minds—to ensure these perfectly normal urges were never carried out.

The down button stared at him, and his finger shot out and pressed it, officially bringing Bobby to the point of no return. *Goodbye, world. Goodbye, life,* he thought as the building started to hum with the sound of a distant motor. The ground trembled like a light earthquake before a crack of light appeared from the edges of the floor.

The descent was slow and steady, the light growing brighter

until he reached the lower level. Immediately, four Road Runners greeted him with guns drawn just a few feet away. He saw at least two dozen others crouched behind their desks, guns also aimed at Bobby's head.

"Don't shoot!" Bobby screamed, waving the remote in front him. "This is tied to my pulse and will detonate if I flatline."

A lie, but one he knew no one wanted to take the gamble of finding out for sure.

"Shoot his sorry ass!" someone from the back of the room cried out, and Bobby was certain a bullet would pass through his brain within seconds, leaving him a dead, flopping fish who would never get to blow up the Road Runners. Death had become the only obvious exit to this situation, and Bobby wanted to make sure it was on his terms.

"Don't shoot!" he pleaded again, arms shaking as he held them above his head, sliding his thumb over the trigger. "Chris sent me here to do this—I don't want to. Please help me."

"Then hand over the remote," the Road Runner in the front barked. He was a large man who could easily wipe Bobby off the planet with his bare hands.

"I can't!" Bobby cried. "The remote is what's connected to my pulse. Please just get me out of this thing." He offered a quick stream of tears that weren't exactly fake.

The four Road Runners who were closest—clearly their version of soldiers, judging by their military-grade outfits and assault rifles—looked at each other in confusion. Surely this specific situation had never arisen in all of their preparation.

"Don't move a fucking muscle!" another shouted before leaning in to whisper with his team.

Bobby obliged, remaining frozen as he looked out to the several guns pointing at him. They weren't going to shoot him, that much he'd decided because they would have done so already. He studied the back of the room, judging it to be roughly one hundred feet to the back wall. Chris assured him the bombs covered a seventy-five-foot radius.

It didn't appear anyone was outside of that range. The Road Runners were too defensive to simply back away like cowards, and this would work against them.

One of the four soldiers stepped forward, rifle still locked on Bobby's forehead. "Okay. If what you say is true, we can help you out of that vest. Lower your hands slowly and let us come to you."

The words fell deaf on Bobby's ears. He couldn't stop thinking about how this room would fall completely silent in just a few seconds. How his own bones would become part of the lethal shrapnel blasting across the room to pierce organs and arteries.

They say your life flashes before your eyes just before you die, and Bobby experienced this phenomenon as his hand holding the detonator steadied. He saw his teenage self, kicked out on the streets after telling his parents he wanted to date other boys. He saw himself crying next to a storm drain, rain beating down on him as he contemplated sliding into the drain with no intent on coming out. Then he saw when he joined the United States Army, turning his life around after learning how to live independently at the age of eighteen. These memories, along with countless others seemed to flood his mind in unison, dizzying his head, the room spinning.

His throat tightened to the point of barely being able to swallow, but he managed his final words through gritted teeth.

"Long live the Revolution," he said, and pressed the trigger.

35

Chapter 35

Antonio had slipped into the living room for an urgent phone call while Martin rehearsed his speech for the fourth time. He liked it, and they did fantastic work in making it sound like things he'd actually say.

"Let's go, people!" Antonio commanded when he stepped back into the kitchen, his cell phone clutched in a death grip. "We have to leave right now."

Urgency clung to every word, and everyone sensed it, wasting no time as they snapped their laptops shut and stuffed papers into their backpacks.

"What's wrong?" Martin asked.

"I'll explain in the car, but we need to leave right now. Don't ask questions—just grab what you need and get out of the house."

Martin obliged, dashing up the stairs to snag his flask of Juice, speech papers still clutched against his chest. *Is this really my only prized possession?* he thought as he returned downstairs.

"Move, move, move!" Antonio barked, forcing the campaign

team out of the house like a mother rushing her kids out the door to get to school on time. "We will meet at the downtown office. Do not enter the building until Everett and I have a chance to sweep the property."

They all nodded as they jumped into the car they had rented, Martin and his two guards leaving the house last.

Antonio broke into a light jog toward their car still parked on the curb from the night before. It was a few minutes past eleven in the morning, the sun nearly directly above their heads as it beat down on them.

They filed into the car, Antonio wasting no time starting the engine and skidding away.

"What the hell is going on?" Everett asked, the slightest tinge of fear audible in his voice.

"They attacked us."

"Who?"

"The cocksucking Revolters, who else? They just blew up the Alaska headquarters."

Martin gasped, struck by memories of being held a no-restraint prisoner in Chris's mansion, to his sprint through the woods until he found safety in the form of Bill and Julian looking to bring him back the aforementioned headquarters. Bill and Julian were both dead now, due to an ugly turn of events that the organization was still recovering from today.

"Did anyone survive?" Martin asked from the backseat. He had spent enough time there to know everyone by name. Alaska housed the Road Runners' sharpest minds. That particular group worked continuously to ensure the organization's safety, and he wondered how many of that team had gone into hiding after the attacks in New York.

"Twenty-seven dead, plus the Revolter. Zero survivors.

Suicide vest."

"What does this mean?" Everett asked.

Antonio shrugged as they reached the freeway, moving the vehicle to a tick above eighty miles per hour. "I don't know what this means long-term, but we have a major problem. Our New York *and* Alaska offices are out of commission. Our two main hubs. New York kept us afloat with guidance, Alaska had our best people. We're in trouble."

"Chris is moving to end the war," Martin said. "We can't give him any more daylight. We have to retaliate or all of our buildings will be gone. Once that happens, do we have faith that we can rebuild again, or will people just try to live normal lives and spend the rest of their days looking over their shoulder, waiting for a Revolter to wipe them out?"

Martin's voice had turned grave at this prospect, leaving Antonio and Everett with no viable response.

"Do you think they know about the speech today?" Everett asked.

"I don't know, Ev," Antonio snapped, growing frustrated. "They shouldn't, but who knows anymore? This has turned into a real shitshow."

"I'm going to add some things to my speech that address this," Martin said, more of a declaration.

"I don't know what your little team will think about that, but it's your speech, so you should do what you want."

Martin glanced at the dashboard and saw their speed now at ninety, the world blurring by through the windows. Downtown was already in sight, and it had taken them a whole fifteen minutes to arrive, record time thanks to Antonio's lead foot and the lack of traffic in the late morning.

"We need you to stay in the car while we check inside the

office," Everett explained over his shoulder. "You got your gun?"

"I don't. It's still in the bag in my bedroom—didn't think to grab it because we left so fast."

Good one, Martin. Now you can just chuck your flask at anyone trying to kill you. How can a commander be so stupid? Clearly you're not cut out for the job.

"There's a spare in the glove box," Antonio said as they exited the freeway and crept toward the office building now less than a mile away.

Everett pulled it open and handed the black pistol to Martin. He studied it like he had never held a gun before, praying he wouldn't have to use it on this beautiful morning.

"You don't think they're actually here in Denver? At the office?" Martin asked.

"It's highly unlikely," Everett said. "The only reason they would be is if they know about the speech you are set to deliver today. They're attacking us where it hurts. Denver is a big hub, but not a crucial one to the organization's overall operation. We are tightening security as best we can in offices like Chicago, L.A., and Houston—the more heavily populated locations."

"Funny hearing all those cities listed next to Barrow, Alaska," Everett said with a chuckle.

"Strike wanted to set up there to keep an eye on Chris. Looks like we were a little too close," Antonio said, no humor in his voice.

They reached the office building. The windows provided a glimpse of an abandoned workspace: lights off, not a single person in sight. Their front as a marketing firm had a sign posted on the door that explained the business was closed indefinitely due to unfortunate circumstances, and to keep posted about when they would re-open.

"Doesn't look like anyone is here," Everett said.

"No shit, they're not exactly going to sit on the front steps and wait for us. Let's go in. Martin, why don't you go for a walk? It's almost lunch time—the sidewalks will be crowded with people in a few minutes to blend in with."

Martin nodded and let himself out, soaking in the downtown surroundings as he had so many times in his life. Sixteenth Street Mall was three blocks south, and he thought back to the day he had roamed the mall with Sonya by his side, pockets full of money, not a thought in the universe that his new love interest was pulling him along for her job.

The nostalgia smacked him like a tree branch, enough to move him down the sidewalk where he took a whole ten steps before stopping.

A car horn honked across the street, startling Martin as if someone had tossed a bucket of water on his head. To his relief, it was Tony Jenkins and the rest of the campaign team, Tony grinning through his partly-open window. He stuck out an arm and waved Martin over.

He had to wait for a line of cars to pass before jogging across Blake Street.

"You can wait with us," Tony said. "Let your boys do their thing and we can all head inside together."

"Alright."

The back door swung open, and Lila slid over to make room, Madison on her other side, and Dylan riding shotgun. Martin settled in and asked the question that had been burning since they all left the house. "Does this attack in Alaska change anything in my speech?"

"It does," Tony said, looking into the rear view to meet

Martin's eyes. "Not much, but we decided to make some small adjustments. If anything, it makes the message we already had written more relevant, don't you think?"

Martin nodded. "I can see that. I just worry that our organization is too on edge to even handle an election. How can we expect everyone to vote in their right mind when they're all worried about getting killed?"

"I study the population," Lila said from beside him, crossing her hands as she turned to face him. "We still conduct pre-election polls, and it seems this will compete for our best voter turnout. We usually turn in votes in the low 90's, but the trends so far suggest that ninety-five percent plan to vote. The population is eager for a leader and some guidance."

Martin wanted to ask which candidate was the front runner since he had yet to formally enter the race, but bit his lip. It didn't matter, and he'd have an endorsement from Europe soon after his speech.

"It's hard to predict exactly how the people will vote," Lila continued. "But we expect you to pull out a close race."

"Close? Everyone has made it sound like a slam dunk. Why the skepticism now?"

"These attacks do change things. Now, I haven't had a chance yet to run numbers, but based on my general knowledge, something like this will make voters long for someone with experience. There are a lot of factors in play, but I don't foresee it being anything that kills our chances."

Martin nodded and looked out his window, surprised to find Antonio and Everett already standing on the front steps of the office. "They're done?" he asked, more to himself, but getting everyone in the car to swivel their heads toward the building.

"Let's move, people," Tony said, wasting no time opening

his door and crossing the street, the rest of them lagging behind.

Antonio had his arms crossed as he waited at the top of the steps, undisturbed.

"What's the word?" Tony asked, huffing for air as he climbed the few steps, not used to the Denver altitude.

"Abandoned," Everett said. "Doesn't look like anyone has been in there for at least a week."

"Coast is clear," Antonio confirmed. "You can all get set up, I don't foresee any issues today."

"You heard the man," Tony said, brushing by them as he barged into the office and disappeared down the long hallway as if he'd been there hundreds of times. The Road Runners tried to make each office with a similar layout, for ease of familiarity when traveling across the world.

The rest of the team rushed into the building. "We're going live in thirty," Lila said over her shoulder, and hearing the formal countdown begin made Martin's stomach sink.

Antonio and Everett remained in their positions, looking like two guards again with no imminent worries, much like when Martin had first arrived to Crooked Island.

"Thank you both," Martin said. "For everything. I'll be honest, I'm surprised to still be alive after all that's happened."

"Just doing our job, and that will continue if you win this election," Antonio said, not breaking his gaze from the street and sidewalks. "I think they need you in there, though."

Martin nodded and entered the building, feeling like a visitor despite having been there several dozen times already. He trudged to the back and down the steps that led to the soon-to-be headquarters, should he win this thing.

When he reached the bottom landing Martin saw his campaign team hurrying through the furthest conference room door, the one where he had been examined on camera for his Warm Soul. His nerves settled, and everything came into clear focus. He heard the words of his late mother, rest her soul, urging him to do something meaningful with his life.

Martin shuffled toward the conference room, entering to his team setting up the podium and prepping a backdrop that showed the Denver city skyline.

"We're going to start as soon as we're ready," Tony explained. "We don't want to be in this building any longer than we need."

"But Antonio said we'll be fine."

"And I'm sure we will. But have you ever seen an empty Road Runner office? This place gives me the creeps. Makes it feel like we all died from a nuclear bomb or something."

Martin hadn't considered this, but there was an eeriness lingering in the abandoned air of the office.

"Ten minutes," Dylan said, tapping on the microphone he had just set up on the podium. Madison sat at the table a few feet away with an earpiece and offered a thumbs up to ensure the mic was hot.

Dylan nodded before running back to a storage closet along the side wall, holding a teleprompter in each hand that he set up a few feet in front of the podium. "Let's get a camera check!"

Lila ran to the teleprompters and connected their wires to her laptop. She rapped furiously on the keyboard. "Camera is on, stand in position."

Dylan dashed behind the podium, standing exactly where Martin would in just a few minutes. Lila squinted at her screen as Madison inserted herself behind the camera.

"To the left," Lila instructed. "And just a nudge downward."

Madison moved the camera, prompting Lila to pull back the teleprompters a couple of inches to get them out of the view. "We're all set!"

"Martin, come on over," Tony said, starting toward the podium.

Martin followed, and Lila ran back to the closet where she returned with a dark gray suit jacket.

"Put this on," Tony said, helping his new candidate into the blazer. Martin had on a solid black t-shirt to round out his outfit deemed "professional enough" once Tony helped button up the jacket. "How do you feel? You ready?"

Martin drew a long inhale. "Let's do this."

"Have we confirmed we have the feed still?" Tony barked over his shoulder.

"We have it," Dylan replied. "We're ready to go live."

"Good luck, Martin," Tony said, taking a step back. "Follow the script, but make it come out in your voice. You did great in our practice session."

Martin slid behind the podium, dropping his hands on its smooth wooden surface, adjusting the mic to reach his mouth.

Tony settled behind the camera, crossing his arms as he watched the feed on the small monitor. "Launch the feed."

"We're live. Thirty seconds," Lila said, the lights around the conference room dimming with the exception of the one on Martin and the backdrop behind him, making him appear like he was standing on a balcony somewhere with a view of the city behind him.

The teleprompter showed the countdown, and Martin imagined all of the scared Road Runners at their homes, watching their televisions countdown in anticipation of what the next wave of news might be for their organization.

"Three . . . two . . . one," Tony said, pointing his finger to Martin.

"Good afternoon, my fellow Road Runners. My name is Martin Briar, and I'm broadcasting live from Denver, Colorado to announce my candidacy to be your next commander."

Off and running, good pace, keep it flowing, Martin told himself.

"I want to first address the situation with Commander Strike. I understand many of you out there are upset with me, but please understand I had nothing to do with Commander Strike's death. Chris used both her and myself as bargaining chips in his twisted game. I knew Commander Strike on a personal level—she even swore me in as a Road Runner right here in the Denver office. She was a friend and trusted confidant, and her death makes me sick. That's why I'm entering this race.

"We're nearing the end of this war with the Revolution, if you can believe it, and right now, things are looking bad for us. If we don't take swift action, our entire group is at risk of going extinct. Our Council is hiding, and for good reason. No one knows who to trust. We must remain diligent and aware of our surroundings.

"I first entered the time travel world through Chris Speidel. He offered me the opportunity to go back in time to learn what happened to my daughter, who went missing in 1996 without a trace. I did what any grieving father would have done and accepted the offer, understanding I was putting myself at risk for a painful experience. I was prepared for that, but not the onslaught of constant pain I've had to endure.

"My payment for my Juice was to witness my mother fall

victim to Alzheimer's disease. I was expecting a broken back, perhaps, not an emotional pain that spun me back toward the depression I've battled my entire life. I know many of you have similar stories about Chris taking matters too far, and that's why we're at war with him.

"If you look back at the events of the past several years, it has consisted of Revolters killing Road Runners, and vice versa. We need unity. We're on the same team with our unique abilities, and should be working together to make the world a better place. Unfortunately, Chris doesn't see things that way, and only wants to further his own agenda, weaponizing those innocent lives who fall for his antics, and using them against his own people if he has to. The man—if you can bear to call him that—has no boundaries or moral compass. He's also made the mistake of narcissism, believing he is the only person in the world who can keep the Revolution alive.

"Because of this, our mission is simple: kill Chris and the Revolution collapses into itself. And I have great news for those of you who don't know much about me: I'm a Warm Soul. This is an extremely rare ability to resist the freezing of time. Through an international agreement made during our last peace treaty more than four decades ago, the use of freezing time during a war is prohibited, but do we really think Chris cares about our laws? He will do anything to win, including freezing time, but that will have no effect on me. With me, you'll have a commander who can continue working no matter what Chris tries to throw our way.

"My running mate is an outstanding gentleman named Gerald Holmes. He was supposed to be here, but we had to move up the start time of this speech. I met him on my mission to the future to obtain a cure for Alzheimer's, and working alongside Gerald showed me a man hungry for an end to the war, not to mention a brilliant strategist who grew up in the unpleasant future, surviving every day in a horrific culture where the poor and minorities are executed in the streets for fun.

"I've been to that future and witnessed it for myself, and that's why I'm making this announcement today. Not only are we, as Road Runners, in grave danger – the entire world as we know it faces the same trouble, only they're not aware of it. The Road Runners have always vowed to keep the world a safe place for both ourselves and innocent civilians, and that is exactly what I plan to do if elected.

"I have one advantage over anyone else in the world—I've been inside Chris's mansion. I've roamed the halls, met his goons, and even sat down in his office."

Martin paused, took a sip of water, and saw he had his closing paragraph on the teleprompter. He decided to ignore the script and end his message on his terms.

"If you're a Road Runner—new or old—please know that I'm like you. I've lost everything I ever cared about in this world. With nothing further to lose, I will not stop until Chris Speidel is dismembered and dead. Two years is a short term, but it's plenty of time to finish this fight. A vote for me is a vote for a return to peace. Thank you."

Tony nodded to Lila, who promptly pushed a button on her computer, cutting off the live feed.

"Well done," Tony said, stepping in front of the camera with a grin. "Was our closing not good enough?"

"It was," Martin said. "But I wanted something a little stronger—to make the people remember me."

"Oh, they're going to remember you, no doubt about that.

Let's wrap this up and grab a celebratory lunch. Commander Blair is expected to release his endorsement for you later this evening, then we'll officially be off and running to start a mini tour across the continent. Three weeks until election day, can you believe it?"

Martin nodded, unsure what else to say. He felt accomplished after the speech, truly ready to tackle the next three weeks and win over the hearts of his fellow Road Runners. He didn't know what his life would look like at the end of this road, win or lose, but things would never be the same.

He watched his campaign team pack up the conference room as quickly as they had set it up, and Martin wondered if he'd ever be back in this building again. He wondered how many viewers had tuned in, and what they thought about his speech. He had started the day as a man hated by half of the organization, and could only hope he gained new supporters.

His mind raced with these thoughts until the team—Antonio and Everett included—was ready to head to lunch, blending into society during the rush where restaurants had lines of business workers out the door. Martin didn't currently sense any danger, but knew there would be plenty coming his way, likely delivered from his old friend in Alaska.

That was here nor there, and for the rest of the day Martin and his team did exactly what Tony had suggested, celebrating a successful day and speech. The real work would begin tomorrow, setting into motion a month-long blur to the finish line.

They found a restaurant with an outdoor dining area, and Martin toasted a glass of whiskey to the rest of his team as they basked in the beautiful day.

Meanwhile, nearly 3,000 miles away, Chris Speidel sat in

his office, staring at his monitor that had just shown Martin's speech. He smirked, fists clenched and shaking with rage, and threw his head back, howling maniacal laughter.

Zero Hour (Wealth of Time, Book #5)

Zero Hour is the fifth installation of the *Wealth of Time* series. This book continues the story from where *Keeper of Time* ended, continuing the story line between Martin and Chris.

You can order your copy by CLICKING HERE!

GET EXCLUSIVE BONUS STORIES!

Connecting with readers is the best part of this job. Releasing a book into the world is a truly frightening moment every time it happens! Hearing your feedback, whether good or bad, goes a long in shaping future projects and helping me grow as a writer. I also like to take readers behind the scenes on occasion and share what is happening in my wild world of writing. If you're interested, please consider joining my mailing list. If you do so, I'll send you the following as a thank you:

1. A free copy of *Revolution*, a prequel story that goes back in time before Chris Speidel ever knew about the mysterious world of time travel.
2. A free copy of *Road Runners*, a prequel story that visits the origination of the Road Runners organization.

You can get your content for free, by signing up HERE.

https://dl.bookfunnel.com/zb03c72679

Acknowledgments

I can't believe this is my tenth published book. It just seems like yesterday I was publishing my first book, Followed Home, with no clue what I was getting myself into. It's amazing how much you can grow in a short period of time. Every day since hitting that publish button for the first time has been a constant thirst for growth and improvement. This industry has its ups and downs, like any I suppose, but one constant has always been the network of supportive authors. It's truly a blessing to be in a business where you essentially have no competition. We're able to team up with like-minded authors and promote each other and see each other have success.

I've been lucky to have a close group of colleagues who have paid it forward, and am now enjoying my first experiences of having new authors reach out to me for advice. It's the ultimate compliment, and one I'll cherish forever. On that note, I'd like to thank my tight group of friends, the Dizzy Dragons. Of all the available resources us authors have, this group is the one I call "home" and will always turn to when stuck in a bind.

At this point, my team is pretty much the same crew working on my books for each release. Thank you to Dane Low, my cover artist, who has been putting together my covers since day one. And a major thank you to my editor, Stephanie Cohen. You always know how to keep my books on track and clarify my message when I can't quite get it right. We didn't start working together until this Wealth of Time series, but I can't imagine working with anyone else at this point!

Thank you to my Advance Readers Team, you all read so quickly (I'm truly jealous), and always help make launch day just a little bit more special!

For Arielle, Felix, and Selena. I hope by the time you're reading this, you've understood the importance of chasing your dreams. Don't ever let anything get in your way, and take the leap of faith to get it done.

Lastly, thank you to my foundation, my motivation, and my world. The "light of my life" and wife, Natasha. I know neither of us had this envisioned during our emotional conversation at the kitchen table. But look at us now! Onward and upward!

Andre Gonzalez
November 1, 2019-August 16, 2020

Enjoy this book?

You can make a difference!

Reviews are the most helpful tools in getting new readers for any books. I don't have the financial backing of a New York publishing house and can't afford to blast my book on billboards or bus stops.

(Not yet!)

That said, your honest review can go a long way in helping me reach new readers. If you've enjoyed this book, I'd be forever grateful if you could spend a couple minutes leaving it a review (it can be as short as you like) on the Amazon page. You can jump right to the page by clicking below:

mybook.to/KeeperOfTime

Thank you so much!

Also by Andre Gonzalez

Wealth of Time Series:

Time of Fate (#6)
Zero Hour (#5)
Keeper of Time (#4)
Bad Faith (#3)
Warm Souls (#2)
Wealth of Time (#1)
Road Runners (Short Story)
Revolution (Short Story)

Amelia Doss Series:

Salvation (#3)
Nightfall (#2)
Resurrection (#1)

Insanity Series:

The Insanity Series (Books 1-3)
Replicate (#3)
The Burden (#2)
Insanity (#1)
Erased (Prequel Short Story)

The Exalls Attacks:

Followed Away (#3)

Followed East (#2)
Followed Home (#1)
A Poisoned Mind (Short Story)

Standalone books:

Snowball: A Christmas Horror Story

About the Author

Born in Denver, CO, Andre Gonzalez has always had a fascination with horror and the supernatural starting at a young age. He spent many nights wide-eyed and awake, his mind racing with the many images of terror he witnessed in books and movies. Ideas of his own morphed out of movies like *Halloween* and books such as *Pet Sematary* by Stephen King. These thoughts eventually made their way to paper, as he always wrote dark stories for school assignments or just for fun. Followed Home is his debut novel based off of a terrifying dream he had many years ago at the age of 12. His reading and writing of horror stories evolved into a pursuit of a career as an author, where Andre hopes to keep others awake at night with his frightening tales. The world we live in today is filled with horror stories, and he looks forward to capturing the raw emotion of these events, twisting them into new tales, and preserving a legacy in between the crisp bindings of novels.

Andre graduated from Metropolitan State University of Denver with a degree in business in 2011. During his free time, he enjoys baseball, poker, golf, and traveling the world with his family. He believes that seeing the world is the only true way to stretch the imagination by experiencing new cultures and meeting new people.

Andre still lives in Denver with his wife, Natasha, and their three kids.

Made in United States
North Haven, CT
31 August 2023

40988518R00161